A CAROLINE

TO KILL
A KING

MARY V. WELK

KLEWORKS PUBLISHING COMPANY
CHICAGO, IL.

Also by
Mary V. Welk

A Deadly Little Christmas
Something Wicked in the Air

To Kill A King
Published by Kleworks Publishing Co.
First Printing August 2000

Publisher's Note: This is a work of fiction. Names, characters, places, and
incidents either are the product of the author's imagination or are used
fictitiously, and any resemblance to actual persons, living or dead, events, or
locales is entirely coincidental.

ISBN 0-9665157-2-2

Printed in the USA by
Morris Publishing
3212 East Highway 30, Kearney, NE 68847
1-800-650-7888

FOR THE FOSSILS -- ESPECIALLY MO

When you strike a king, you must kill him.

Ralph Waldo Emerson

PART ONE

We die -- does it matter when?

The Revenge
Alfred Lord Tennyson

CHAPTER ONE

April 12th, 1980

Dr. Jack Melmann slipped a third white tablet under his tongue and silently prayed that the pain in his chest would stop. The first doses of nitroglycerin had done nothing to relieve the feeling of pressure on his sternum, and that worried County Hospital's Chief of Staff. He'd suffered through bouts of angina before, but in the past the attacks had always eased after one or two tiny pills. This time the medicine was having no effect on his heart.

He wondered fleetingly if he shouldn't revise his self-diagnosis.

"Jack, perhaps we should discuss Truman's retirement some other time. You seem preoccupied today."

"Hmm?" Melmann glanced over his shoulder at the man whose soft baritone voice had interrupted his private musings. "Ah, yes," he muttered, dragging his thoughts back to the matter at hand. "Bill Truman. Bill's had a long and illustrious career as County's Director of Emergency Medicine. I'm going to miss him."

He palmed the brown glass bottle of nitro pills into the side pocket of his jacket and turned from the window overlooking the hospital parking lot. "Would you like some coffee?"

"Decaffeinated?"

"Of course." Melmann filled two mugs with steaming brown liquid from a small electric pot standing on a shelf below the window. He handed the first mug to his visitor, then stood sipping from his own while surreptitiously studying the other man.

Dressed in blue scrubs and a carefully pressed lab coat bearing a plastic tag with the letters M.D. emblazoned behind the name, Melmann's guest lounged lazily in one of the black leather armchairs gracing the tenth floor office. He was considerably younger than Melmann, but his demeanor implied equality with the man who was his boss. He carried himself with an aplomb that bordered on insolence, and although he now feigned an expression of amiable concern, his dark eyes were laughing at the Chief of Staff.

Melmann was not beyond caring. He noted the look, filed it away in his memory, and snapped, "Bill's leaving the end of next month. You're angling for his job, aren't you, Scotty?"

The rancor in his voice caught the other doctor off guard. Scotty straightened in his chair and responded cautiously.

"I've paid my dues, Jack. I've worked ER longer than any other doc in the department, and I've been Truman's right hand man for the past ten months. I know that position inside out."

Melmann fought down a sudden wave of nausea. "I'm aware of that," he murmured. "I'm aware of everything that goes on in ER."

Intent on pressing his case, Scotty barely heard Melmann's words, much less the menacing tone of his voice. He plunged on.

"I'm a fine diagnostician, as you well know. Plus, I don't make legal blunders. My charting is a work of art, and no claim against me has ever stood up in court. It's only logical that I be appointed the next Director of Emergency Medicine for County Hospital."

He leaned forward anticipating a reply, but the Chief of Staff seemed unimpressed. His only response a raised eyebrow, Melmann turned his back on Scotty and crossed the room to his desk.

Walking proved too much of an effort for the senior doctor. The tightness in his chest increased, and he drew a deep breath to quell the rising queasiness in his stomach. He told himself again that his discomfort was due to simple angina, but like a mantra repeated too often, the words had lost their ability to reassure him.

Jack Melmann began to suspect he was in real trouble.

"Look," Scotty continued. "If you're not going to support me on the Director's job, just say so. You called this meeting, so I figured you wanted to talk about it."

When Melmann still didn't respond, Scotty got to his feet and picked up his briefcase. He walked to the door, then paused and looked back.

"I've been pulling down twelve hour shifts for over a month, and I'm exhausted. When I get home from work, all I want to do is sleep. I was hoping this promotion would allow me to see more of my wife, but I guess that's not to be."

His hand lingered on the doorknob. Just when he thought he might have guessed wrong, the other man stirred.

"Ah, yes. Barbara."

The tenderness in Melmann's voice betrayed him. Scotty moved in quickly, eager to score another point.

"I'd like to spend more time with her during her pregnancy. She's very excited about the baby. I am too," he added with a laugh.

You bastard, thought Melmann. The attempt at emotional blackmail infuriated him and sent his pulse rate soaring. He told himself to stay calm, to remember that his duties as Chief of Staff preceded his own personal desire to throttle Scotty.

And if truth be told, fulfilling his responsibility to the hospital would wreak greater havoc in Scotty's life than any act of physical harm he could inflict on the man. Not only did he intend to deny his subordinate the directorship he so coveted, but he was also about to end the young doctor's career at County Hospital, perhaps even his career as a medic.

"Sit down," Melmann commanded, waving Scotty back to his seat. "There's something else you and I need to discuss."

Sheer will power allowed Melmann to conceal his physical distress from his adversary. The pain in his chest was now radiating upward into his neck and jaw. He felt oddly lightheaded, almost dizzy.

"Does this concern the budget? I've been meaning to..."

"It's a personal matter," Melmann interrupted. He shook his head, the movement intended to clear the cobwebs from his brain. Instead, the gesture precipitated a sharp stabbing sensation between his shoulder blades that caused him to catch his breath. His hands trembled as he gripped the edge of the desk to steady himself.

"There are rumors circulating through ER," he continued shakily. "The word is you're sleeping with a student nurse by the name of Witterson, a young girl who's not even eighteen years old."

He massaged his neck muscles with an open palm while observing Scotty for some overt sign of panic.

There was none forthcoming. The other doctor wore a mask of innocence that transformed itself into mild surprise, then disbelief.

"You must be kidding," Scotty laughed. "You know this place is a rumor mill, but ninety-nine percent of the gossip has no basis in fact. Frankly, Jack, I'm shocked you'd put credence in such talk."

He shook his head, a sad little smile curving the corners of his lips. Melmann had seen that smile before, been taken in by the sincerity of it time and again, but now he refused to let it sway him.

"This is not the first time you've been the subject of gossip, Scotty. In the past I chose to ignore the talk as nothing more than vicious backbiting. In this instance, though, I believe what I've been told."

Even so brief a statement left Melmann short of breath. He sucked in a mouthful of air and leaned forward to pick up a thick manila folder lying on the corner of the desk. A sharp pain knifed down his left arm, and he winced involuntarily. Scotty noticed it.

"Are you all right, Jack? Jack!"

Melmann had fallen back in his chair, his skin ashen and his eyes wide with fear. Perspiration beaded his forehead and trickled down his face and neck. He felt as if a great iron weight had descended on his chest crushing every inch of air from his lungs. He struggled to control his labored breathing, determined to finish what he'd started.

"I've...had you...investigated, Scotty," he gasped. Clawing at the neck of his shirt, he fumbled with his tie, then ripped open his starched white collar. "There...were...way...too...many...rumors. Too...many...inconsistencies." With numb fingers he kneaded his throat, milking words from vocal cords too rigid for speech. "Now...I know...who...and...what...you really...are."

Shadows filled the corners of the office, sealing the room in twilight shades of gray as Melmann's vision dimmed. He fought to remain conscious, furious that death had caught him so totally unprepared. He needed more time. Time to punish Scotty. Time to save Barbara.

The Chief of Staff's failing eyesight sought and found the face of the man he'd grown to hate. Scotty had risen from his chair and was standing statue-like on the opposite side of the desk. His left hand rested on the telephone, his right on the brown manila folder lying beside it.

"Help...me," Melmann moaned. "Please, Scotty...call...a code."

But Scotty made no move to lift the receiver and punch in the numbers that would have brought help. Instead, he picked up the folder and scanned the attached cover letter. When he looked up again, his face was rigid with anger.

"It's a pity you chose to follow this path," he said stonily. "A man as sick as you has no business antagonizing a fellow doctor, especially one who could possibly save your life."

Melmann's face contorted in one last spasm of pain and rage. He had no strength to lash out physically, but before the final darkness washed over him, he managed to pass judgment on Scotty.

"Murderer," he whispered. "Murderer!"

PART TWO

Was he devil or man? He was devil for aught they knew.

The Revenge
Alfred Lord Tennyson

Chapter Two

June 13th

Noon

.   Caroline Rhodes pulled off the Kennedy Expressway with a distinct sigh of relief. The drive from Rhineburg to Chicago had been a pleasant one until she'd hit I-90 where construction was once again underway. Roadwork had forced lane closures from Belvidere to Huntley, then again just west of Elgin. Congestion eased east of the city, and Caroline had accelerated to a respectable seventy miles per hour until a three-car pile up near Schaumberg brought cars on the Chicago-bound lanes to a screeching halt. After thirty minutes of stop-and-start driving, she'd finally arrived at the Des Plaines oasis only to find traffic crawling from there to the O'Hare Airport cutoff. Bracketed by a semi spouting diesel fumes, a gaudily painted tour bus, and a white stretch limo, she'd had plenty of time to ponder the reason for her trip as traffic crept towards the final booth on the tollway.

The email from Molly O'Neal had been carefully worded to avoid any details of the nurse manager's problem, although previous letters had mentioned a growing tension among the ER staff of Ascension Hospital. There was a hint of desperation in her plea that Caroline return to her old stomping grounds. Since Molly was not the sort to beg, Caroline's curiosity had been aroused, and she'd phoned her old friend soon after receiving the odd message.

"Thanks for calling," Molly said upon hearing Caroline's voice. "I hope this means you're coming home."

"I am home," Caroline replied. "I've lived in Rhineburg for almost a year now, and I like it here."

"Nonsense," Molly snorted. "I can't believe a woman like you, born and raised in the big city, would be satisfied with a hum-drum existence in some little backwoods town."

"Rhineburg is not a backwoods town," Caroline protested. "And I don't lead a hum-drum life. Actually, I've had more than my share of excitement lately."

Unaware of Caroline's role in the recent murders in Rhineburg, Molly remained unconvinced.

"But all your friends are here in Chicago."

"I've plenty of friends in Rhineburg, Molly. You just haven't met any of them."

Caroline could almost hear Molly shrug.

"Whatever you say, Cari. I've enough on my plate to worry about without adding you to the list. If you're content to while away your days in Farmland, USA, then so be it."

"You're mixing your metaphors."

Caroline wondered was wrong with Molly. Normally good-natured, it was unlike the woman to speak so sharply to a friend, especially to one who'd been like a sister to her. Her unexpected criticism was troubling, and Caroline gently but firmly told her so.

There was a brief silence on the other end of the line, then Molly replied, "I'm sorry, Cari. I've been under a lot of pressure lately, and I guess it's beginning to show. I didn't mean to snap at you."

"It's not the snapping I mind. What bothers me is the fact that you're obviously disturbed, and I don't know why."

"It's a complicated story."

"I'm used to complicated stories. Remember, I have kids."

Molly laughed. "We've always been there for each other, haven't we, Cari. I guess that's why I wrote to you. I figured if I asked politely, you might come galloping back to town and rescue me from this mess at the hospital."

"I'm a little old for galloping," Caroline retorted. "And I'm not quite sure from what mess you need rescuing. Still, I'm willing to do what I can if you'll explain the problem."

Molly hesitated. When she spoke again, her voice was subdued. "I'm losing staff. They're leaving the department in droves."

"Droves? You mean they're quitting en masse?"

"You could say that. Five nurses and a tech have moved to other hospitals since January, and two more people tendered their resignations this week. You'll know some of the names, Cari. They're all good workers, and I really can't afford to lose them."

"But why are they leaving? What in the world is going on at Ascension?"

"We have a new Director of Nursing, Angela Horowitz. She arrived in November, and she's a friend of Roger MacGuffy."

Caroline groaned.

"What happened to Olivia?"

"She retired at the end of last year, lucky dog. Olivia stayed long enough to show Angela the ropes, then she skedaddled down south for a well-earned rest in Florida. I hear she bought a house in the Keys where she spends her days lolling on the beach under a palm tree."

"Nice," Caroline commented. "Right now I could do with a few rays myself."

"We have sun in Chicago. We also have beaches, and lots and lots of water." Molly paused before plunging into what sounded like a prepared speech. "I only need you for a couple of months, Cari. Just until the new kids are broken in. They're not familiar with the routine, and they can't direct the paramedics yet. I simply don't have enough experienced staff to fill in for all the people going on vacation. And to top it all off, there's some construction work being done in the Emergency Room."

Caroline thought about it for a moment. Her shifts at St. Anne's were being cut to the minimum due to the summer holidays. With Bruck University shut down until August, there was less need for coverage in ER, the department where she'd worked since arriving in Rhineburg last autumn. And since the nursing students were out of the dorm, her job as housemother was also on hold. She could use the extra cash a full-time job would provide, and she'd enjoy the chance to visit with her daughters who lived in the Chicago area. All in all, Molly's request was coming exactly at the right time. There was only one thing bothering her, and that was something Molly had said.

"Hold on a minute, Molly. What's all this about 'new kids'? Are you telling me the hospital's hired new grads for the ER?"

"They come cheaper, Cari. The bottom line is money, and the pay rate for new nurses is much less than for experienced ones."

"That's wrong, and you know it. Your patients deserve to have nurses who know what they're doing."

"Tell that to the bigwigs who run this place. I agree with you, but I have no choice in the matter. I take the people they send me."

Caroline drew a deep breath to calm herself. "OK," she said at last. "Tell me about your current Director of Nursing. You said she was tight with Roger."

"Tighter than my mother's new girdle," Molly quipped. "She was Assistant DON at Bridgeview Community, the hospital Ascension acquired last year in that deal with Trovan HMO."

"Roger was Medical Director of Bridgeview's ER, wasn't he?"

"Yeah. He was brought over here to replace Dr. Simmons shortly after the deal was finalized. It was a step up the ladder for him. Ascension's ER is bigger and busier than the one he left."

"I don't remember the details of that acquisition. When did you say it happened?"

"About the same time Ed died. You weren't paying much

attention to hospital gossip back then."

How true, Caroline thought. Her husband's sudden death fourteen months before had thrown her into a state of depression that eventually led to a brief but necessary hospitalization. She'd gone back to work after her release from the psychiatric unit, but remained at Ascension only a few months before relocating to Rhineburg, the small Illinois town where her son and daughter-in-law lived.

"Roger was Director when I left AMC," Caroline recalled. "He could be a real charmer with patients and their families, but I never quite trusted him. There was something phony about the man."

"I've heard that a cobra's eyes are hypnotic," Molly replied cryptically. "Stare at it long enough, and you'll be lulled into letting down your guard. Then it will strike before you can defend yourself."

"You're saying Roger MacGuffy is a snake in the grass."

"He was manageable when Olivia was DON. She let the doctors know in no uncertain terms that nursing was an entity beyond their control. Angela Horowitz, on the other hand, bends over backward to meet their every need. She's especially mindful of Dr. MacGuffy, both in and out of the hospital."

"I take it Roger and Ms. Horowitz are an item."

"Roger was very active in promoting Angela for the DON position. They're careful about their relationship at work, but whatever Roger wants, Roger gets. Right now, Roger wants total control of the ER staff, nurses included. I'm fighting him every step of the way, but I'm not sure I can outlast the man. He runs to Angela with complaints about my management style, my scheduling of staff, even the dress code I've established in the ER. You name it, and he'll find something wrong with it."

"Sounds like he's trying to force you out. Does he think another nurse manager will bend to his will?"

Molly laughed grimly.

"Two nurses transferred here from Bridgeview's ER. They're very ambitious people, and both are friends of Roger MacGuffy."

"Are they undermining your authority?"

"What's left of my authority. Angela has been rewriting ER policy, adapting it to Roger's demands. She's gradually stripping me of any power I hold as nurse manager."

"Is she doing the same thing in other departments?" Caroline asked, aghast.

"Not yet," Molly conceded. "She's floating a trial balloon under the pretense that the ER staff has run amok under my leadership. She claims we're too independent, too privileged, too used to calling the shots. She wants us to knuckle under and be good little nurses."

"Regular Florence Nightingales."

"The doctor's handmaiden, to be seen but not heard."

"Sounds like you have real trouble on your hands."

"That's why I need your help. Do you think you could possibly come back to Ascension? Even for a few weeks?"

Caroline told her she'd have to clear it with her own boss at St. Anne's, but she thought the trip was possible.

"You don't know what this means to me, Cari. What I've told you is only the half of it. Have you got the strength to hear more?"

When Caroline hung up the phone ten minutes later, it was with a sense of incredulity. Molly's problems seemed overwhelming. She now knew why her friend so desperately needed her back in Chicago. She also knew why she couldn't refuse the plea.

The two women had been friends since childhood. They'd grown up on the same block in the old Kelvyn Park neighborhood of Chicago, going their separate ways only after high school when Caroline married Ed while Molly entered nursing school. It had been Molly who'd urged Caroline to give nursing a try after Ed was settled in his job as a firefighter, and Molly who'd coached her through exam after exam until she earned her license as a Registered Nurse. Afterwards, it seemed only natural for her to apply for a job at the same hospital where Molly worked. Starting out on a medical floor at Ascension, she'd transferred to ER a year later on the recommendation of her friend. She'd never regretted the move, even when Molly was named nurse manager of the ER and officially became her boss.

Molly was a career nurse, a woman who chose medicine over marriage and dedicated her every waking moment to the ER. In that way she and Caroline differed, but their friendship never faltered. Godmother to Caroline's son Martin, Molly was an unofficial member of the Rhodes family, loved by both Caroline and Ed.

When Ed died, Molly had done her best to help Caroline through her depression. Unfortunately, even her best friend could not ease the pain of Caroline's loss. It had taken a new friend, a white-haired professor of history at Rhineburg's Bruck University, to do that.

"And almost getting myself killed," muttered Caroline as she nosed the Jeep into a steady stream of traffic on Cumberland Avenue. The past winter had proven a turning point in her life, a time for healing and growth. She was a new person, a different woman from the one who had slunk out of Chicago licking her wounds only a few short months ago.*

"Or am I?" she asked herself as she drove north through the suburb of Park Ridge. She could have exited the expressway farther east at Harlem Avenue. Instead, she'd unconsciously avoided her old Chicago neighborhood by opting for a circuitous route to Ascension Medical Center in the nearby town of Niles.

The realization of what she'd done stung. Perhaps she wasn't as strong as she'd thought. Memories of Ed's death and her subsequent emotional breakdown were inexorably entwined with the house in Norwood Park. Seeing it again would be like plunging a knife into her own heart, opening wounds that had only recently healed.

But avoiding the house was a sign of weakness, a concession to the pain that had haunted her past. Did she have the courage to face the demons awaiting her on Marigold Street?

'Not today,' she thought as she zigzagged east to Waukegan Road. 'I'm not up to it today.'

Grimly, she wondered if she'd ever be up to it.

---

* See A DEADLY LITTLE CHRISTMAS

CHAPTER THREE

June 13th
5 P.M.

.   Caroline unpacked the last of her clothes and stowed them in a battered but serviceable dresser in the spare bedroom of her daughter's Evanston apartment. The middle child of the Rhodes clan, Krista taught art in a Chicago public high school but lived north of the city less than a stone's throw from the sandy shores of Lake Michigan. The suburb of Niles was only a few miles west of Evanston, and when Krista learned of her mother's plans to return to Ascension Medical Center, she'd invited her to share the second floor flat in the roomy old house on Oakton Avenue. Caroline gladly accepted the offer. The summer promised to be a hot one, but the proximity of the lake offered some relief from the heat, especially at night.

Krista had been using the spare bedroom as a studio, and there were still traces of paint on the rag rug covering the worn linoleum floor. Outside of that, no one would have guessed that the room had recently been crowded with the tools of an artist's trade. Trays of paint and chalk had been moved to shelves in the small walk-in pantry, and newly stretched canvases were deposited in neat rows behind the living room sofa. Krista's easel now stood in her own bedroom while her collection of art-related catalogs and books had been transplanted to a hallway closet. The room had been newly painted, and framed samples of Krista's pen-and-ink drawings hung in groupings on the cream colored walls. An old pottery wheel with bits of clay clinging to its base still sat in the corner farthest from the door, but it now served as a repository for a luxurious Dallas fern in a speckled ceramic pot.

"Ready for a cool drink?"

Krista stood in the doorway, a glass of lemonade in each hand. Taller than Caroline and already deeply tanned, the young woman had inherited Ed's blond hair, blue eyes, and witty sense of humor. Unlike her father, who considered a flat tire to be a major disaster, Caroline's eldest daughter was born with an innate pragmatism that reduced life's little difficulties to quite manageable levels. In Krista's opinion, no issue was so complex, no problem so overwhelming, that it couldn't be addressed calmly, quietly, and with a view to a practical solution. She simply couldn't fathom the meaning of the word impossible, and was genuinely puzzled by people who reacted to minor obstacles as if they were major catastrophes.

This trait stood Krista in good stead in her chosen profession. Aware of the unpredictability of both teenagers and school boards, the hijinks of neither group caught the young teacher off stride. She approached her students with the confident expectation that they would -- come hell or high water -- master the material she taught. She took the same approach when facing the school board, and to the surprise of older and more cynical teachers, she was as successful at getting her way with the administration as she was with teaching art to a roomful of hormone-driven youths.

Caroline was secretly amazed at her daughter's Kiplingesque ability to keep her head while all about her were losing theirs. It was a quality she greatly admired in Krista, and she had no doubt the girl would apply the same levelheaded approach to the problems at Ascension when apprised of the situation.

"Just what I needed," Caroline remarked as she and Krista clinked their icy glasses in a silent toast. "I can't believe I brought so much clothing with me. You'd think I was staying for a year rather than a couple of months."

Krista sank down on the bed, one eyebrow raised in mock

disbelief.

"Did you forget all the wonderful shops we have here in Evanston? I thought we'd spend next weekend shopping for some new summer duds, but it looks like you packed everything you own."

Caroline shrugged her shoulders. "I don't know what got into me. Actually, I could use a few things. Most of what I have is pretty old."

"Let's take a look," said Krista, jumping to her feet. "There's no time like the present, right?"

Caroline opened her mouth to object, but shut it just as quickly. It was futile to argue with Krista once she'd made up her mind to do something. Apparently all the items Caroline had so carefully placed in the drawers were about to be dragged out and examined.

"Oh, mother! You can't still be wearing this old thing!" Krista held up a faded blue tee shirt with a giant red letter 'C' plastered across the front.

"But I love my Cubs shirt," Caroline protested as Krista waved the tee in her face. "Your father bought me that when we won the division title."

"And do you remember how long ago that was? Mother, really!" Krista sighed and threw the offending piece of apparel on the bed. "We'll head over to Wrigley Field and get you a new souvenir shirt, OK? One that says, 'When Hell Freezes Over!'"

It was Caroline's turn to raise an eyebrow. "They'll do better this year," she sniffed, then added with a growl, "Don't you dare touch my Bears sweatshirt. I'll need that if the evenings get cool."

Krista rolled her eyes, but placed the beloved garment on top of the dresser and continued digging.

"This can stay. And so can these shorts. But this has gotta go," she muttered as she unfolded one piece of clothing after another, relegating some to the growing pile on the bed and replacing others in the dresser. After ten minutes of muffled comments and exasperated sighs, she finally closed the last drawer and turned to Caroline.

"A woman in your position should dress better," she said with a knowing nod.

Caroline threw up her hands. "And just what position am I in? I've got my uniforms for work, comfortable jeans for relaxing at home, and a couple of nice outfits for when I go out. I don't need any more clothes cluttering up my closet."

Krista took her mother by the arm and led her into the living room where she indicated with a swish of her hand that the sofa was available if Caroline chose to sit. She then picked up a folded newspaper from the end table and opened it to an inner page.

"Take a look at this," she said, handing Caroline the paper.

"Oh, good grief!" Caroline wailed as she scanned the neighborhood news section of her old community newspaper. In half inch headlines, the paper announced the return to Chicago of "Caroline Rhodes, The Woman Who Kicked Crime In The Pants". An article followed detailing the Christmas bombing at St. Anne's Hospital and the springtime murder of Rhineburg's postmistress, two cases in which Caroline had played a significant role.

"Who gave them this story?" Caroline asked in dismay. "How did they find out about...oh, no! Don't tell me." Like a neon sign blinking madly in the night, a name flashed through her brain. "Only one person would think I'd be pleased by this," she snarled, crumpling up the newspaper and throwing it on the floor. "It had to be..."

"Now, mom. She really thought..."

"...Kerry."

Caroline leaned back on the couch and closed her eyes. Krista attempted to plead her sister's case, but Caroline silenced her with an upraised hand.

"I know your sister is well-meaning," she said, rubbing her

temples with the fingertips of both hands. "But this time she's gone too far. What if this story gets back to Ascension? You think they're going to employ a nurse who has a habit of stumbling across dead bodies?"

"Now, mom…"

"If you 'now, mom' me one more time…" Caroline glared at her daughter, and for once, Krista held her peace. "You don't understand how loath hospitals are to associate themselves with bad publicity. I might have been viewed as a heroine in Rhineburg, but Ascension is another kettle of fish. They're very big business, and the last thing they want is a nurse with a reputation."

Krista waited for her mother to finish. Then, without a word, she picked up Caroline's empty glass, walked to the kitchen, and refilled it. When she returned, Caroline was standing by the open window glumly watching the next door neighbor cut his lawn. Krista glanced down at the man before speaking.

"Mr. Wilton mows his grass every single evening. He's obsessed with the way his yard looks and with keeping up appearances. As if anyone truly cared," she added. She moved to the sofa and sank down on the cushions with a sigh. "He's kind of like you, you know. Way too concerned with what other people think."

Caroline whirled around. "And what's that supposed to mean?" she demanded.

Her display of temper didn't faze Krista.

"You haven't contacted anyone in the old neighborhood since moving to Rhineburg. You've let all your good friends just slip away."

"I have not," retorted Caroline. "I've kept in touch with Molly."

"Not often enough, or you would have known what she was facing at the hospital. And what about Sharon and Janie? You three were best buddies, the Magnificent Moms of Marigold Street, back when we were kids. How come you haven't written to either of them in almost a year?"

"I sent them each a Christmas card."

"Big deal!" sputtered Krista. "A lifetime of friendship deserves more than a measly holiday greeting."

Anger blazed in Caroline's eyes. "If you recall, I was a little busy this past Christmas dealing with a murderer. Just ask Kerry. It's obvious from the newspaper article that she remembers all the details."

"Kerry wasn't to blame for that story, mom. She stopped by Sharon's place to say hello and..."

"Kerry saw Sharon?" Caroline was taken aback. She'd no idea her youngest had gone anywhere near their old home since Ed's funeral.

"We've both visited Sharon. And Janie, also. Kerry talks with the two of them more often than I, but it's something she needs to do. She's fortunate in that she's never been self-conscious about expressing her feelings. I take after you, though. I'm more reserved emotionally."

This last bit of news left Caroline totally confused. She sunk into a chair opposite her daughter and shook her head.

"I thought we'd cleared this all up when you and Kerry came to Rhineburg for Christmas. Apparently I was wrong."

"We made a good start," Krista said with a shrug. "But nobody heals that fast. You haven't healed completely, or you wouldn't be so upset over that article. I don't think you're worried about Ascension's reaction to your success as a sleuth. I think you're afraid they'll find out about your nervous breakdown."

Their eyes met and held. Krista, the ever-practical child, had grown into a woman who understood her mother's imperfections and had a plan to overcome them. Caroline melted under her daughter's steady gaze.

"I couldn't say no to Molly, but yes, I have been nervous about returning to Ascension. It's true I went back to the ER after my hospitalization, but I never told any of the other nurses why I'd been off the job for so long."

"You didn't think your coworkers would understand?"

"I was more concerned with what the administration would think if they found out I'd been confined to a psychiatric unit," Caroline confessed. "They tend to look twice at crazy nurses."

"You weren't crazy, mom. You were depressed."

"It's the same thing in some people's eyes, Krista. I couldn't afford to take that chance."

"And you were afraid Sharon and Janie would react in the same way."

"I wasn't thinking clearly when I left Chicago," admitted Caroline. "Carl helped me pull my head together, but I've never been comfortable explaining my situation to former friends."

"Carl Atwater is an old dear," said Krista, veering off track at the mention of the septuagenarian professor who'd befriended her mother soon after her arrival in Rhineburg.

Caroline had met the elderly professor of history through her son Martin, a PhD candidate at Rhineburg's Bruck University, and Martin's wife Nikki. Carl had lured her into a scheme to unmask a murderer, and in the process had saved not only her life, but also her sanity. She owed him a debt she could never fully repay.

"Nikki wrote that she and Martin are spending the summer in West Virginia with the Professor."

"That's right, Krista. They're doing research for a history of early twentieth century mining towns. Carl's past books have sold well, and I'm sure this one will prove equally successful."

"Hmmp." Krista dismissed the Professor's adventures with a grunt. "Let's get back to the subject of Sharon and Janie. Are you going to visit them?"

"While I'm in town? Of course I will." Caroline fidgeted with the hem of her skirt. "After I'm settled at the hospital, that is."

Krista rolled her eyes.

"Going to put it off until August, are you?"

"Look, Krista..."

"No, mom. *You* look." Krista leaned forward and reached for her mother's hand. "A long time ago you taught me that the only way to get through life was to face up to it. You told me never to make excuses for myself, and now I'm telling you the same thing. What happened, happened. It's over and done with, and none of your real friends are going to think less of you because you had difficulty dealing with dad's death. Just because you could handle every other problem you came up against..."

"Superwoman," Caroline mumbled.

"Superwoman?" A frown creased Krista's forehead. "What's that all about?"

"It's just something Carl once mentioned during a conversation. He told me I was a natural-born fixer, always around to clean up somebody else's mess. Your father's death was something I couldn't fix, and it was disappointment in myself that induced the depression."

"I see," said Krista, treading more carefully now. "Nothing stops Superwoman in her quest to save the world."

"Something like that. I guess I felt guilty because there wasn't a thing I could do to help Ed after the accident. There I was, an ER nurse used to dealing with trauma cases, and my own husband dies before he can even reach the hospital. I felt like I failed him. And all of you children, too."

"Oh, mom, don't say that! We don't blame you for dad's death."

"I know that, dear. I'm only telling you how I felt back then."

Caroline stood up and walked to the window overlooking the Wiltons' front yard. Krista's elderly neighbor had finished with his lawn and was now trimming the hedges between the two buildings. Sweat darkened the old man's shirt and dribbled down the back of his neck. Strands of thinning gray hair were plastered to his beet-red forehead.

"That man's going to have a heart attack one of these days," Caroline commented. "He should know better than to work outside in this kind of heat."

"I imagine he'll drop dead with his hedge clippers in one hand and his pruning saw in the other. At least the funeral procession will have something to admire when they pass by his house."

Caroline turned and smiled at her daughter. "Keeping up appearances can exact a heavy toll. It's really not worth it, is it?"

"Doesn't make sense to me," Krista replied lightly. "What does make sense is a trip into town for dinner. I don't know about you, but I'm starving."

"I could go for a nice plate of pasta and a glass of wine. How about that little restaurant over by the railroad tracks?"

"Tony's? I absolutely adore that place. I'll give them a ring and make a reservation."

"While you do that, I'll go and change into something more comfortable. Maybe we could take a walk down by the lake after dinner."

"Sounds like a plan." Krista rose and headed for the kitchen. "Now don't go getting glamorous on me, mom. Shorts are perfectly acceptable at Tony's."

Caroline stood watching as her daughter dialed the phone. Krista had grown into a confident young woman with unlimited potential in her field, and Caroline was justifiably proud of her. The only thing that seemed to be lacking in the girl's life was romance.

There's plenty of time for that, Caroline told herself as she headed for the bedroom. Krista had been out of school only two years.

Still, she wondered if Krista would ever find Mr. Right. She'd dated a lot of different fellows in college, but most of them were put off by Krista's strong will and independent ways. Krista brooked no nonsense from her boyfriends, expecting them to be as straightforward as she was. Few men lived up to her expectations, and boyfriends fell by the wayside like dandelion puffs on a windy day. As far as Caroline knew, Krista was dating no one at the moment.

Well, that's another thing I can't fix, she mused.

Much the same could be said for Molly's predicament. Caroline's return to Ascension would have an impact on the staffing problem in ER, but one nurse could only work so many hours. As for her friend's quarrel with Roger MacGuffy, that was another matter altogether. Caroline could support Molly's efforts to keep nursing an independent entity in the ER. Still, she had no power to resolve what appeared to be an increasingly personal conflict between the Medical Director and the department's nurse manager.

Caroline pondered the situation as she changed into khaki shorts, a white tank top, and a long sleeved blue denim shirt. She slid her feet into soft leather sandals and buckled the straps, then swiped a comb through her short brown hair. She was hanging her traveling clothes in the closet when Krista appeared in the doorway.

"Are you ready for some suburban style fun before you start work tomorrow?" Krista quipped.

"I sure am," Caroline replied, then added darkly, "God only knows what I'll be walking into at Ascension. Going back to that ER could be one of the worst decisions I've made lately."

"Oh, mom!" Krista laughed. "You worry too much. You're going to have a wonderful summer. Just wait and see."

For some reason, Caroline doubted it.

CHAPTER FOUR

June 14th
6:30 A.M.

.   Dr. Roger McGuffy brushed a speck of dust from the lapel of his lab coat before stepping back to examine himself in the office mirror. What he saw pleased him, and he allowed a brief smile to cross his face before his naturally critical nature resurfaced. Turning, he gazed at his profile pensively.

While his body was running to fat, from the neck up Roger considered himself handsome. An expensive cut had tamed his unruly curls into a raven cap that barely scraped the collar of his immaculate white shirt. Silvery wisps highlighted his temples, the contrast lending a certain dignity to his appearance that he cultivated through surreptitious visits to a colorist. His salt and pepper eyebrows needed no such touch-ups. Thick and natural, they accented a lean face made angular by high cheekbones and a hawkish nose and bronzed beneath the tanning lamps of an exclusive North Shore health club.

The problem with Roger was his stomach. Wine, rich food, and a lack of exercise had taken a toll on his once trim physique. A lab coat hid his increasing paunch when he was at work, but one couldn't wear a lab coat while golfing at the country club. Roger knew he'd have to bite the bullet and go on a diet. The extra weight was affecting his confidence, not to mention his heart.

He drew a deep breath and sucked in his gut. Checking the mirror out of the corner of one eye, he watched his chest expand as his belly retracted to meet his belt. Perhaps liposuction was the way to go, or perhaps…

"Dr. MacGuffy?"

Caught off guard, Roger exhaled so quickly that his throat closed in a spasm. He doubled over, choking on his own breath.

"Doctor!"

Erlinda Torres ran into the room and began beating on Roger's back with the palm of her hand. He pushed her away furiously.

"Stop!" he gasped between coughs. "I'm all right!"

The spasm subsided. Roger sank into a chair and ran a hand over his face. His cheeks burned, and his skin felt clammy to the touch.

"Get me some water. Now!"

The nurse ran from the room, returning moments later with a large paper cup filled with ice water. Roger snatched it from her hands.

"That's better," he said after downing half of the frigid liquid. The water had revived him, and he sipped the rest slowly as the worried nurse watched.

Those few extra seconds gave him time to compose himself. When he felt totally in control, he crushed the empty cup and handed it to the nurse, then stood up, rising to his full height.

"Don't you know you're supposed to knock before entering my office?"

The words were spoken with such vehemence that Erlinda was taken aback.

"But your door...it was open," she stuttered. "I saw you looking in the mirror, and I thought..."

"You thought what? You thought you could come barging in here and startle me half to death?"

"I didn't mean to startle you." Confused, Erlinda retreated to the doorway. "I thought you'd want to know. About the pipes, I mean. It looks wrong, but I'm not sure..."

Roger threw up his hands in disgust. "Dammit, woman! Spit it out."

Erlinda's eyes widened. She'd never expected to hear a doctor swear at a nurse. It hurt more than offended her.

"Those construction people made a mistake," she murmured unhappily. "They put the pipes too close to each other."

"What you talking about?" Roger growled, taking a step towards the girl. "What pipes?"

"The pipes in the new ER. The ones for the oxygen." The young nurse's voice quivered. She was seeing a side of Dr. MacGuffy she hadn't known existed, and it frightened her. "If you don't believe me, go see for yourself!"

Erlinda fled, leaving Roger in a state of fury. What the hell had gone wrong now? The Emergency Room renovations were already behind schedule due to a series of screw-ups with the blueprints. If it turned out another mistake had been made, someone's head would surely roll.

Roger mentally examined the possible list of victims. The architect and the construction company were covered by iron-clad contracts, so they had nothing to fear. Equally well protected was Ascension's Vice-President of Development, a twenty-year employee of the hospital and a man with more connections than the telephone company. One would be a fool to think he'd lose his job over a misplaced pipe.

Next in line was Ascension's Superintendent of Buildings and Grounds. Jerry Sands had been around for fifteen years and reported directly to the VP of Development. His quick thinking and even quicker tongue had saved him in previous crises. It was useless to think he'd take a fall this time.

That left only two people to take the blame.

The first was Roger himself.

As Director of Emergency Medicine, it had been his responsibility to oversee the medical end of the renovations. It was a duty he hadn't minded in the beginning. But once the improvements were decided on, Roger grew bored with the planning process and began absenting himself from the weekly meetings with the architect, content to let Molly O'Neal attend the sessions in his stead.

"Our precious Miss O'Neal."

A grin spread over Roger's face. Molly was the last person on his list, the low man on the don't-blame-me totem pole. She'd gone to every single meeting, checked out every single blueprint, and annoyed him no end with her suggestions for changes. If there'd been a mistake, the ER's nurse manager should have caught it.

Pleased with the chance to discredit her in the eyes of the administration, Roger set off to examine the construction site. His mood had lightened considerably, and his thoughts wandered easily from Molly to the other women in his life.

Angela Horowitz was his most current conquest. Angela was smart, savvy, and very good in bed. Her ambitions rivaled his own, and she'd proven herself a valuable ally in his bid to control the ER.

Then there was Michelle Devine, the cute little tech with sparkling brown eyes and hair the color of coal. The divine Miss Devine made no bones about her desire to marry a doctor. Roger strung her along because she knew how to please a man.

He also had his eye on Susan Kane, a newcomer to the department. Having abandoned the uncooperative Patrice Woodson, Roger had moved Susan to the top of his pursuit list. So far his charm had failed to dent her armor, but he would not be denied twice. He was a determined man, and Susan was a divorced woman. He figured it was only a matter of time before she gave in.

Life is sweet, he thought as he entered the construction area. Very sweet indeed.

CHAPTER FIVE

June 14th
6:45 A.M.

Susan Kane gripped the upper rim of the steering wheel with both hands and rested her forehead on the cool surface of the air bag lock. Her eyes burned from lack of sleep, and the muscles in her neck sent shock waves of pain coursing through her shoulders as they stretched to accommodate her awkward position. Susan had had a bad night. If all went as expected, the day would be no better.

"Why did I ever think I could do this?" she wondered aloud. "I should have resigned as soon as I saw what I was up against."

She wanted to cry, wanted desperately to scream and shout and stamp her foot. It wasn't fair. It wasn't fair at all. She'd worked hard to regain her skills, studying her nursing books and asking questions of her instructors until she was sure she understood the new methods addressed in the refresher course. It hadn't been easy working full time at the grocery store and going to school at night, but she'd managed to get it done, finishing first in her class just like back in nursing school.

But I was nineteen then, she thought bitterly. I was young, and ready to conquer the world.

Today she felt powerless to conquer anything more demanding than a checkout line at First Foods. Of course Gary would be thrilled if she washed out at the hospital. He'd go home to his twenty-year-old bride and tell her what a failure wife number one was. Why, the woman couldn't even hold down a decent paying job! It wouldn't be the first time he criticized her, and it certainly wouldn't be the last.

But what did it matter what Gary thought or said? He was out of her life, and she was better off for it. Little Gina Morelli, a blessing in blue jeans and a tank top, had waltzed into their lives exactly one year ago today. It took her only six weeks to make her mark on Gary. When he walked out on Susan, she felt nothing but relief. She was finally done being abused by that jerk.

She squeezed back a tear, angry with herself for wallowing in unpleasant memories. She had enough problems without thinking of her ex, problems that couldn't be banished by will power alone. If she'd only known he'd be working here...

"Hey! Wake up in there!"

Susan snapped to attention at the sound of knuckles rapping on the car window. She turned jerkily to stare at the intruder, then let out her breath as she recognized Michelle Devine's impish face grinning down at her.

"Michelle, you startled me." Susan pushed open the door and swung her feet to the pavement. She fumbled momentarily with her purse, avoiding Michelle's inquiring eyes as she added, "I must have dozed off for a minute. Guess I'm more tired than I thought."

"Hot date last night?"

Susan laughed shakily. "Don't I wish! No, I just didn't sleep well." She locked the car and slipped the keys into the cargo pocket of her scrub pants, then switched the conversation to a safer subject. "Do you know who the docs are today?"

"Aleene Del Greco and Dr. MacGuffy."

Susan's heart sank.

"Roger's working the room?" She could hear the desperation in her voice, and hurried to cover her mistake. "I didn't think the Director would find time for patients what with all his other duties."

Michelle's eyes narrowed. "I've noticed you're not very

comfortable around Dr. MacGuffy. Has he done something to make you dislike him?"

"I hardly know the man," Susan protested. "After all, I only started at Ascension a couple of weeks ago."

"That's right, you haven't been here long. Funny, then, that you're already on a first name basis with our boss."

The girl made it sound like an accusation. Susan felt trapped, but responded as casually as possible, "Oh, come on. All the nurses call Roger by his first name. I was just trying to fit in."

Michelle hesitated, then said begrudgingly, "I guess that's true. We are kind of a family around here."

"And a nice family at that. I feel quite at home in this ER."

What a lie, she told herself. She'd actually come to hate the place. Each day it became harder to even walk through the doors.

Afraid the other woman might read her thoughts, Susan stooped down to survey her face in the car's side mirror.

"My goodness. I look like a total wreck this morning."

Michelle shrugged her delicate shoulders. "Does it matter how you look? You're only going to work."

Susan glanced up sharply. The ER tech had turned away and was walking towards the hospital entrance. Her shapely little butt swayed in her tight fitting white jeans, and her long gleaming hair sparkled in the sunlight.

"Obviously it matters to you," Susan muttered. "No baggy blue scrubs to hide Miss Devine's fine figure."

She ran her fingers through her own auburn curls as she hurried across the parking lot. Unlike Michelle, she needed a rinse to keep the gray at bay and daily workouts to ward off the extra pounds that had magically appeared after her thirty-fifth birthday. Two years of nightly visits to the YMCA had turned fat into muscle, but she was still no match for the svelte ER tech.

The realization that she was mentally comparing herself to the twenty-something Michelle only added to Susan's gloom. She didn't like the girl, hadn't liked her since she first saw her flirting with Dr. MacGuffy. It was none of Susan's business, of course. Michelle could flirt with anyone she liked. But it reminded Susan of another time, another place, and that was what made her uncomfortable.

At least she wouldn't have to work with the girl today. Michelle was wearing street clothes, a sign she was subbing as unit receptionist. Unlike the techs in their scrubs, URs were allowed to wear whatever they wanted on the job. While a hospital dress code existed, the receptionists rarely paid more than lip service to the rules. Michelle was the worst of the bunch. She wore skin-tight jeans and see-through blouses to work, much to the displeasure of their boss, Molly O'Neal. Molly wanted to put the URs in uniform, but the receptionists were fighting her tooth and nail.

For Molly, it was a losing battle. Roger MacGuffy supported the URs, and Susan, better than anyone else, understood why.

CHAPTER SIX

June 14th
6:50 A.M.

.   Molly O'Neal slammed down the phone and pounded her fist on the desk. The sound of her anger reverberated across the crowded room, bouncing off the thin walls separating her office from the triage area and echoing out into the hallway. She was aware that Vic Warner, the day shift nurse assigned to triage, had overheard at least part of the heated discussion between herself and Roger MacGuffy, but frankly, she didn't care. Vic was Roger's man, and he'd probably arrived early at his post at the Director's suggestion. Roger would want a report on Molly's reaction to his phone call, and who better to spy on her but his old buddy, the gossip mongering Mr. Warner? At least he hadn't heard all of the conversation. She'd seen him lingering in the hallway, and pushed the door closed before the argument with Dr. MacGuffy got totally out of hand.

"I'm not a complete fool," she muttered in disgust.

It had been a mistake to lose her temper with Roger, but this time the Medical Director had pushed her too far. Blaming her for the construction errors was like blaming Mother Theresa for the legions of poor sick people in India. After all, Molly had a department to run. She couldn't spend every minute of her day looking over the shoulder of some dim-witted architect. The firm of Dawkins, Olowski, and Grasso had been hired to draw up the plans for the ER renovations. If their junior partner couldn't understand the need for a twelve-inch gap between the oxygen and the suction outlets, the company didn't deserve the huge contract it had been awarded.

She'd pointed out the problem the last time they'd reviewed the blueprints. In words of one syllable she explained how large the suction canisters were, and how, once fitted to the walls, they would overlap the oxygen ports, rendering those outlets useless. The distance between the two, now only three inches, had to be increased.

The architect had smiled, nodded, and promised to make the necessary changes, but of course he hadn't. Over the weekend the pipefitters had begun working in the patient cubicles using the defective blueprints as their guide. The job was half completed when a sharp-eyed night nurse spotted the blunder while taking a midnight tour of the deserted site. She'd told Roger what she'd seen, and he'd immediately checked out her story. It hadn't taken him long to decide who was at fault. Molly barely had her foot in the hospital door when Dr. MacGuffy called and raked her over the coals.

Now, alone in her office, Molly snatched up a piece of paper and began writing a letter of resignation. Sick of the constant confrontations with the egotistical Medical Director, she gave a vivid account of their most recent arguments, then listed the reasons she'd opposed Roger's ideas. She was penning a second page when a knock on the door jolted her back to the present. She swept the papers into a desk drawer and snapped, "Come in!"

The door edged open and Caroline glanced into the room.

"Hope I'm not disturbing you. Just thought I'd check in before I go upstairs to fill out the paperwork."

The wrinkles in Molly's brow disappeared when she spied her old friend in the doorway. She rose and walked over to embrace her.

"I'm so glad you're here." The nurse manager backed off and gave Caroline the once over. "Lordy, you're looking fit. Must be all that clean air and good country living."

"Pfhh! I've gained weight, and you know it."

Molly shrugged. "Haven't we all? It's called aging, Caroline.

We're thickening like old oak trees."

"I'm not sure I like the comparison," Caroline retorted. "I prefer the term 'maturing' to 'aging'. It's less damaging to my ego."

"Let's not quibble over semantics. Anyway you look at it, we're not kids any more."

"No, we're not. But we aren't ancient relics either. I, at least, have a few good years left in me."

"Then you're doing better than I am," Molly laughed, her voice trembling slightly. "Ten minutes ago Dr. MacGuffy called me an old fossil. I don't think he meant it as a compliment," she added.

"An old fossil? What's his problem?"

"Outside of the fact that he's a megalomaniac, Roger has no problems." Molly waved Caroline to a chair and went to sit behind her desk. "Perhaps I should amend that statement. Roger has *one* problem. Me."

Caroline studied Molly as she described the Medical Director's early morning phone call. Her friend had visibly aged in the months since Caroline's departure from Ascension, and the change was shocking. Molly's green eyes lacked their previous sparkle, dark smudges beneath the lower lids telling a story of sleepless nights and worrisome days. Once her pride and glory, her hallmark halo of red-orange hair had been cropped short and shaped for minimum care. Invaded by dull strands of gray, it barely edged her forehead and ears where before it had curled in fiery waves down to her shoulders.

The change was even more noticeable when one looked closer. Worry lines now streaked Molly's brow, and her skin bore a sallow unhealthy sheen. She'd lost weight, a considerable amount of weight, and it showed in the hollows of her cheeks and neck. Her uniform blouse hung loosely, no longer accentuating the curve of her breasts, and her white slacks looked two sizes too large. Caroline tried to conceal her dismay as she listened to Molly's tale of woe.

"Sounds like the good doctor is covering his rear," she said when Molly at last fell silent. "You say he hasn't attended many meetings with the architect."

"He's left those to me." Molly leaned an elbow on the desk and massaged her forehead with one hand. "I try my best, Cari. I really do. But I can't catch every mistake that's made."

"There have been others?"

Molly nodded. "Too many to enumerate. Some I found on the blueprints. Others were discovered only after the contractors started working. The renovations are now well behind schedule."

Caroline shifted in her chair. "Molly, there must be someone else in this hospital who knows how to read blueprints. Can't you ask for help?"

Molly looked at her wearily. "There are others who can read blueprints, but no one else who understands what's needed in an ER. Roger complains to Angela Horowitz if I ask him to attend a meeting. He says I'm pulling him away from his patients for no good reason." She glanced at the telephone resting on her desk. "I get two to three calls a day from that woman. It's always about Roger," she said, then added grimly, "Everything's about Roger."

It sounded to Caroline like Angela was conducting a campaign of harassment. The question was why?

"As long as we're talking about the construction, I was wondering why you didn't mention it in your phone calls. Afraid I'd back down on the deal if I found out about the working conditions around here?"

"Sorry, Cari," Molly said with a weak smile. "I thought I told you we were having a little work done on the ER."

"This is not 'a little work'. This is a tear-down-to-the-bare-walls, build-it-back-up-from-scratch job. I took a tour of the temporary ER yesterday and..."

"You were here yesterday?"

"I dropped in on my way to Krista's place. Thought I'd say hello to some of the old gang. Chan Daley was on duty, and when he heard I was coming back to work, he insisted on giving me my employee physical. He saved me some time today."

"So you saw the department."

Caroline made a face. "It's pretty cramped in there. Looks like they just tore out some walls and combined old office space with portions of the Out-Patient Department."

"That's exactly what they did," Molly said, nodding. "Out-Patients isn't any happier than we are. They lost four examining rooms and part of their lobby."

"It's a strange set-up with that corridor dividing the ER."

The temporary department was a distorted H-shaped area. Curtained off cubicles for patients filled the vertical legs of the H, called wings by the staff. The east wing extended farther south than the west and held more patients than its counterpart. The crossbar of the H was a corridor connecting the east wing to the west one. Storage and utility rooms occupied the area north of the corridor between the wings. The main desk was situated in the east wing just north of the corridor. A smaller desk for the doctors stood behind it. The telemetry radio, used to maintain contact with in-coming ambulances, sat on a shelf across from the main desk flanked by policy manuals and miscellaneous small equipment. The ER lobby and waiting room lay beyond the west wing, sealed off from the patient area by a thin plasterboard wall.

The crossbar corridor extended beyond the east wing and ended in a maze of hallways that led to the main hospital on the north, the triage area, Molly's office, and the lobby and waiting room on the south, and offices for the Medical Director and the Emergency Medical Services coordinator on the east.

Beyond the Medical Director's office stood two doors. The first opened onto a makeshift hallway lined with unpainted plasterboard. Approximately eight feet in length and four feet wide, the hallway ended at yet another door, this one opening into the old ER construction area.

The second door opened onto a staircase that wound its way up to the fifth floor of the hospital. Beneath the first level of stairs stood a large walk-in closet containing plaster casting material, canes, crutches, and knee braces, and a variety of metal splints and elastic bandages.

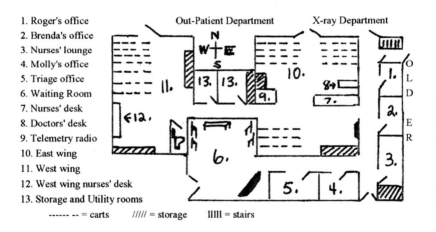

1. Roger's office
2. Brenda's office
3. Nurses' lounge
4. Molly's office
5. Triage office
6. Waiting Room
7. Nurses' desk
8. Doctors' desk
9. Telemetry radio
10. East wing
11. West wing
12. West wing nurses' desk
13. Storage and Utility rooms

------ -- = carts   ///// = storage   lllll = stairs

"The layout is poor," agreed Molly. "It was the best they could do, though, under the circumstances. We'll be in the temporary ER at least a year, probably longer."

"A frustrating situation." Caroline glanced at her watch, then bounded to her feet. "Oh, no! It's after seven already. I was due at Human Resources five minutes ago."

"And I was due at the desk five minutes ago." Molly rose and accompanied Caroline to the door. "Check back with me when you're done with all the paperwork. We'll go over the schedule and plug in your shifts. One other thing, Cari," she added, halting outside the office, "I want to say how grateful I am you've returned to Ascension. You're a real life saver."

Molly's voice quavered, and for a moment Caroline thought her friend was going to break down. They needed to get away, get out of the hospital and go to some safe, quiet place where Molly could feel free to talk, cry, get it all out of her system. Caroline recognized the symptoms. The nurse manager was close to a nervous breakdown.

"I wouldn't go that far," she said, giving Molly a hug. "Let's just say I'm a sucker for a hard luck story. Now, off to work with you." She pointed towards the ER, and Molly dutifully saluted, then turned on her heel and strode up the corridor.

"See you later in the Room," she called over her shoulder.

The Room, with a capital R. An innocent synonym for a far from innocent place, a term that belied the harsh realities of the department and provided instead a false but soothing sense of security to those who sought help there. People feared ERs, but no one feared a Room. "Step into my parlor," said the spider to the fly.

To the ER staff, the Room meant more than their physical surroundings. It was a password of sorts, a means of communicating information. When someone asked, "How's the Room?" what they really meant was, "How busy are we today? How sick are the patients?" Rooms could be good or bad, dead or messy, but never, ever quiet. It was considered bad luck to label a Room quiet, even when there was a paucity of patients. Many a day had gone right down the drain after a nurse had uttered that unfortunate word.

Ascension's Room was seldom dead, and today was no exception. A dozen people sat in the waiting room with another two currently being triaged by Vic Warner. He appeared absorbed in his work, but he got up and came to the door when he saw Caroline.

"Can I help you?"

"No," she said, throwing a halfhearted smile in the male nurse's direction. "I was just thinking what a busy hospital this is."

She turned with a wave of her hand and walked rapidly towards the main part of the hospital. Her thoughts still on Molly, her mind didn't register the look of pure contempt in Vic's eyes.

CHAPTER SEVEN

June 14th
7:30 A.M.

. Perspiring freely, Brenda Berlein shrugged off her linen jacket and draped it over the back of her chair. The tiny EMS office was so crowded with filing cabinets, cardboard cartons, and miscellaneous equipment that the air conditioning had little effect on the stuffy atmosphere of the room. Earlier in the month, Brenda had requisitioned a fan from maintenance, but the antique model they'd provided rattled in protest when asked to perform above anything but the lowest speed. Perched on one of the cabinets, it circulated more dust than air, and the Emergency Medical Service coordinator rarely bothered to use it.

This morning was different. Despite its high-pitched whine and constant clanking, the fan was switched to high. Brenda was prepared to put up with the noise if it meant an end to the fishy aroma permeating the room. The pungent odor of rotting flesh had assaulted her nose when she'd unlocked the office at seven o'clock. The source of the smell was evident once she'd recovered from her initial shock. A dead catfish lay decaying on her desk, its glassy eyeballs fixed and staring directly at her as she stood in the doorway.

She'd promptly shut and locked the door again. A security guard was stationed in the ER lobby, and after a brief but explicit conversation with Brenda, he radioed his supervisor for instructions. Minutes later the chief of the security department arrived on the scene with two members of the housekeeping staff in tow. The fish was bagged and removed, the desk wiped clean of scales, and the office sprayed with disinfectant. The security chief filed a report that Brenda dutifully signed, knowing, when all was said and done, that nothing would ever come of it.

Brenda was pretty sure she knew who had placed the fish on her desk. What she wasn't sure of was how the culprit had broken into the room. Outside of herself and Molly O'Neal, the only people with keys to the office were members of the security department. It was hard to believe one of them would risk their job over a childish prank. Still, the possibility had to be explored.

She was about to dial the security chief when her eye was drawn to a long, white envelope lying in her in-box. It bore the signature of Angela Horowitz, the hospital's Director of Nursing, and had evidently been delivered late Friday. Curious as to its contents, Brenda replaced the receiver and reached for her letter opener.

The envelope contained a single sheet memo drafted by the DON and dated Friday, June 11th. The gist of the memo was that paramedics working in the ER would no longer be allowed to triage patients, start IV's, or perform any other duties not normally reserved for unlicensed ER technicians. A formal policy up-date on the matter was to follow by the end of the week.

Brenda tossed the message down in disgust. She'd known Angela would launch a retaliatory strike after their meeting Friday afternoon, but she hadn't guessed the woman would move so swiftly. She wondered if Molly had seen the memo. Grabbing up the phone, she dialed the main ER extension. The charge nurse picked up on the second ring.

"Mavis? It's Brenda. Is Molly there?"

"She's in a meeting with Roger and the architect. There's been another screw-up with the construction work."

"Not again. What happened this time?"

Mavis' southern drawl deepened as she gleefully reported the latest crisis and Dr. MacGuffy' reaction to it.

"I'll tell you, honey, he looked like a Sunday mornin' drunk when he came stompin' into the Room this morning. Why, I was ready to call Security and slap him in leather restraints, he was carryin' on so. Like a man possessed, he was."

"And looking for someone to blame, I'll bet."

"Well, of course," Mavis harrumphed. "You ain't gonna' see him takin' responsibility for anything that goes wrong. His main delight in life is slappin' people down."

"Be careful what you say, Mavis," Brenda warned. "Roger has friends in the department."

"You think I don't know that? Both of 'em are workin' today, and they're flutterin' around the desk like two pickled butterflies, just waitin' to hear what happened in that meeting." Mavis lowered her voice. "Don't you worry, honey. If the good doctor tries any funny stuff with me, I'll sic the NAACP on him."

Brenda laughed. "I bet you would, Mavis. When you see your boss, tell her I called. I'm going up to Angela's office, but I shouldn't be there long."

"Bearding the lioness in her den? Hope you've got your armor on. I hear she's in a lousy mood today."

"And how would you know?"

"Oh, I've got my sources," Mavis replied loftily. "Roger ain't the only one around here with spies."

Brenda shook her head as she hung up the phone. Mavis never ceased to amaze her. Married to a banker, the woman held a Master's degree in nursing, was certified in every ER specialty, and ran a computer consulting service on the side. She taught literacy classes to immigrants on Saturday mornings, and volunteered one day a week at an inner-city free clinic. Despite all this, she preferred to play the role of a good old girl from the South when at work.

Brenda had run into Mavis at a Chicago Symphony Orchestra charity event the previous year. The charge nurse was there with her husband, a gray-haired man with the classical features of a Nairobi prince. Mavis had been dressed in a flowing white caftan with pearls scattered across the neckline and down the long sleeves. Diamonds glittered on her brown fingers and earlobes, and her husky voice, so well known to Brenda, held not a trace of an accent as she discussed the expertise of the orchestra's first violinist with the senior partner of a downtown law firm.

When Brenda cornered her in the ER the next day, Mavis shrugged off the disparity between her at-work and off-duty personalities.

"St. Paul once wrote, 'Be all things to all men'." She paused, then added with a twinkle in her eye, "And my mama used to say, 'It's easier to catch a fly with honey than with vinegar'."

Brenda recalled those words of wisdom as she entered the elevator and pushed the button for the first floor. Perhaps she should go easy with Angela, try to reason with her on this latest issue. It wouldn't help to aggravate the woman since she seemed to be holding all the cards.

She waited ten minutes in the outer office before being ushered into the DON's inner sanctum by an elderly secretary with worried eyes. The Director of Nursing's welcome was less than warm.

"I expect you're here about my memo," Miss Horowitz said frostily as she motioned Brenda to a chair. "I thought it was clear both in content and meaning."

Brenda pushed a lock of brown hair behind her ear, then adjusted her glasses, nudging them higher on her nose with one slim finger. Petite to the point of tiny, she always felt like a midget in Angela's presence. The other woman was twice her size and wore boxy suits with padding that accentuated her already broad shoulders.

Angela was everything that Brenda wasn't. Well heeled and well connected, she'd spent her nursing career gathering degrees and climbing the corporate ladder. No bedside nursing for Miss Horowitz; the down-and-dirty side of medicine was clearly beneath a person of her stature. Real nurses hated the woman, and Brenda understood why.

"I wondered why you felt it necessary to change the policy," the EMS Coordinator said with a forced smile. "We've been utilizing the skills of paramedics for years in the ER, and no one's had a problem with it up to now."

"Our lawyers might disagree with you on that." Angela's glance shifted impatiently to her jeweled watch. Brenda hurried on.

"I realize you're busy, but this will only take a few minutes to straighten out. As Emergency Medical Services coordinator, it's my job to work with the various fire departments servicing this area to assure that the paramedics who bring patients to this hospital are adequately prepared to deal with any medical problem they encounter. I also oversee the ER nurses who are certified to give orders to paramedics in the field."

"I'm aware of your duties, Miss Borlin," Angela said with a bored sigh. "Please get to the point."

"It's *Berlein. Mrs.* Berlein," Brenda replied crisply. My God, she thought. She doesn't even know my name! Controlling her irritation, she continued with her argument. "The point is, our paramedics are among the best trained people in the country. Their chief duty is to triage people on site, then decide the most appropriate course of action to take regarding their patients' health and welfare."

"You seemed to have memorized that right out of the book. You're so good, in fact, that the fire department could hire you for an ad campaign. Perhaps I'll recommend that to them." Angela's lips twitched in silent mirth. Pointedly ignoring the look on the EMS coordinator's face, she picked up a file and began flipping through it.

"Miss Horowitz," Brenda said, recovering slightly from her shock, "I don't consider myself a walking advertisement. I'm simply telling you the facts. Your new policy forbids paramedics working part time in the ER from doing the things they know best. They are trained to triage patients. They..."

"Not...at...Ascension...Medical...Center. Not any longer, Miss Borlin."

Angela's words cut through the room like a scalpel cutting through flesh. Brenda winced at the stony inflection in her voice, the clipped sentences pronounced so precisely. The DON was truly a first class bitch.

"You're doing this because of Patrice Woodson, aren't you? Patty is the only paramedic currently working in the ER."

"Really?" Angela's pencil-thin eyebrows soared in mock surprise. "I hadn't realized that."

"Come off it, Miss Horowitz. Don't pretend this isn't a vendetta aimed at her." Brenda had a sinking feeling she'd let her temper get in the way of common sense. Having gone this far, though, she figured there was no turning back. "Molly O'Neal and I brought Patrice to your office on Friday because she made a serious accusation regarding Dr. Roger MacGuffy."

"You should have gone through proper channels. Miss O'Neal is aware of normal hospital procedures, yet she chose to bypass them."

"We thought it best to meet with you directly rather than risk a leak of information. You know how easily talk gets around this place."

"Miss O'Neal obviously doesn't trust her superiors."

"Let's leave Molly out of this. The point is, Patrice Woodson says Dr. MacGuffy is harassing her. If that's true, she has a right to voice her complaint and have it investigated. This new policy of yours is aimed at intimidating the girl into silence."

Angela leaned back in her chair and stared at Brenda.

"Are you accusing me of a cover-up, Miss Borlin?" she asked coldly.

Brenda refused to back down. "You don't control my job, Miss Horowitz. I don't have to be afraid to speak the truth."

"But I do control this interview, and I think I've heard enough." Angela pushed back her chair. Rising, she tipped her sun streaked blond head to one side and glared at Brenda. "I also control nursing in this hospital. If I decide to update certain policies, I expect to have my decisions respected and enforced." She pointed to the door. "If you or Miss O'Neal are unable to comply with hospital policy, you are free to seek employment elsewhere."

Brenda stood up. "I came here to discuss this matter reasonably and with a view to saving the hospital from embarrassment. We both know that if Patrice Woodson goes public with her accusations, there'll be hell to pay in the press. Unfortunately, you seem more interested in saving Roger MacGuffy's hide than in performing your duty as Director of Nursing. That's a real shame."

"Good day, Miss Borlin. Please shut the door on your way out."

Brenda purposely left the door open as she passed through to the outer office. Angela's secretary was making a pretense of typing, but Brenda guessed the woman had heard at least part of her conversation with the DON. By lunch time, the news would be all over the hospital.

There was nothing left to do but find Molly and tell her what had happened. She had to be warned, for clearly Angela was taking aim at the ER's nurse manager. Molly's immediate superior was Mrs. Josephine Rose, the Assistant Director of Nursing for Critical Care Services. The ADON was an insecure little woman promoted well beyond her capabilities. Her decisions often bordered on foolishness, and because of that Molly had purposely bypassed her on Friday.

It had seemed the intelligent thing to do at the time, but the EMS Coordinator now saw it as a mistake. Angela Horowitz was no fan of Mrs. Rose, and it was well known that the ADON's job was in jeopardy. Josephine would do anything to retain her position, including fronting for Angela in her attack on Molly. Given what she knew, Brenda was sure Josephine would happily rip Molly to shreds if ordered to do so by her boss.

Brenda was also sure of something else. Roger MacGuffy was still unaware of Patty's accusation.

Roger had been out of town over the weekend, incommunicado since two o'clock Friday afternoon. Supposedly he hadn't flown back to Chicago until late on Sunday. Angela had written her memo only hours after hearing Patty's story. She'd obviously decided to handle the matter without consulting the accused, confident her heavy-handed ploy would silence the young paramedic.

There was always the off chance that the Director of Nursing had contacted Roger over the weekend, but Brenda doubted it. Dr. MacGuffy never gave out a phone number when he left town on one of his jaunts. He guarded his privacy with a passion bordering on paranoia, and the hospital and his medical colleagues weren't the only ones kept in the dark as to his whereabouts. Girl friends were also firmly excluded from Roger's private excursions.

This Brenda knew for a fact. After all, she'd lived with the man for almost a year.

CHAPTER EIGHT

June 14th
8:30 A.M.

    .   Glynnis Milburn selected yet another form from her capacious file cabinet and slid it across the broad desk separating her from Caroline Rhodes.

"This is our New Employee Service Agreement," she trilled. "We in administration view NESA as a progressive approach to the employer/employee relationship. Just initial each paragraph and sign your name at the bottom of the page."

"Mind if I look at it first?"

Caroline snatched up the paper, barely able to conceal her growing irritation from the bureaucratic Miss Milburn. If the perky little Nurse Recruiter launched into one more gushing endorsement of hospital policy, Caroline would be tempted to reach over the desk and strangle the woman.

"You call this progressive?" she yelped in disbelief. "It says here that I can be terminated at any time, with or without cause, and with or without notice, solely at the discretion of the hospital."

"That's correct, Mrs. Rhodes," Glynnis chirped. "Our new policy reflects a cutting edge concept in labor management. By controlling the size of the work force, we're able to keep costs down, thereby assuring our clients a continuum of valuable services."

"Apparently one of those valuable services will not be nursing care."

"Come now, Mrs. Rhodes." Miss Milburn's saccharin smile slipped a fraction. "That's not the kind of talk we like to hear from prospective employees of Ascension Medical Center. As I told you when I explained our Mission Statement..."

"Pardon me, Miss Milburn, but I'm quite familiar with the hospital's Mission Statement. I was a nursing staff representative on the committee that formulated that document twelve years ago. I don't think it was intended to strip workers of their rights."

Glynnis ducked her head. "I forgot that you were employed here previously. Since you were part of the Mission team, though, you should realize how much time and effort are given to perfecting policies of this sort. It's not a task we take lightly."

"I'm aware of that," replied Caroline. "It took us six months of knock-down, drag-out meetings to draft a simple statement of purpose." She shook her head. "All that time spent on three little paragraphs. It makes you wonder how old Abe managed to write his entire Gettysburg Address in less than two hours."

Miss Milburn failed to see the connection between hospital policy and the penmanship problems of some senior citizen. Being a woman of impeccable manners, though, she mustered a reply.

"Poor fellow," she murmured. "Perhaps he forgot his zip."

"His zip?"

Glynnis nodded sagely. "The elderly often have difficulty recalling their zip codes. That may be the reason it took your friend two hours to copy down his address."

Caroline collapsed in a knee-slapping fit of giggles, utterly confusing the normally unflappable Miss Milburn. But then the Nurse Recruiter recalled a tidbit of gossip gleaned from the hospital grapevine. Mrs. Rhodes, it was said, had a history of mental instability.

Glynnis decided to humor her disturbed guest. In a voice usually reserved for her senile aunt, she asked sweetly, "And where is this Gettsyburg, Mrs. Rhodes?"

CHAPTER NINE

.   Caroline plucked a tissue from the box sitting on Brenda Berlein's desk and passed it to her friend.

"Control yourself, Brenda," she said in mock disapproval. "What will people think if they see you sitting in your office with tears rolling down your face?"

The EMS Coordinator dabbed at her eyes. "Who cares what they think? I deserve a good laugh after the morning I've had." She balled up the tissue and tossed it at the wastebasket, missing the container by a good six inches. Rocking back in her chair, she grinned at Caroline. "So tell me. What did Glynnis do next?"

"She asked me where Gettysburg was."

"And your reply?"

Caroline shrugged. "I told her it was a small town in Pennsylvania. A small town with a very large cemetery."

Brenda doubled over in another attack of unrestrained glee. Her raucous laughter filled the tiny room and echoed off the walls of the adjoining corridor. Caroline was forced to jump up and close the door for fear of someone overhearing them.

"You're going to hurt yourself if you keep this up," she warned as she slumped back down in her chair.

"I'm sorry," Brenda gasped. "It's just...so funny!" She smothered a final chortle with a hand pressed to her lips. "That woman is very odd. I can't believe the hospital trusts her to hire new staff."

"She has a lot of letters behind her name. That always

impresses the bigwigs in administration."

"I think she graduated from the University of Utter Nonsense with a major in Paper Pushing. The woman's a nut case, Cari."

"Now, Brenda, be nice. Glynnis is one of those rare people who actually believe in the value of bureaucracy. She probably stays up nights memorizing memos from the Administrator."

"Or framing them," Brenda grinned. A lock of curly brown hair drifted across one eye and she tucked it back in place with her fingertips. "I'm so glad you're back in town, Cari. I'd almost forgotten what it was like to have a little fun at work."

"People do seem a bit up-tight around here. I haven't noticed a lot of smiling faces in the department."

"That's because no one knows what will happen next. We're all walking on eggshells, waiting for the bomb to drop." Brenda glanced at her watch. "I hate to cut this conversation short, Caroline, but Molly should be back in her office by now and I need to talk to her."

"I won't keep you then," Caroline said, getting to her feet. "I dropped by mainly to check on my ECRN status. We work under a different set of SOP's in Rhineburg, and my certification from there won't cover me here."

"Standard Operating Procedures are more or less the same throughout the state," commented Brenda as she began rummaging through a side drawer of her desk. "It's true there are slight variations in each system, but basically you should have no trouble passing...Ah! Here it is." She handed Caroline a four-page question and answer sheet. "When Molly told me you were coming back to Ascension, I got clearance for you to retest here rather than sit through the entire ECRN course again."

Caroline was grateful she wouldn't be stuck in a classroom. The Emergency Communications Registered Nurse course was lengthy and demanding. Without certification, though, she'd be unable to direct paramedics in the field using the ER's telemetry radio.

"You can use my office to take the test," Brenda continued, slipping into her jacket. "When you're done with it..."

She stopped short as the door burst open, and a giant of a man in blue scrubs strode into the room. Behind him in the doorway stood an attractive black woman dressed in street clothes.

"Brenda, we have to talk. I can't find Molly, but you..."

"Mr. Jones!" Brenda's voice was sharp with anger. "I do not appreciate you storming into this office without knocking."

"But this is important!"

Ignoring him, Brenda motioned to his companion. "Come in, Patrice. I gather you've heard the news."

The woman nodded as she entered the room. "Keeshon saw the memo on Molly's desk and called me. I figured I'd better get over here and talk to you about it."

"It's not fair!" raged the man, pounding one dark fist against the palm of his other hand. "You know why she did this, don't you? She's determined to protect that bastard."

"Calm down, Kee," Brenda demanded. "Losing your temper isn't going to help."

"Right now I could kill them both."

"Keeshon!" The woman laid a restraining hand on the muscular arm of her companion. Her touch seemed to affect him, for his shoulders drooped, and his hands, balled into tight fists, relaxed and fell to his sides. Taut lines still creased his brow, but he appeared subdued, even sheepish, as he gazed into the worried eyes of Patrice.

"I'm sorry, Patty. I don't mean to make things worse."

Caroline felt like an eavesdropper as she stood there listening to the conversation. She edged towards the door, but the EMS Coordinator held her back with a silent shake of her head.

"I was going to call you, Patrice, but I had a few things to attend to first." Brenda motioned towards her guest. "I'd like you both to meet Caroline Rhodes. She's going to be working in the ER this summer, filling in for vacationing staff."

Two sets of eyes swung in Caroline's direction. It was apparent that neither Keeshon nor Patrice had noticed her before, and both people appeared unnerved by her presence. Caroline felt equally ill at ease, but she extended her hand to Patrice.

"Glad to meet you, Patrice. Are you a nurse also?"

"A paramedic," Patrice mumbled, shaking hands. "I work here part-time as a tech."

Caroline nodded and turned to Keeshon. "I've heard of you," she said with a smile. "Molly says you're one of her best nurses."

Ignoring her outstretched hand, the man regarded her warily.

"Molly told you that? How strange. Our boss usually doesn't confide in newcomers."

Kee's behavior strained Brenda's patience.

"Give it up, Kee. Mrs. Rhodes isn't your enemy. She's been a friend of Molly's for years."

"That's right," agreed Caroline. "We've known each other since we were kids. I worked with her here in the ER until I left Ascension about a year ago."

"Oh, lord," Patrice sighed, rolling her eyes. "We're so sorry, Mrs. Rhodes. We didn't mean to be rude. It's just that...well, we're kind of suspicious of strangers around here."

"You never know who's a spy," Keeshon added darkly.

"Spies at Ascension? Hey, man. You've been watching too many movies."

All four heads turned as Vic Warner strolled into the room. Caroline craned her neck to peer over Keeshon's shoulder as he spun around to face the other male nurse.

"Listening in on private conversations again, huh, Vic?" Kee growled.

Vic Warner threw up his hands in mock surrender. "Now don't be getting on my case, Mr. Jones. I came here to talk to Mrs. Berlein, and since the door was wide open..."

Keeshon took a step forward, but Brenda intervened.

"Back off, Kee. This is a hospital, not a boxing ring." She turned to Vic. "What do you want, Mr. Warner?"

Vic sidestepped Keeshon and walked over to the desk. "I got your note about the monthly review test. Seems I forgot to hand it in on time again." He pulled a wrinkled set of papers from the cargo pocket of his scrub pants and handed it to Brenda with a grin. "Better late than never, right?"

Brenda glanced at the top sheet. "This is last month's test."

"Really?" Vic feigned concern. "I guess I must have lost the one for this month."

Brenda reached into a drawer and pulled out a new set of forms. "Here," she said, handing it to Vic. "I'll expect it on my desk this afternoon."

"Not giving me much time, are you?" he said with a pained expression. Suddenly he wrinkled his nose and sniffed the air. "What's that odor, Brenda? Smells kind of fishy in here."

"Get out, Mr. Warner." Brenda walked to the door and pointed. Vic sauntered past her, then turned and gave her a wink.

"I'll be back."

Brenda slammed the door in his face. "Damned fool," she muttered, turning back to the others. "Patrice, have you talked with Molly today?"

"She wasn't around when I arrived."

"Why don't you go wait in her office? I'll find her and we'll meet you there in a few minutes."

Patrice hesitated, but Keeshon wrapped his arm around the worried girl and offered to stay with her.

"No way, Kee," Brenda said, shaking her head. "You get back to work where you belong. We don't need you and your hot temper messing things up any more than they are already."

Anger flared in Keeshon's eyes, but it died almost as quickly. With a quick nod in Brenda's direction, he flung open the door and ushered Patrice out of the office. Brenda watched them go, then closed the door and turned to Caroline.

"I suppose I should tell you what that was all about."

"Not if it's confidential."

Brenda shrugged. "Everyone in the department knows what's going on, so there's no reason to keep you in the dark."

Caroline waited as the EMS Coordinator settled herself once more behind her desk.

"According to Patrice Woodson, Roger MacGuffy has been sexually harassing her. He wants her to go out with him, and apparently he won't take no for an answer."

"Is she dating Keeshon?"

Brenda nodded. "Yes, but another man's presence never stopped Roger in the past. Patty claims he made unwanted phone calls to her at home. At work, he's made comments about her figure that she finds offensive."

Caroline's eyebrows shot up. "Doesn't he understand that kind of thing can get you in trouble nowadays?"

"Roger's one of a kind," Brenda replied dryly. "He doesn't see his actions as demeaning to women. He's always on the prowl, always looking to put another notch on his belt. Patrice isn't the first female employee he's gone after here in the ER. There have been others."

"But how does he get away with it? If he's been accused before..."

"No one's had the guts to file a formal complaint until now. You have to understand something, Cari. Roger is a clever man. He targets young inexperienced women, and he never hassles them in front of witnesses. These girls are nurses just starting out in their careers, or techs working their way through school, not self-assured old pros like you and me. They're afraid no one in administration will believe them, so they either keep quiet and put up with Roger's advances, or they quit and go elsewhere."

"What made Patrice come forward?"

"She was afraid of what Keeshon would do if he found out Roger was trying to date her. Last Friday, she confided in Mavis Taylor. Mavis persuaded her to speak to me, and I took her to Molly."

Brenda told Caroline about the decision to bypass the Assistant Director of Nursing and go straight to Angela Horowitz.

"Angela treated Patrice like dirt. She asked her why she'd want to stir up trouble for a well-respected doctor like Roger MacGuffy. When Patty persisted in her accusations, Angela said she'd give her the weekend to reconsider her story. There was no mention of an investigation of the complaint, just an implied threat that if Patty didn't retract her statement, she would be the one in trouble, not Roger.

"Molly was livid, but outside of counseling Patty to pursue the matter with the Human Resources Department, there was nothing more she could do at the time. Then this morning I found this memo on my desk." Brenda gave Caroline the slip of paper that had precipitated her early morning meeting with the DON. "Patrice is the only paramedic currently employed in the ER, so she's the only person affected by Angela's new policy."

Caroline read the memo with growing amazement.

"Your DON has incredible audacity," she remarked, placing the paper face down on Brenda's desk.

"She's very secure in her position."

"But if the hospital does nothing, and Patrice files a complaint with the EEOC, Angela's tactics could backfire on her. The Equal Employment Opportunity Commission might look askance at a Director of Nursing who threatens her employees."

"I tried to explain that to Angela when I saw her earlier today." Brenda outlined her meeting with the DON, concluding wryly, "She wasn't very receptive to my ideas. She's bound and determined to protect Roger, whatever the cost."

"She may be arrogant, but I don't think Angela is stupid. If Human Resources investigates Patty's claim and comes up with a conclusion supporting her, Angela will abandon ship faster than the proverbial rat. She won't give up a high profile job for the likes of Roger MacGuffy."

Brenda rose and moved slowly to the door.

"I hope you're right, Cari, but I wouldn't bet on it. Roger has a way with women, and right now Angela Horowitz is under his spell. I have a feeling there's more trouble to come before all this is over."

With a sad little smile, she walked out of the office, leaving Caroline alone with her thoughts.

CHAPTER TEN

June 14th
9:45 A.M.

"Paramedics are called to the home of a 54-year-old man who complained of a sudden onset of pain between the shoulder blades while dancing with his wife. On arrival, they find the man alert and oriented and sitting in a chair. His only other complaint is profuse diaphoresis. Vital signs are within normal range; lungs are clear. What would you direct the paramedics to do?"

Caroline read the question for the third time. The answer was simple, but she couldn't keep her mind on the ECRN test. Visions of the morning floated through her brain like clips from a bad movie. Molly, troubled and tired, looking lost in her office. Patrice Woodson, caught between a rock and a hard place, watching her life unwind. Keeshon Jones, verbalizing his hatred for Roger and Angela.

Even Brenda flitted in and out of her thoughts. She heard again the contempt in the young woman's voice when she mentioned Roger's name, saw once more the parting glance that communicated more sorrow than the situation justified.

Caroline leaned back in her chair and stared pensively at the calendar on the wall. Almost a year had passed since she'd last set foot in Ascension Medical Center. Change was to be expected, but not the kind of changes that had occurred here. This was not the friendly workplace she'd left last August, not the ER she'd once called home. Old colleagues had vanished, and some of the new faces weren't all that welcoming. She'd stick it out - she owed that much to Molly - but she already knew she wasn't going to enjoy the summer.

With a discontented sigh, she forced her thoughts back to the test. "Our 54-year-old man is having a heart attack," she mumbled as she scrawled the appropriate answers across the page. "IV, oxygen, aspirin, etc. Call in the cath lab, folks; we've got us a live one." Refraining from writing that last comment on the paper, Caroline glanced at the next question. It concerned a 67-year-old woman who'd fallen out of a tree while trying to rescue a cat.

"What the heck was she thinking of?" Caroline yelped. "A woman her age has no business climbing a tree. Leave that to the kids."

The kids. That's what Molly had called her young nurses, the ones who'd replaced the old veterans of the ER. If Brenda could be believed, Roger was already setting his sights on at least one of these new employees. More trouble in the ER, more trouble for Molly. But it wasn't only the young who'd left Ascension and gone elsewhere. Older nurses had quit also, women who weren't Roger's type. Had Angela made life so miserable in the ER that staff who'd worked there for years felt compelled to resign? And why were Roger and Angela doing a hatchet job on Molly? Caroline shook her head. So many questions, and she had no answers for any of them. There was only one thing she knew for sure. Something out of the ordinary had caused the drastic change she'd seen in Molly. Something deep and abiding, something deadly to the heart and soul of her friend.

"Molly's holding back on me."

The thought struck Caroline with such certainty that she wanted to leap up and confront Molly immediately, but she couldn't. She had a test to finish, and Molly was busy with other matters.

Glynnis Milburn's pinched face suddenly superimposed itself on the desk. Her lips were drawn back in a ghastly grin, and business forms circled her head like a spinning paper halo.

"Go away," grumbled Caroline even as a new thought struck

her. Keeshon Jones might be outraged over Angela's latest move, but the Director of Nursing had an even deadlier weapon in her arsenal, a weapon she might be tempted to use on Patrice. She had the New Employee Service Agreement.

Glynnis had hailed NESA as the ninth wonder of the modern world, but Caroline saw it as a means for the hospital to rid itself of troublemakers. By accusing Roger of impropriety, Patrice had entered the ranks of undesirable employees. That obnoxious piece of paper would allow Angela to fire the paramedic regardless of the results of any inquiry.

It was enough to make Caroline swear.

"Damn!" she snarled, angry with herself for not thinking of the document earlier. At this very moment, Molly and Brenda were closeted with Patrice in the nurse manager's office. If NESA's existence had slipped their minds, they'd be unable to warn the girl of her possible fate.

"Damn, damn, damn!" Caroline said even more fiercely. She picked up her pen and hurriedly finished the test, then placed it squarely in the middle of Brenda's desk and headed for the door. Rushing into the corridor, she collided with Michelle Devine.

"Oops! Sorry about that." Caroline smiled an apology, but the unit receptionist was having none of it.

"Watch where you're going!" Michelle yelped. "You almost knocked me down."

"I'm sorry," Caroline repeated as the girl rubbed an imaginary injury to her arm. "I hope you're not hurt."

Michelle cast a look of exasperation Caroline's way, then turned without a word and stalked off in the direction of Roger's office. She was met at the door by Susan Kane, a relatively new nurse in the department. Susan was just leaving the office, and she scurried past Michelle head down without speaking.

Caroline thought the woman's behavior was odd, but she put it down to preoccupation with work. Michelle didn't seem bothered by Susan's manner in the least. She favored the nurse with a brief up and down look, then walked into the Medical Director's private sanctuary without knocking, leaving the door ajar.

Caroline's natural curiosity had proved both an asset and a curse in the past. Now it nudged her to follow the footsteps of the younger woman. She stopped just short of the doorway, alert to the sound of angry voices within the room.

"What do you want with her anyway? Don't you think I'm good enough?"

Michelle was obviously in a bad temper. Her words spilled out in a shrill whine, the clipped sentences grating on Caroline's ears. A man's voice intervened, the tone less strident but equally compelling.

"You're reading too much into one little incident. I can't help it if women pursue me."

"You should have put a stop to it."

Caroline could imagine the look on the girl's face, her lips pursed in a sulky pout, her dark eyes flashing annoyance.

"That's exactly what I was trying to do," the man said smoothly.

Michelle apparently relented. She murmured something, but Caroline couldn't make out the words. Then the man laughed, a clear ringing laugh of vindication. Caroline's skin crawled, and she backed away from the doorway.

She'd heard enough to guess what was going on between Roger MacGuffy and Michelle Devine. Whatever else their relationship might be, it surely wasn't platonic.

CHAPTER ELEVEN

June 14th
2:30 P.M.

.   Caroline replaced the receiver on the telemetry radio and swiveled her chair in a half circle.

"MVA coming in," she said, leaning back and facing Mavis. "Two greens and a yellow with a possible broken wrist."

"Two walkin' wounded and one hurt but not dyin'. What's with all the multi-vehicle accidents today?" Mavis grumbled. "Everyone forgotten how to drive? Jack! Shake loose three more carts."

Jack Nickerson, a tow-headed college-aged kid with a ready smile, gave Mavis the thumbs up sign and ambled away, ostensibly to locate more gurneys.

"And don't get lost!" Mavis called after him. Turning to Caroline, she rolled her eyes. "That boy does a great vanishing act. Gotta watch him every minute of the day."

Caroline grinned. "I noticed he's quite interested in your new unit receptionist. He's been using every excuse in the book to get near her."

"Wendy Moss?" Mavis glanced over her shoulder to where Michelle Devine was instructing a young woman on the intricacies of the hospital's computer system. "Good lookin' blond, isn't she? Nice kid, too. Comes from some little town in England."

"England?"

"Yeah. She's taking time off from school before starting college. Guess that's the latest rage over there. Send the kids to work for a year so they mature a bit."

"That's not such a bad idea. How'd Wendy end up here?"

"She has relatives in the area, an aunt and an uncle. She has computer skills, and when Kelly up and quit last month, we were desperate to fill her position. Wendy fit the bill, so here she is."

Caroline remembered Kelly as a conscientious worker and a friendly young woman. She asked Mavis what had caused the girl to leave the ER after four years on the job.

"Well now," drawled Mavis. "That's kind of a long story. Let's just say Kelly had a choice. She could put up a fight, or she could walk out. She chose to walk out." The charge nurse slid a chart into its slot on the desk. "Now tell me, Cari. What we gonna do with that old gentleman on cart five? I need that cubicle for a live one, but Mr. Gone-To-His-Just-Reward is smack dab in the middle of the room, and I hate to move dead folks past sick ones. Tends to shake their confidence in the ability of the doctors, if you know what I mean."

Caroline laughed. "Leave it to me. I'll move him to the morgue without anyone noticing." She waved to Michelle and Wendy. "Can I tear one of you away from that computer for a minute?"

Michelle looked reluctant, but Wendy was more than ready to abandon her job. After listening carefully to Caroline's instructions, the girl broke into a broad grin.

"I took some acting classes back in England," she said in a confident voice. "I'm sure I can pull this off."

"Then follow me," replied Caroline as she headed towards the back of the east wing. Passing Susan Kane midway through the room, Caroline called out, "Hey, Sue! We're taking your patient on cart five upstairs."

Susan was starting an IV on a woman on cart two. She looked up in alarm and stuttered, "But...but...he's..."

"I know," sang out Caroline. "No need to worry. We'll take good care of Mr. Gone."

Three minutes later Wendy pulled back the curtain encircling cart five.

"There now, sir. Are you warm enough under that blanket?"

The elderly dead man sat upright on the cart staring blindly at the ceiling. Propped up by pillows, an oxygen mask hid most of his lower face and a towel draped over the top of his head shielded his forehead and ears. A thick blue blanket covered the rest of his body.

"Let me pull it up a bit. Can't have your chin getting cold now, can we." Wendy tugged on the blanket, tucking it under the edge of the oxygen mask. Ten toes suddenly appeared at the end of the cart.

"Forget the feet, Wendy. Let's go," whispered Caroline as she nudged the gurney out of the cubicle and into the walkway between the other patients' carts.

Unfortunately, Wendy wasn't listening.

"Oh, dear," the girl exclaimed. She yanked on the blanket, forcing Caroline to pull up. "Mustn't have our piggies sticking out."

"Let's go!" hissed Caroline as several patients sat up to stare in their direction. She smiled at them reassuringly while motioning to Wendy to back off. The girl never moved.

"You'll like your room," Wendy went on in a booming voice, reaching over to pat the dead man's arm. It promptly slid from beneath the covers and fell to his side.

"Enough!" Caroline muttered through clenched teeth as Wendy grabbed for the offending extremity. Ignoring the unit receptionist, she leaned against the cart, gave a mighty shove, and ran right over Wendy's foot.

"Oowww!"

A male medical student raced up, eager to assist the pretty young woman staggering about the room on one foot. Stumbling in his haste, he slammed into Wendy, ricocheted sideways into the cart, and fell headlong across the dead man's legs.

"Son of a...!"

Caroline threw her weight against the cart as it rocked backwards, slamming into her knees. Her action had an opposite effect from the one she'd desired. The pillow propping the dead man's chin toppled to the left and slid to the floor. Unsupported, the heavy skull pitched forward.

"He's not alive!" The medical student gazed up in horror. The oxygen mask had fallen away exposing the waxy features of the corpse. Hovering only inches above the boy's head, the dead man stared down through sightless eyes, his wrinkled face frozen in a toothless grin.

"Oh my gawd!"

His legs spinning uselessly off the end of the cart, the medical student tore at the blanket, struggling to right himself. The thick blue material slithered through his fingers and wadded up against his face, throwing him even further off balance and causing the corpse to bounce up and down in a silent jig.

The hairless head bobbed ever closer to the boy. He scrambled blindly to find purchase on something solid, and after what seemed like an eternity but was only a second, his hand brushed against a knobby object. In desperation, he closed his fingers over it and pulled. As he did so, the last bit of blanket fell away.

Caroline leaped to the side of the cart, but she was too late to avert disaster. The body tumbled over, bent at the waist, the torso flattening the medical student.

Fortunately, the young man never felt the blow. He'd fainted dead away after seeing his fist wrapped around the most private part of Mr. Gone's anatomy.

As for the corpse, he seemed no worse for the wear. His face turned to the side, the old man's head rested squarely on the medical student's soft buttocks.

CHAPTER TWELVE

June 14th
3:15 P.M.

.   "I hate heat waves," Mavis Taylor said as she directed a pair of Niles paramedics to the west wing of the room. "People are just plain stupid, working on their yards when the temperature's ninety-five. Don't they know they're gonna keel over when it's that hot outside?" She slammed a chart into the rack on the desk and sat down with a sigh.

Caroline turned away from the radio. "Another one's coming in now. I just took the run report." She stood up and walked over to the desk. "I'm really sorry about what happened with that body, Mavis. I'll tell Molly it was my idea, not yours."

Mavis waved a fat brown hand in Caroline's direction. "Lordy, girl, it isn't Molly we have to worry about. It's Josephine Rose, that poor excuse for an Assistant Director of Nursing. Josephine's bound to get her shorts in a knot over this one."

"You think she'll take it to Angela Horowitz?"

Mavis nodded. "You can bet on it. Oh, oh. Here comes trouble."

Caroline looked around, expecting to see the ADON. Instead, she saw a young nurse in lavender scrubs marching towards them, her face screwed into a frown. The woman was in her late twenties or early thirties, tall and anorexic looking with a long, narrow face and prominent cheekbones. Her hair was the color of honey, and she wore it tied back in a loose ponytail. She might have been pretty except for the stern set of her mouth and the coldness in her deep-set blue eyes.

"I can't take another patient back there, Mavis," the nurse complained. "There's only myself and Judith."

"It's a simple heat exhaustion, Fawn. The guy gets some IV fluids and it's goodbye, Charlie. Ask Jack to help you."

"I don't need a tech! I need another nurse."

Mavis shrugged. "Keeshon and Susan are workin' this end of the room. Caroline just started today, and she hasn't finished orientation. I don't have anyone to give you, Fawn, unless you want to pull Vic out of triage."

"I'll take the patient," Caroline offered. "It may be my first day back, but..."

"I don't want to baby-sit another newbie," Fawn snapped. She turned and stalked back to her station, flinging a parting shot over her shoulder. "Don't you send me any more patients, Mavis. I refuse to take them."

"Whoa!" whistled Caroline. "What an endearing personality!"

"Yeah, the Lady of Charm herself." Mavis motioned to a team of paramedics just walking in the door. She pointed down the hallway. "Follow the purple people eater, boys. Miss Phillips will be thrilled to see you."

One of the paramedics groaned.

"Give us a break, Mavis. That woman has a heart of stone."

"Hey!" Mavis retorted with a grin. "Didn't your momma tell you there'd be days like this? Now get moving!"

Caroline watched the men obediently wheel their patients towards the west wing.

"Aren't you being a little hard on Fawn?" she asked. "She may not be the most likable person on earth, but saddling her with another new arrival is a bit much."

"Fawn Phillips is a royal pain in the butt, Cari. I wouldn't have given her that case if she'd kept her mouth shut and done her work."

Mavis pulled three pages of lab results off the printer, glanced at the numbers, then tossed the sheets on the doctors' desk. Turning back to Caroline, she continued, "Take my advice and watch your backside when you're around Fawn. She'll rip you apart when you least expect it."

"You really don't like the woman, do you?"

"The girl is book smart, but she doesn't have the heart of a nurse. She lacks compassion, and in my book that's a mortal sin."

Caroline recalled something Molly had told her.

"Did Fawn transfer here from Bridgeview's ER?"

"Yeah," said Mavis, wrinkling her nose. "She and Vic Warner came over after Dr. MacGuffy was made Medical Director. They're his spies in the department."

That was the second time Caroline had heard the word 'spy' used by a member of the ER staff. Either paranoia was setting in here, or the problem was worse than she'd originally thought. She was about to ask Mavis another question when the very doctor just mentioned walked up to the desk.

"You're overcrowding Miss Phillips' end of the room, Mavis," MacGuffy said without preamble. "Move those last two heat victims to this side."

"I'd love to, doctor," Mavis replied smoothly. "Unfortunately, Kee is preparing a patient for the cath lab, and Susan is handling the other six cases on her own. She has one chest pain, a GI bleed, two kids with fevers, a fractured hip, and a probable stroke. Fawn, on the other hand, has the fast track patients today. If she'd like to trade two heat exhaustions for a chest pain..."

"I get your point, Ms. Taylor," Roger snarled. "Now where are those lab result on Mrs. Marchetti? I've been waiting for them for over an hour."

"They're on your desk, doctor, exactly where they should be."

Mavis reached for a large white envelope sitting in a rack to her right. "And here is Mr. Williams' X-ray."

She held out the envelope. MacGuffy snatched it from her hand, and for a split second their eyes met and held. Then Roger wheeled and walked away.

The charge nurse winked at Caroline before turning back to the pile of orders accumulating on the desk.

"I love it when I win a round," she chuckled. "Makes me feel invincible."

But you aren't, thought Caroline. None of us are.

She glanced across the room. Roger had slipped the X-ray out of its cover and placed it on the viewing box. He was standing with his arms folded across his chest, studying the film. Suddenly, his gaze shifted to the charge nurse.

If looks could be carving knives, Mavis would have been sliced to pieces right there in the ER.

CHAPTER THIRTEEN

June 14th
3:45 P.M.

.   Caroline left a message on Krista's machine explaining she'd be late getting back to the apartment.

"My first day back at in the ER, and I've screwed up already. I have to meet with the Director of Nursing, and that could take a while. Then I need to talk to Molly. Go ahead and eat without me, Krista. I'll pick up a bite on my way home."

Caroline thought of her old friends in Rhineburg as she made her way up to Angela Horowitz's first floor office. Madeline Moeller and her Chief of Police husband Jake were probably barbecuing ribs tonight on the grill behind their Victorian on Wilhelm Road. The Archangels, Michael, Rafael, and Gabriel Bruck, would be going home to dinner with their triplet wives after their security shifts ended at Bruck University. Alexsa Stromberg Morgan probably wasn't even thinking about food; Elvira Harding would be cooking Alexsa's meal this evening, just as she did every other night of the week. As for Carl Atwater, she needn't bother to worry that he'd go hungry. The way that man consumed food, supper would probably be his sixth or seventh meal of the day.

"Looks like I'm the only one whose stomach will be growling tonight," she muttered as she entered the outer room of Angela's office.

"Talking to yourself again?" Mavis waved her over to a chair near the secretary's desk. "Come sit next to me. and I'll protect you from the big bad wolf."

"Where's Molly?" Caroline asked as she slipped into the chair. "I thought she left the ER before I did."

Mavis shrugged. "Maybe she's having a good stiff drink down at the corner bar. She's going to need it to control her temper over this one." She thumbed towards the door leading to Angela's office. "Roger's already in the inner sanctum. Been there a good ten minutes." Lowering her voice, she added, "Long enough for a little fun and games with our esteemed Director of Nursing."

"Behave yourself," Caroline admonished. "This is serious business."

Mavis rolled her eyes. She started to say something but quickly clamped her lips shut as Angela appeared in the doorway.

"Where's Miss O'Neal?" The Director's voice was sharp, and she was not smiling. The look she gave them bode ill for the coming interview.

"I'm here."

Caroline turned in her seat. Molly stood in the entranceway, her chin held high and her eyes glittering. She'd combed her hair, put on new make-up, and exchanged her uniform for street clothes and a lab coat.

"Will Mrs. Rose be present at this meeting?"

"I have her report of the incident, Miss O'Neal. I'll handle matters from this point on." Turning, Angela strode back into her office. The other three women followed, Molly in the lead.

Roger was standing at the window, gazing down on the parking lot below. He turned wordlessly and sank into a chair near Angela's desk as the nurses seated themselves.

"I understand this fiasco was your idea, Mrs. Taylor. Just what did you think you were doing?"

"Actually, Miss Horowitz..."

Angela's eyes swiveled towards Caroline.

"I don't believe I was speaking to you, Mrs. Rhodes."

"But I was the one who suggested..."

"My question was directed at Mrs. Taylor," Angela snapped. She silenced Caroline with a cold stare, then returned her attention to Mavis. "I'm awaiting an answer."

Mavis laced her fingers across her ample stomach and cocked one eyebrow at Angela. "I asked Cari to move the gentleman from cart five to the morgue. Due to all the personnel cutbacks, there aren't enough transporters in this hospital. Those are the people we call on in these circumstances, but no one answered my page. Since I needed the space for another patient..."

"You could have waited," Roger interrupted with a sigh of exasperation. "You see, Angela, that's the very thing I've been complaining about. Nobody in the ER follows rules. They just go about blaming all their little problems on administration."

"I waited one hour, Dr. MacGuffy." Mavis' voice hardened as she glared at Roger. "One solid hour elapsed between the time I called transport and the time I asked Caroline to move the body."

Angela raised her hand. "That's enough, Mrs. Taylor. Regardless of the time involved, Ascension does have policies and procedures concerning expired patients. You did not follow the policy, and I have no choice but to discipline you in this matter. You will write letters of apology to every patient present in the ER during this incident, and you are suspended for three days without pay, effective immediately."

"What!" Mavis sprang from her chair, but Molly grabbed her arm and pulled her down.

"Just a minute, Miss Horowitz," Molly said angrily. "The incident was unfortunate..."

"That's putting it mildly," Roger muttered.

"...but your response is inappropriately severe."

"Inappropriate? In case you've forgotten, Miss O'Neal, I had to revive a medical student," Roger said sarcastically. "And Wendy Moss, your unit receptionist, was injured."

"Caroline ran over her toes," Molly snapped. "The girl was perfectly fine when she left work. As for your medical student, none of this would have happened if he'd minded his own business and not gone crashing into the cart."

"So you approve of Mrs. Taylor's decision to disregard hospital policy and move the patient?" The Director of Nursing fixed Molly with a look that dared her to say yes.

Accepting the challenge, Molly replied, "I approve of Mrs. Taylor's decision to use all available space to treat living patients. If hospital policy cannot be carried out in a reasonable manner, then, yes, I do approve of improvising as necessary."

Roger's hand strayed to his mouth in a poor attempt to hide a smile. Infuriated by his smug behavior, Caroline interrupted Molly.

"This whole mess was my fault," she blurted out. "I thought we could move the body to another area of the room where he'd be out of the way until the transporters arrived. This is not Mavis' fault. And Molly knew nothing about it until it was over."

She might as well have kept silent for all the good her speech did. No one was listening to her.

"I refuse to write any letters," Mavis said stubbornly. She stood up and stalked to the door. "Suspend me if you like, but I won't apologize for my actions."

Angela pointed a manicured finger at Mavis. "You, Mrs. Taylor, will do as I say or face termination of your employment."

Mavis whipped around. "Fire me, will you, you bitch? I won't give you the satisfaction. I quit!" That said, she walked out of the room, slamming the door behind her.

"Happy now, Roger? Or would you like my resignation also?"

Molly rose from her chair. "Sorry, but I'm not ready to leave this place yet." Turning to Angela, she said, "Ascension has just lost one of the best ER nurses it ever had. It's a pity you chose this course."

"Mrs. Taylor made a choice, Miss O'Neal. I didn't force her to quit." Angela glanced down at Josephine Rose's report. "Although you weren't in the room at the time of this affair, as nurse manager, I hold you responsible for everything that happened. We'll discuss this matter further tomorrow morning." Rising from her chair, she continued, "I'll expect to see you here in my office at ten o'clock sharp."

They hadn't anticipated Molly's stand, Caroline realized. Since she hadn't up and quit, they needed time to plan a new strategy. The whole situation was unbelievable.

"What about me?" she asked, unable to keep the sarcasm from her voice. "Am I fired, suspended, or what?"

"You'll hear from me in due time, Mrs. Rhodes." Angela walked to the door. Opening it, she waved the two nurses out of the room.

"Another rational meeting of the minds," Molly murmured as they walked down the corridor to the elevator. "Now that you've met our beloved DON, perhaps you understand why my staff has been leaving in record numbers."

"I certainly do," Caroline said with a nod. She also understood why Molly had dark circles under her eyes and wore a perpetual frown. Working under these conditions would stress out a saint. She was amazed that her friend had withstood the pressure for so many months.

Caroline suspected she herself would have cracked and gone screaming off to the looney bin long ago. If not that, she would have been arrested for strangling Miss Horowitz.

"How about dinner at some nice quiet restaurant? You need to talk, and I'd be glad to listen."

Molly shook her head. "Not tonight, Cari. I appreciate the offer, but I think I'll drive over to Mavis' place and make sure she's all right."

"She'll never reconsider, you know."

"Of course she won't. I know Mavis inside out. Backing down on her principles is not something she'd ever do."

"She was one angry woman when she walked out of the meeting."

"Yes," Molly agreed. "And that's what worries me. I don't want to see her do something foolish."

"Like smacking Angela alongside the head with a two-by-four?" Caroline joked. She'd meant to lighten her friend's load with humor, but Molly reacted in a way she hadn't expected.

"Exactly," the nurse manager said soberly. "That's exactly what I mean."

CHAPTER FOURTEEN

June 14th
5:00 P.M.

.   Caroline stood by the living room window of Krista's apartment and let the air conditioner work its cooling magic on her tired muscles. The afternoon sun beat a relentless tattoo on the pavement outside. It glanced off the windshields of passing cars and blinded drivers scurrying westward to the suburbs. Bouncing through the treetops, it stabbed at the necks of unlucky pedestrians who fought back with open shirt collars and discarded ties, sleeves rolled to the elbow, and the occasional open umbrella. Like an army on a search and destroy mission, the sun showed no mercy in its attack. It engulfed the city in shimmering waves of heat and left the citizenry wilted in body and spirit.

A few foolhardy souls continued to challenge the power of the sun despite the warnings of city officials. Krista's neighbor was one of them. Caroline watched as, oblivious to the power of the sun's rays, Howard Wilton pushed his lawnmower over the scorched grass fronting his house. He jockeyed it around the base of a withered apple tree and between fading hydrangea bushes before steering the machine towards the back yard, sweat streaming down his neck and face.

Shaking her head over Wilton's reckless disregard for nature, Caroline turned from the window and switched on the televison set.

"...and temperatures will remain in the upper nineties throughout the week, possibly breaking one hundred on Tuesday and Wednesday. The mayor's office continues to warn residents to take sensible precautions when..."

Caroline hit the power button and the room plunged into soothing silence. Except for the hum of the air conditioner, all was quiet in the little apartment. The stillness was a welcome change from the noisy activity of the ER, and Caroline relished the opportunity to relax. Stretching out on the sofa, she closed her eyes.

"Hey, mom! Are you home yet?"

The back door banged open as Kerry, Caroline's youngest daughter, came bouncing into the kitchen. She swept through the apartment like a tornado through a Kansas cornfield, a blur of motion that finally came to rest in the living room.

"There you are," she exclaimed. "It's about time you got home from work." Knocking the magazines off the coffee table, Kerry deposited two white bags on the wooden surface. "Chinese. Hope you like it."

Caroline sat up and smoothed the hair from her face. "Where's your sister?"

"Right behind you," Krista called from the kitchen. The back door banged again, this time, Caroline suspected, as it was being closed. If there was one thing her daughters weren't, it was quiet.

Kerry must have noticed the pained expression on her mother's face because she yelled for Krista to keep it down.

"I think she was sleeping," she called to her sister. "You know how these old people are, Krista. Always needing a nap before dinner."

Caroline punched her daughter's arm. "Watch how you talk about your mother. I can still write you out of my will, you know."

"Yeah, sure," Kerry laughed. "Leave everything to Krista, especially that ratty old Cubs shirt and that Bears jacket with the holes in the pocket."

"Those are antiques," chided Krista as she entered the room with three bottles of cold beer. "Who knows how valuable they may be some day?"

Caroline dug into the sweet and sour pork, content to listen to her daughters' raucous jokes as they pulled box after box of steaming food from the bags.

"Think you bought enough?" she asked between mouthfuls.

"I haven't eaten all day," Kerry complained. "My stomach thinks my throat's been cut."

Krista piled rice on her plate and covered it with a mixture of vegetables. "So what's all this about a meeting with the Director of Nursing? Your message was a little vague, but I gather something went wrong today."

Caroline groaned. "Yes, something did go wrong, but," she added with a stern look directed at Kerry, "I don't want to read about it in the neighborhood news."

"Mother!"

"I mean it, Kerry. I'm in enough trouble already. I don't need any more."

Kerry held up both hands. "I promise not to say a word, but it's not me you have to worry about. Krista's the blabbermouth in the family. She tells that new boyfriend of hers everything, and I mean everything."

"Kerry!" Krista frowned at her younger sister, then seeing her mother's raised eyebrows, she explained, "He's just a friend, mom. Another teacher from my school."

"Really?" Caroline murmured. "You will invite me to the wedding, won't you?"

Krista's face reddened, and Caroline took pity on her. Turning back to Kerry, she sketched out the events of the afternoon.

"I wish I'd been there," Kerry howled as she wiped a tear of laughter from her eyes. "I'd have loved to see that medical student flat on his face, a dead guy's head on his butt. What a riot!"

"Angela Horowitz didn't find it so funny," Caroline assured her daughter. "She fired Mavis."

"Mavis Taylor? But she's a friend of yours, isn't she?"

"I've known her for years, Krista. She's a top-notch nurse and a very bright lady. Actually, though, she wasn't fired. Angela pushed just a little too hard, and Mavis up and quit."

"Your Miss Horowitz sounds like a head case," muttered Kerry. "I'm glad I don't work for her."

"You'll run into her kind one day, honey. I'm sure the theater attracts women like her, ambitious, clever, on the make."

Kerry, a third-year theater major at a local university, considered the matter before shaking her head. "No, mom, I don't think so. It's more fun playing a bitch than being one."

The telephone rang and Krista jumped to answer it. "It's for you, mom," she called from the kitchen. "A woman."

Caroline got to her feet, hoping it was Molly calling with news of Mavis Taylor.

"Cari? It's Madeline."

"Well, hello there, old friend," Caroline said, a smile lighting her face as she pressed the receiver closer to her ear. "How's everything in Rhineburg?"

"Humming along at its usual pace. The tourists are beginning to dribble in now that the weather's turned warm. Business is picking up at the store, but I'm closing up shop for a couple of days. Jake and I are taking a mini vacation!"

Mad Moeller's Antiques and Collectibles was a drawing point for bargain hunters across the county. The pumpkin-haired wife of Rhineburg's Chief of Police was a shrewd woman when it came to picking up merchandise for her store, and because she wasn't greedy, her prices were always fair.

"But I thought summer was your best season for sales."

"It is," Madeline agreed. "Normally I wouldn't leave town at this time of year, but I have to make arrangements for the sale of Emma Reiser's furniture. Even though the will is still in probate, it's not too early to schedule an auction. I'm determined to get the best price possible on everything in that apartment."*

"So this is a working vacation. Where are you off to, Maddy. New York?"

"No, Cari. We're coming to Chicago! Jake's going to check out the sights while I haggle with the folks at the auction houses. I'll probably be tied up during the daytime, but I was hoping to see you at least one of the evenings we're in town."

"Of course, Maddy. I'll introduce you and Jake to the nightlife here in Chicago. I know some hot little spots downtown."

"Hot little spots, huh? I'll remind Jake to pack his blood pressure medication. We wouldn't want the poor man to keel over from excitement!"

Caroline was still laughing when she hung up the phone. After the day she'd had, she'd needed the pick-me-up provided by the irrepressible Maddy Moeller. It reminded her that all was not wrong with the world.

The phone rang again as she was leaving the kitchen, and Caroline turned back to answer it. This time it was Carl Atwater calling.

"How's the research going?" Caroline asked after the two friends had exchanged greetings.

"Slowly, Cari. Very slowly. The records I was looking for were stored in the basement of the old mining company headquarters. They reek of mildew and God knows what else."

"I take it the books are in a sorry state."

* See SOMETHING WICKED IN THE AIR

The professor snorted in disgust. "The ink is so faded that half the pages are indecipherable."

Caroline knew how important this project was to Carl. The professor had stumbled across a town in West Virginia that exemplified the early twentieth century mining communities of America. The author of a number of best sellers, Carl had planned to feature the place in his next book. It would be a shame if his hopes were dashed due to poor housekeeping techniques.

"To top it off, the house I rented hasn't lived up to the realty agent's description. What he portrayed as quaint is actually decrepit."

"Pretty bad, huh?"

"That's putting it mildly. It's been raining for over a week here. Last night the roof sprang a leak, and we awoke to a flood in the kitchen. The day before last, the toilet backed up, and the back door fell off its hinges."

Caroline couldn't help but laugh. The professor didn't sound like a happy camper. Knowing how the man treasured his creature comforts, she bet Carl would be checking out train schedules back to Rhineburg by week's end.

Changing the subject, she told him about Madeline's call.

"The Moellers are vacationing in Chicago?" he said, his voice perking up a bit. "When are they arriving?"

"Sometime tomorrow. Maddy's going to call me after they settle into their hotel."

"Hmm," mused the professor. "Sounds like you three are going to have some fun."

"I wish you could join us, Carl, but I know you're up to your ears in work. I wouldn't even think of pulling you away from... what's the name of that town?"

"Heaven," muttered Carl gloomily. "A real oxymoron, if you ask me."

With a few encouraging words, Caroline bid the professor adieu. He promised to call again soon, and she said she'd hold him to it.

Sitting in the kitchen in the early evening twilight, Caroline let her hand linger on the phone long after the line went dead. She'd enjoyed hearing Carl's voice. She could visualize the rotund professor turning heads in the little West Virginia town. Dressed in his usual costume of plaid shirt, suspender pants, and hunting boots, his white hair and beard only added to the woodland Santa image Carl chose to cultivate among friends and strangers alike.

The professor was one of a kind, and Caroline sorely missed him.

CHAPTER FIFTEEN

June 14th

Midnight

.   The killer moved quietly about the apartment arranging and rearranging items until all was as it should be.

An empty champagne bottle was retrieved from the kitchen garbage bin and carefully wiped free of debris. Together with two glasses used earlier that evening, it was placed on the wet bar in the dimly lit living room.

The thermostat was lowered to a chilly sixty degrees. The air conditioner clicked on, and cool air quickly flooded the apartment.

In the bathroom, a man's electric razor was positioned on the marble sink alongside an impressive brand of aftershave. Damp towels rescued from the hamper were carried to the master bedroom and thrown carelessly in one corner.

An address book removed from a desk in a back bedroom was opened to the letter 'M' and placed face down by the kitchen telephone. A scratch pad with the words 'call R' scrawled across the top piece of paper was pushed next to the book.

Satisfied with the changes, the killer walked back to the bedroom for a final check of the body. The corpse lay face up on the bed, the still form tangled in a lavender silk sheet. One arm dangled over the side of the mattress while the other rested V-shaped on the pillow above the head. The second pillow, the one used to smother the victim, had been tossed to the floor and was now wedged between the little bedside table and a chair.

The killer moved closer to the bed and brushed the victim's

lips with a piece of gray material. The resultant smudge was carefully examined and found sufficient for its purpose.

One simple task remained to be done.

There was a small anteroom between the front door and the main part of the apartment. In this area stood an antique mirrored hallstand with side hooks for coats and curled appendages for holding umbrellas or canes. A windbreaker dangled from one of the four gleaming brass hooks. Below the jacket rested a tightly furled blue umbrella constrained by a semicircle of wood.

A quick tug on the snap loosened the umbrella's tie string. The aluminum ribs relaxed outward, and folds of bright material fell away from the center pole. Into this exposed space the killer dropped a rectangular piece of plastic.

Moments later, the heavy outer door of an old Chicago brownstone swung open. A figure clad in a knee length, gray cotton coat emerged onto the stoop and hurried down the worn cement steps. It moved cat-like through the midnight shadows dappling the tree-lined city sidewalk, dodging in and out of doorways until it reached the end of the block. Stopping near a trash can chained to a streetlight, the figure peeled off the thin coat and tossed it on top of the accumulated garbage in the container.

Dressed now only in a green hospital scrub suit, the killer turned and fled down a side street, vanishing silently into the darkness of the hot summer night.

PART THREE

He was a Prince of lust and pride;
He showed no grace till the hour he died.

The White Ship
Dante Gabriel Rossetti

Chapter Sixteen

June 15th
7:10 A.M.

Dawn brought a renewed wave of heat to the city after a brief respite punctuated by thunderstorms the night before. A few wispy clouds clung stubbornly to the horizon, but even they couldn't resist the sun as it climber higher in the heavens. By seven o'clock they'd disappeared, leaving the sky the color of faded denim.

The thermometer read eighty degrees when Caroline arrived at Ascension Medical Center. It was going to be another scorcher of a day, the fifth in a row with temperatures above ninety, and the ER was preparing for the worst.

"I've ordered cooling blankets from Central Supply," Molly O'Neal told the nurses gathered for morning report. "We've been lucky so far, but this weather shows no sign of letting up."

Vic Warner rolled his eyes. "Aren't you overdoing it, Molly? 1995 isn't going to happen again."

"You hope not," Molly shot back. "I don't know where you were back then, Vic, but we at Ascension treated more than our share of hyperthermia cases during the heat wave of '95. Too many people died that summer. There were close to two dozen in the Chicago area alone."

She glanced at the other members of the staff. "Some folks just don't take intelligent precautions. Then they end up in here, sick as dogs from the heat. We already had two mild cases yesterday."

Vic didn't reply, but Caroline could tell by the look on his face that he wasn't buying Molly's line of reasoning. She glanced at Fawn, expecting to see a similar expression of contempt. To her surprise, the blond nurse was nodding in agreement with her boss. Fawn wasn't a fan of the nurse manager, but obviously she wasn't as stupid as Vic.

"Mavis won't be in this morning, so Fawn will be acting charge nurse. Caroline will take the east wing of the room with Susan, and Keeshon will cover the west wing with the help of Patrice. Vic will triage and fill in where needed. Michelle Devine is your tech today. Wendy has the computer, and since it's her first day working alone as UR, I expect you to take mercy on the girl. No orders for ovarian tubes from Central Supply," Molly concluded with a smile.

The group broke up, and Caroline drew Susan Kane aside.

"Mavis' absence has created a problem for Molly. She's short on nurses, so I'm off orientation as of today. So are you."

Susan's eyes widened in surprise.

"While I'm used to the routine at Ascension," Caroline continued, "I'm not all that familiar with this temporary ER. It's still foreign territory to me, so I may have to ask for your help at times."

"My help? But I've only been here a few weeks myself." Susan glanced over at the charge nurse, then lowered her voice to a whisper. "I graduated from school in the eighties, but I haven't worked as a nurse in almost fifteen years. This is my first job since taking a refresher course, and to tell you the truth, I'm a nervous wreck."

Caroline smiled in sympathy. "I'll tell you what, Susan. I'll help you find your confidence if you help me find supplies. Seems like nothing's where it ought to be around here."

"It is a bit confusing, isn't it?" Susan laughed. "OK, Caroline. It's a deal. In between patients, I'll give you the grand tour of all the cabinets, closets, and hidey holes in this place. In exchange, you teach me some of the tricks of the trade."

The two women shook on it while Fawn Phillips looked on in displeasure.

CHAPTER SEVENTEEN

June 15th
10:25 A.M.

.   "Back so soon?" Caroline said when Molly entered the break room later that morning. "I thought you'd be tied up with Angela for at least an hour."

Molly poured herself a cup of coffee, then slumped down at the table that occupied most of the space in the tiny lounge.

"Angela never showed up." Rubbing her forehead with the fingertips of one hand, Molly stared wearily at the stained Formica surface of the table. "She didn't come to work today."

"That's strange," remarked Caroline. "She doesn't seem like a woman who'd set up a meeting and then skip out on it."

"She isn't," Molly replied. "It's totally out of character for her to miss work and not even call in. That's why the Administrator decided to notify the police."

"The police? Do you mean to say he thinks something's happen to Angela?"

Molly nodded. "Her secretary started calling her apartment around seven-thirty this morning. When she didn't make it in for a nine o'clock meeting with the department heads, people began to worry. Then she missed the meeting with me.

"Angela's secretary phoned Josephine Rose, and Josephine phoned the Administrator. Not wanting to appear derelict in his duty, Mr. Bradford asked the Chicago police to check out Angela's apartment."

"Was she there?"

Molly shrugged. "I didn't wait around to hear. I noticed Roger didn't make it in on time either today. Maybe the two of them stayed up late celebrating, and Angela decided to play hooky and sleep in."

Caroline frowned at her friend. Molly looked like she hadn't had much sleep herself. Her eyes were red-rimmed and dull, and the hand holding her coffee cup trembled.

"Hi, you two." Brenda Berlein walked through the door and headed straight for the coffeepot. "How'd the meeting go, Molly?"

"You tell her, Cari," Molly said as she dragged herself to her feet. "I have to go check the Room."

Brenda carried her cup to the table, then thumbed over her shoulder at the departing figure of the nurse manager. "She's totally burned out, you know."

"I noticed that yesterday. I'm worried about her, Brenda. She needs to get away from this place for a while."

"That's impossible," Brenda said with a shake of her head. "You've seen the schedule. We're short on people for every shift. Molly will never take a day off while the department's understaffed." She took a sip of her coffee. "So tell me what happened at the meeting. I already heard about Mavis quitting."

Caroline repeated what Molly had told her. Brenda expressed amazement at Angela's absence.

"That's not like the woman at all. She's a workaholic, the first person in the door every day."

"I have to get back to work," Caroline said, rising from her chair. "If I hear anything about Miss Horowitz, I'll pass it along to you. Although with your connections, you'll probably get the scoop on her disappearance long before I do."

Brenda drained her coffee cup. "I'll walk back with you, Cari. Vic Warner still hasn't handed in this month's test, and I'm determined to see that he does."

"Vic doesn't like continuing education classes, does he?"

"Not my classes," Brenda admitted as they left the break room. "Vic would prefer a beer tasting course to anything I teach. But he has no choice in the matter. If he's going to keep up his ECRN certification, he has to take the monthly review test like everyone else in the department." Brenda stopped short in the hallway. "Good grief, Cari. Where's all that noise coming from?"

The noise she referred to was a mixture of guttural animal sounds and raised human voices. The two women picked up their pace just as a security officer rounded the corner and raced into the ER.

"What's going on here?" Brenda demanded as she and Caroline entered the room.

Fawn Phillips was standing in front of the desk nose to nose with a cab driver, the two of them surrounded by an assortment of expensive looking luggage. The driver, a short burly man with hairy arms and tattoos running from wrist to elbow, was waving his finger in the face of the much taller woman.

"It ain't my affair," the man shouted. "This junk belonged to that guy, and I don't want nothin' to do with it."

"This is an Emergency Room for humans, not for animals. Get them out of here now!" Fawn pointed to the door, but the man was having none of it.

"Are ya deaf, lady? You don't hear what I'm tellin' ya?" The driver shook his fist in the air. "That stuff don't belong to me!"

"What's the problem?" Brenda repeated, thrusting her body between the charge nurse and the cabbie. "Perhaps I can be of some assistance, sir."

The man continued to glare at Fawn, but eventually his gaze swung to the EMS Coordinator. "You the boss around here?"

Brenda looked around for Molly. Not seeing her, she answered, "At the moment, yes, I am."

Fawn's lips tightened into a thin line, but she contented herself with dagger looks aimed at Brenda's back. Caroline saw the hatred in the young woman's eyes and pitied Brenda. The older nurse had made a serious mistake by usurping Fawn's authority.

"Then you get to take charge of all this." He pointed to the objects on the floor. "They came with the guy, and they're stayin' with the guy. All I want is my fare, and I ain't leavin' till I get it." That said, the cabbie crossed his arms over his chest and planted his feet in a just-try-to-throw-me-out stance.

Caroline glanced at the security officer, a man she'd known for years. He raised his eyebrows, straining to contain a grin.

"Would someone please explain what's going on here?" Brenda snarled. An unearthly wail punctuated by sharp whining noises had erupted from a large plastic carrying case jammed between two pieces of luggage on the floor.

"This man brought a patient to the ER," Fawn began.

"A patient? Ya call that guy a patient?" The cab driver raised his eyes to heaven and sighed. "A patient is a live person, lady. That guy ain't no patient. He's dead!"

Caroline shot a look at Wendy who sat watching the proceedings from her station at the computer. With a nod of her head, the girl confirmed the man's statement.

"He picked him up at the airport," Fawn continued more firmly. "Apparently the man collapsed in the cab, and instead of calling his company and requesting paramedic assistance," -- here Fawn looked accusingly at the driver -- "he chose to drive the man here himself. The patient was dead on arrival."

"And these are his belongings?" Brenda asked, her control returning as she assessed the problem and found it solvable.

Fawn nodded. "I have no difficulty with storing the luggage, but the dogs have to go."

Brenda's gaze fell on the plastic carrying case. "Dogs?" she murmured. "Like in more than one?"

"A whole damn litter of puppies," the cabbie gloated. "And the mama, too."

"You know the rules," Fawn said to Brenda. "The Public Health Department would have a fit if we kept them here."

Caroline knew Fawn was right. Still, they couldn't put the dogs outside in their carrier. Thirty minutes in this blinding heat and every pup would be dead. It was no use asking the cabbie for help. He was obviously not interested in taking the poor things to a vet.

"Was the man from Chicago?" Caroline asked, thinking that relatives might be on their way to the hospital even as they spoke. If so, the dogs could be given to them along with all the luggage.

"Guy lived in Florida," the cab driver stated. "He was some kind of breeder, and he came up to deliver them dogs to a customer. Told me all about it before he croaked in my back seat."

"Have you notified the police?"

"Not yet," Fawn told Brenda. "I haven't had a chance with all this commotion."

"Why don't you call them while Joe" -- Brenda motioned to the officer -- "moves this luggage to the Security Office. As for the dogs, I'm not quite sure where we'll put them."

Caroline had walked behind the cabbie and was now hunched down in front of the carrying case. After pushing the luggage away to let air flow through the container's vented door, she peered inside at the pups. She quickly pulled her head back as a musky odor assailed her nose. Rising to her feet, she turned to the others.

"They're cute little devils, but man! Do they smell."

"It's not the dogs that stink, lady," the cab driver said. He pointed to a plastic shopping bag half hidden among the luggage behind the carrying case. "It's the fish."

As one man, all three nurses backed away from the luggage.

"Fish!" Brenda exclaimed. "Don't tell me this guy bred fish, too."

"Naw," the cabbie assured them with a wave of his hand. "He just liked eatin' the stuff, and he brought his own supply along. As if we got no fish markets here in Chicago," he added, a pained expression creasing his face. "That guy was one beer short of a six-pack, if ya know what I mean."

Caroline found herself agreeing with the man. Steeling herself, she picked up the bag and opened it. Inside were two round containers, the large kind spread margarine was sold in. One of the lids had fallen off in transport, and the contents of the container, originally frozen, had completely defrosted.

"This goes in the garbage," she said, holding out the bag to the security officer. Joe stepped back, shaking his head.

"Sorry, Caroline. Legally, that belongs to the patient. I can't just throw it out."

"He's right," said Fawn, dialing the Food Service Department. "We'll have to store it in a freezer in the kitchen."

Caroline and Brenda exchanged looks as Fawn made the call. If it had been up to either one of them, the fish would have ended up in the Dumpster in no time flat.

"They won't take it," Fawn reported, slamming the phone into place. "They said if it didn't come from an authorized vendor for the hospital, it can't be stored on hospital property. I guess we'll have to put it in the refrigerator in the break room."

"Uh, uh," said Brenda.

"No way," echoed Caroline.

"It'll smell up the whole place," Wendy added, throwing her two cents worth into the conversation.

"Well, what will we do with it?" Fawn grumbled.

Caroline's face lit up. "I think I've got the answer. Our dead man's from out of town, right? Nobody knows his medical history, nobody knows his doctor, and it's a sudden death. Legally, no doc in this department can sign the death certificate. Add it altogether, and that makes this a coroner's case."

"So? What are you saying, Cari?"

Caroline turned to Brenda. "It could be a while before the cops cart this guy off to the County Morgue. We might as well transport the body to our own morgue, and let him rest in peace until they arrive."

Brenda saw the wisdom in Caroline's suggestion. She turned to the cabbie.

"You said this fellow was from Egypt, didn't you?"

The cab driver looked at her like she was nuts.

"Egypt? I told ya he got off a plane from Florida."

"Egypt, Florida, whatever. Let's just say he has the blood of the Pharaohs in him."

"They used to bury the Pharaohs with items they could use in the afterlife," Wendy informed the driver. "Things like favorite pieces of furniture, and pots for cooking."

"And food to put in those pots," added Brenda.

"Food like fish," grinned Caroline.

"We're going to get in trouble," said Fawn.

"You got a better suggestion?" asked Joe.

It was four to one, so Fawn bowed to the wishes of the others. Picking up the phone again, she dialed the Transport Department.

"I need you to move a body to the morgue. And unlike yesterday when we waited for over an hour, I want you right now!"

"You gonna break that thing," the cabbie warned her when Fawn slammed down the phone for a second time.

"I'm gonna break something before long," she growled. "It just might be your neck if you don't shut up."

"Hot damn," the cabbie whistled in appreciation.

When the transport employee arrived a few minutes later, he found the body bagged and ready to go. A strange odor clung to the plastic sheeting in the area of the victim's armpits.

"Phew!" the man muttered. "Didn't this guy ever bathe?"

Chapter Eighteen

June 15th
1 P.M.

.   "This is our last pair of pediatric crutches," Caroline said as she passed Michelle Devine sitting at the doctors' desk in the east wing. "Would you order some more, please?"

"I'm tech today, not UR. Tell Wendy to do it." Michelle extended her left hand on the desk and grimaced at the chipped nail on her ring finger. "Just look what those dogs did to me. Nearly bit my hand off when I opened the cage to let them out."

Caroline backtracked to the desk as Michelle wiggled her fingers in the air.

"Doesn't look all that bad to me," she said with a shrug. "It was nice of Mr. Bradford to let the puppies roam free in his office. I had no idea our Administrator was such a dog lover."

"He only kept them until the animal welfare people arrived. It was no big deal." Michelle returned her attention to her nails. "And to think I just polished these last night. What a waste of time."

Caroline tore the plastic wrap off the crutches and placed them on the desk in front of the tech.

"Speaking of wasting time, I see you're not busy at the moment, so why don't you take these over to the little boy on cart two. While you do that, I'll speak to Wendy about placing the order."

Annoyed that she was actually being asked to do her job, Michelle took her time getting up from the chair. Caroline stood there waiting until the girl finally rose and grabbed the crutches.

"Don't forget to adjust them to size," Caroline called out as the tech slouched off. "He's only four feet tall."

Michelle pretended not to hear, but that didn't bother Caroline. At least she'd forced the girl to do some work, a triumph of sorts considering the fact that the tech was intrinsically lazy.

"You look like the cat that swallowed the canary."

Susan Kane placed a box of supplies on the doctors' desk and, smiling, slid into a chair. Despite a hectic morning, the novice nurse appeared more relaxed than she had when the day started.

"Just celebrating a moral victory," Caroline stated smugly. "I finally bested our tech."

"Michelle Devine?" Susan's smile faded. She lowered her voice a notch. "She's a real piece of work, isn't she?"

"She'll never make 'Employee of the Year', that's for sure."

"That's not the title she's seeking," Susan said with a touch of bitterness. "She'd rather be known as 'The Rich Doctor's Wife'."

Remembering the conversation she'd overheard between Michelle and Roger MacGuffy, Caroline found it hard to disagree with Susan. Still, what the two of them did on their own time was none of her business. They were both adults, and presumably mature.

"I won't pretend I like Michelle," Susan continued. "She's lazy and conceited. But strangely enough, I feel sorry for her. Roger's running her in circles like a circus pony." She gestured towards the nurses' desk. "Just look how he carries on when she's not around."

Caroline turned and saw Roger standing at the desk hovering over Wendy Moss. The UR was typing orders into the computer, and Roger stood in back of her, his hand resting casually on her shoulder. As Caroline watched, he bent forward to stare at the computer screen, then slowly straightened up again. As he did so, his hand slid up the back of Wendy's neck in a light caress.

Caroline saw the girl shiver.

Over by cart number two Michelle Devine saw it also.

CHAPTER NINETEEN

June 15th
1:15 P.M.

Caroline had just discharged the little boy with the crutches when Josephine Rose stepped into the ER and dropped her bombshell.

"Miss Horowitz is dead! Murdered!"

Caroline dropped the boy's chart on the now empty cart and hurried over to the nurses' desk. Susan and Michelle Devine were already there, as was Wendy Moss. Fawn Phillips, wide-eyed and grimmer than usual, had risen from her chair and grabbed the Assistant Director of Nursing by the arm.

"Keep your voice down," Fawn hissed. "There are patients in the room."

With an apologetic bob of her head, Mrs. Rose sank down on the chair just vacated by Fawn.

"I'm so flustered," she whimpered. "All day I've had this premonition that something was wrong, terrible wrong, and now all my fears have been realized." She reached for a tissue and dabbed at the corners of her eyes.

The dramatic effect of her pronouncement was lost on Fawn. "Somebody get Miss O'Neal," she snapped impatiently. "Michelle, go and find her."

Torn between her fear of the charge nurse and her desire to hear the grisly details firsthand, Michelle hesitated a fraction too long.

"Did you hear me?" Fawn barked. "Go get Molly. Now!"

Michelle stuck out her bottom lip in a sullen scowl, but she did as she was told. The ADON watched her go, then launched into a vivid description of the police activity now taking place at Ascension Medical Center.

"Two detectives arrived about a half hour ago. They went straight to Mr. Bradford's office and told him the awful news about Angela. The Administrator was devastated, of course. Miss Horowitz was one of his most valued employees."

Caroline suspected that the Administrator didn't care a whit about Angela Horowitz. If he was devastated, it was because he feared a swarm of reporters would descend on the hospital seeking inside information on the Director of Nursing.

"I was called to Mr. Bradford's office only minutes after the police arrived," Josephine continued with ill-concealed pride. Stressing her own importance, she added in a murmur, "They asked me to aid them in their inquiries."

"What happened next?" Wendy Moss demanded impatiently. "Do the police think somebody here killed Miss Horowitz?"

Refusing to be hurried, Josephine chose to ignore the question.

"Recalling the wording of our Mission Statement, it occurred to me that 'service' has many meanings. While we at Ascension Medical Center are dedicated to serving our patients, we must at times also serve the state. I saw my duty clearly, and I hope, as employees of this institution, you will do the same."

Caroline wondered if all bureaucrats sounded alike. If she hadn't known better, she would have sworn it was Glynnis Milburn talking. As it was, she had no idea what Mrs. Rose was trying to say.

Evidently no one else did either. Four faces stared blankly at the ADON until Fawn Phillips had the guts to speak up.

"What the hell do you mean?"

"I mean," Josephine said sternly, "I expect you all to cooperate with the police when you're asked about Miss Horowitz's relationship with Dr. MacGuffy."

"What relationship?"

Michelle Devine had returned to the room followed by Molly O'Neal. The tech's eyes blazed as she stared angrily at Josephine Rose.

"Why, dear!" Josephine responded with surprise. "Everyone knows the two of them were...close. There could only be one reason why the detectives asked to be shown to his office. Obviously, Dr. MacGuffy is their prime suspect."

"I don't think it's wise to voice such thoughts."

Molly O'Neal circled the desk in four quick steps.

"Reputations are at stake here, Mrs. Rose. Dr. MacGuffy's reputation for one, and the hospital's reputation for another. Accusations of guilt should be left to the police, although I do agree with you that everyone in this department should cooperate if questioned by these detectives."

The Assistant Director of Nursing got to her feet.

"And when did you become a fan of Roger MacGuffy," she asked waspishly.

"I don't have to be a fan to insist on fairness. I'd want the same for myself if I were the subject of a police investigation."

"As well you may be, Miss O'Neal. It's common knowledge that you were called on the carpet several times by Miss Horowitz. In fact, she was considering firing you today."

"That's enough," Caroline said sharply. She moved to Molly's side. "I doubt that Michael Bradford would be pleased if informed of your accusations, Mrs. Rose. The Administrator has only one thing on his mind right now, and that's to keep this hospital free of scandal. You're not helping him by voicing such dangerous opinions."

Caroline could see the wheels turning in the ADON's head. Josephine was not totally stupid. With Angela gone from the helm, someone would have to fill in until a new Director of Nursing was hired. That someone could be her.

"You'll have to forgive me," Josephine murmured, backpedaling as gracefully as possible. "Angela's murder has affected me deeply. In my haste to see her killer brought to justice, I may have said things I really didn't mean."

Caroline kept silent, but Molly was a more generous soul.

"I'm sure no one here will repeat a word of this conversation. We've all been under a great deal of stress, and it appears now that it will only continue."

Josephine inclined her head but said nothing.

"Time to get back to work, everyone." Molly glanced at the assembled staff. "I can't tell you not to talk about what's happened today, but I will ask you to do it in private, away from the patients." She turned to Fawn. "I'll be in my office if you need me."

Caroline watched her friend leave the room with Josephine Rose in tow.

"That was a class act," said Fawn grudgingly.

Yeah, and it took every bit of strength she had to carry it off, Caroline thought. She'd seen the nervous tick in Molly's cheek and the tremor in her hands. She wondered how much more the nurse manager could take before she cracked.

Turning from the desk, Caroline saw Susan talking with Keeshon in the corridor connecting the two wings of the ER. She was filling him in on the news, and the male nurse was listening intently.

Nearby, Wendy sat at her computer, her face expressionless as she stared at the screen saver.

Only Fawn seemed indifferent to Angela's death. With the room nearly empty of patients, and the doctors out of the way, the charge nurse had pulled out the schedule book and was filling in her shifts for the following month.

As for Michelle, she was nowhere to be seen.

CHAPTER TWENTY

June 15th
2:30 P.M.

.   "This is like the calm before the storm," Caroline muttered as she stood hands on hips in the middle of the east wing contemplating the two rows of empty carts. "No patients waiting to be seen, and not a peep out of the telemetry radio in over an hour."

"Kind of spooky, isn't it." Susan dipped her fingers into a cup of ice water and sprinkled the cool liquid on her throat and forehead. "You'd think with the way the temperature's rising, we'd be swamped with heat victims. I guess Molly's precautions were for nothing."

"It's early times yet. All hell could break loose at any moment." Caroline saw Brenda Berlein enter the room. The EMS Coordinator beckoned to her, then turned and walked back the way she'd come. "I'm going to get myself a cold drink, Susan. I'll be back in a few minutes."

A blast of hot air met her in the corridor as the outside doors opened and two uniformed Chicago cops entered the building. They made their way past Caroline and consulted with another officer standing guard outside Roger MacGuffy's office. With a nod of his head, the third policeman opened the door and ushered the new arrivals inside.

It looked like a full-scale investigation was taking place in the ER. Just as Josephine had predicted, police attention seemed concentrated on Roger. But that didn't mean the rest of the staff was above suspicion. Glancing down the hallway towards Molly's office, Caroline saw another uniformed policeman stationed there.

When she stepped across the threshold of the EMS office, she found Brenda Berlein sitting at her desk, her chin propped on the palm of one hand, a bemused expression etched on her face.

"This is simply incredible," Brenda said, raising her eyebrows in disbelief. "God knows I didn't like Angela Horowitz, but I never would have wished her dead."

"The ER is crawling with police."

"I know. They've already interviewed me."

"You? But why?" Caroline collapsed into a chair and stared at the EMS Coordinator. "You had no motive to kill Angela."

"According to Roger MacGuffy, practically everyone in the ER had a motive. Everyone but himself, that is. To prove his point, he told the cops about that argument I had with Angela yesterday morning."

"But that concerned a professional matter. Surely the police understand the difference between a heated discussion of hospital policy and an argument based on personal issues."

Brenda picked up a pen and doodled distractedly on a pad of paper. "Sometimes the lines get blurred. What starts out as a professional disagreement can turn into a personal one. I'm afraid that's what happened yesterday."

"What I'd like to know is why these detectives showed up on Roger's doorstep. They must have found some incriminating evidence in Angela's apartment, something that linked him to the murder."

"These temporary walls are thin," Brenda said, indicating the painted plasterboard separating her office from Dr. MacGuffy's. "I was in here working when the cops arrived. They must have accused Roger of something because he started yelling about people hating him and trying to frame him. At that point, I started paying attention to the conversation, but I only caught a few phrases here and there."

"Anything interesting?"

Brenda shrugged. "Mainly I heard Roger accusing Molly of the murder. Then my name came up along with that of Keeshon Jones and Patrice Woodson."

"He covered the field, didn't he?"

"I'm worried about Molly, Caroline. Roger dragged out every argument she and Angela ever had. He painted Molly as some sort of mad woman who hated the DON's guts." Brenda ran a hand through her curly hair. "I got the impression from the policeman who interviewed me that Josephine Rose backed Roger's claims. They asked me to substantiate some of the things she told them."

"And did you?"

"I tried to explain the situation in the ER, but it seemed like everything I said only made matters worse. Josephine's still furious with Molly for bypassing her on the Patrice Woodson issue. She's too damned stupid to see that her little vendetta could land our boss in jail."

"Where's Molly now?"

"Closeted with the detectives. This is the second time they've interviewed her, and that worries me, Cari."

It worried Caroline, too. There was no denying Molly had a motive for wanting Angela out of the way. The DON had caused nothing but trouble for the nurse manager ever since she arrived at Ascension. If Josephine Rose could be believed, Angela had been planning to fire Molly. That in itself was ample reason for some people to commit murder.

"Brenda, do you know how Angela was killed?"

The EMS Coordinator wrinkled her nose. "She died in bed, smothered with a pillow."

The answer surprised Caroline. Angela Horowitz had been a big boned woman, large but not running to fat. While size didn't always indicate strength, she certainly hadn't looked like a weakling.

Angela's killer had to be strong if he could force her onto a bed and hold her down with a pillow. Unless, that is, she'd been asleep when the intruder entered the apartment. Or knocked unconscious first.

"Keeshon Jones," she muttered.

"What did you say?"

Caroline roused herself from her reverie and shook her head.

"Sorry, Brenda. I was just thinking aloud."

"You were thinking of Keeshon. Don't tell me you suspect he had something to do with this."

"He's a big man, Brenda, and very muscular. Susan told me he served in the Armed Forces, which means he's been trained in hand-to-hand combat."

"He was a member of the Army boxing team. He won a few medals in competition."

Caroline nodded. "So Keeshon's quite capable of subduing an opponent. You know he has a temper, Brenda. You heard him say he'd like to kill Miss Horowitz."

"Now isn't that interesting."

The sound of a third voice entering the conversation caught both women off guard. They turned simultaneously to stare at the stranger standing in the doorway.

With his long ears, fleshy jowls, and barrel chest, their uninvited guest resembled an aging bulldog in a rumpled brown suit. His droopy mustache matched the color of his pants, and his sleepy looking eyes were half hidden behind tinted glasses. He cast a gloomy smile in Caroline's direction as she uttered a low, drawn out groan.

"Thanks for that heartfelt welcome, Mrs. Rhodes. If I may say so, you're the very last person I'd hoped to run into here."

Caroline shot a meaningful look at her old nemesis.

"The feeling is mutual, Mr. Evans. Definitely mutual."

CHAPTER TWENTY-ONE

June 15th
3:00 P.M.

"May I ask why the FBI are involved in this case?"

"We're not involved," Tom Evans said as he ushered Brenda from the room and closed the door. He settled himself behind the EMS Coordinator's desk. "I'm on a training assignment with the Chicago Police Department, teaching a couple of classes at the Academy and doing a little other stuff."

Caroline assumed that the term 'other stuff' covered a host of unmentionable topics. For the life of her, she couldn't see how the murder of a hospital employee fell under that heading.

"And you just happened to tag along with the detectives when you heard about this murder."

Agent Evans permitted a slight smile to crease his face. "You might say that," he conceded.

Caroline knew she'd get no more out of the man. She'd met him before, once when he'd investigated a bombing at St. Anne's Hospital, and then again when he'd been called in on a case involving a murder in Rhineburg's post office. One didn't trifle with Agent Evans. He was a man of limited personality but much experience whose ability to patiently slog through the evidence usually paid off in a conviction.

Unfortunately, their relationship was a stormy one. Caroline had been a prime suspect in the bombing, and Evans had never fully forgiven her for withholding evidence in the case. He'd warned her off the second murder he'd investigated in Rhineburg, but once again her snooping had led to an arrest.

"What are you doing at Ascension?" Evans asked. "I thought you'd become a permanent fixture in Rhineburg."

Caroline told him about her friendship with Molly O'Neal and her temporary role in the Emergency Room.

"I'm here just for the summer," she assured him. "I never met Angela Horowitz before yesterday, so I'm afraid I can't be of much help to you."

"Hmm. I guess there's a first for everything." Someone knocked on the door and Evans called out, "Come in!"

Caroline looked over her shoulder. She broke into a smile when she saw the familiar figure of Detective Dominic Gianni enter the room.

"Dom! How good to see you again." Rising from her chair, she crossed the room and gave the detective a hug. "Not under these circumstances, of course, but..." She shrugged, letting the sentence hang in the air.

"I know what you mean, Mrs. Rhodes. It's good to see you again, too." Gianni stood back and assessed her. "You're looking pretty fit. Life in Rhineburg must suit you."

"I take it you two are old friends," Evans said, a hint of sarcasm in his voice. "Don't tell me she was out catching killers on your turf, too."

The other man's smile vanished. "Actually, her son Martin and I were buddies back in high school. We played together on the varsity baseball team. I was also the investigating officer in the hit-and-run death of her husband last year."

Evans' eyes narrowed.

"The police were unable to find the driver of the car," Caroline explained. "Dom spent a lot of time searching for that man. My children and I appreciated his efforts."

Tom Evans leaned back in his chair and stared at Gianni.

"Perhaps we'd better discuss this current case." He told his partner about the conversation he'd overheard between Caroline and Brenda. "Mrs. Rhodes said this Jones fellow threatened to kill Miss Horowitz."

"Kee was angry when he said that." Caroline told them about Roger MacGuffy's moves on Patrice Woodson. "Kee was upset because Angela refused to act on Patty's complaint."

Dominic Gianni moved around the desk and drew up a chair next to Evans. He unbuttoned the jacket of his gray silk suit exposing a perfectly pressed black shirt and matching tie streaked with silver threads.

"We'll be talking to Mr. Jones again, but right now, Mrs. Rhodes, I'd like your take on the situation here at Ascension. Was Molly O'Neal's job in jeopardy as Dr. MacGuffy and Mrs. Rose claim?" When Caroline hesitated, Gianni added, "Just tell the truth as you know it. You'll be helping your friend."

Caroline wondered about that. Experience told her the truth sometimes backfired, kicking people in the pants when they didn't deserve it. Everything depended on how it was interpreted, and who did the interpreting.

"Molly runs a tight department that's earned a good reputation in the community. Unfortunately, that reputation is slipping due to hospital policies aimed at saving money. Staffing cuts have affected everyone. It can take an hour to get results from the lab. X-rays are delayed because we're short on technicians, and moving patients to beds can take all day. The people who use this hospital don't like that."

Gianni nodded, seemingly interested in what Caroline was saying. Tom Evans, on the other hand, showed signs of impatience.

"The Emergency Room serves as a calling card for the entire medical center," Caroline continued, her words tumbling out one after another. "If people have unpleasant experiences in the ER, they tend to think badly of the hospital as a whole."

"What you're saying is, complaints about Miss O'Neal's handling of the department could have cost her the job."

Caroline shook her head. "No, Mr. Evans, that's not what I'm saying at all. Patients complained *to* Molly, not *about* her. Miss Horowitz didn't seem to understand the problems down here. Molly and she were on different wavelengths when it came to running the department, and Roger MacGuffy's constant interference didn't help."

She told them about Roger's desire to control the nursing staff.

"Roger got nowhere with the previous Director of Nursing, but he seemed very close to Miss Horowitz. When Molly opposed him on issues, he'd run straight to Angela for help. From what I've heard, she sided with him ninety-nine percent of the time."

Evans and Gianni exchanged looks.

"That must have been frustrating for Miss O'Neal," said the detective.

"I think Molly was ready to resign," replied Caroline.

"But she won't have to do that now that Horowitz is out of the picture. A new Director of Nursing may see things from Miss O'Neal's point of view." Evans appeared pleased with his summation. He glanced over at Gianni. "Any more questions, Dom?"

The detective shook his head. "Not at the moment."

"Now wait a minute," Caroline protested. "I know what you're thinking, and you're wrong. Molly had nothing to do with the death of Angela Horowitz."

"I hope you're right about that," Gianni said gently. "Miss O'Neal seems like a nice person. Unfortunately, she's unable to account for her whereabouts last night. She had motive and opportunity, and in my book, Mrs. Rhodes, that makes her a prime suspect."

Chapter Twenty-two

June 15th
5 P.M.

.   The rush hour traffic was in full swing by the time Caroline left Ascension Medical Center. She nosed her Jeep into the right lane on Oakton and headed east towards Evanston, the air conditioner turned on full blast. The temperature outside had dropped to an almost balmy 84 degrees, but after hours sitting in the hospital parking lot, the car's interior felt like an oven. Caroline gripped the sun-baked steering wheel gingerly and tried to concentrate on her driving rather than her discomfort.

The heat wasn't the only thing distracting her as she headed back to Krista's apartment. Images floated through her brain like tangled balloons caught in a breeze. Faces bobbed into view, hovered momentarily, then drifted away as others pushed forward to claim her attention.

Caroline saw again the worried look in Molly's eyes as she emerged from her office flanked by Tom Evans and Dom Gianni. Molly had smiled when she'd seen her old friend, but it was a weak smile devoid of any real cheer.

Vic Warner's reptilian grin crowded out the vision of the nurse manager. Vic had appeared jubilant after his interview with the police, boasting that his testimony would convict a killer. He'd mentioned no names, but made numerous references to a position of power opening up in the ER in the very near future. It didn't take a genius to understand what Vic was up to. Warner wanted Molly's job, and if he couldn't earn it through hard work and ability, he'd steal it from her.

Vic's features faded into the background to be replaced by the face of Roger MacGuffy. The Medical Director's expression wavered between anger and bewilderment. Caroline could accept the first emotion as real, but she wondered about the second. Was Roger as mystified by Angela's murder as he claimed to be, or was it simply an affectation, a front put on for the benefit of the police?

Caroline recalled how he'd wandered about the room questioning nurses while Molly was closeted in her office with Dom Gianni. MacGuffy's usual arrogance had been missing, and he'd seemed genuinely baffled by the fact that few people wanted to talk to him.

"Why does everyone dislike me?" he'd asked Caroline with a perplexed shake of his head. "I'm a nice guy!"

Goaded by concern for her friend, Caroline had snapped, "You're anything but a nice guy, Dr. MacGuffy. You're smug, egotistical, and demeaning towards the staff. You've driven away half the nurses in this department, and you've antagonized the rest with your campaign to discredit Molly. You, sir, have a propensity for causing trouble."

Roger's eyes darkened. "So I'm a pompous ass, am I?"

"Your words, doctor. Not mine."

Caroline had walked away before she could be provoked into saying anything more. Losing her temper with the Medical Director had been a foolish thing to do. Still, looking back on the incident, she felt a certain sense of satisfaction. It was high time someone put Roger in his place.

She wondered how Molly had survived the months of abuse dished out by the tag team of MacGuffy and Horowitz. Her own encounter with Angela had been brief, but she'd formed an instant disliked for the woman. As for Roger, she'd seen enough in the past two days to know what kind of man he was.

But wasn't that the very point she'd been trying to make during her interview with Dom and Tom Evans? Molly had been battling with the Medical Director for over a year and had the scars to prove it. If she'd wanted to kill anyone, it would have been Roger, not Angela. Angela was only the midddleman. True, she was a thorn in Molly's side, but Roger was the thorn tree. Cut down the tree and the prickly thorns would vanish.

An image of Wendy Moss slowly emerged on the windshield. Wendy, with her youthful curiosity. Wendy, with her uncomfortable questions.

"So what do you think, Caroline. Was Dr. MacGuffy sleeping with Miss Horowitz?"

"Why do you ask?"

Wendy's eyebrows soared. "It could explain the murder, couldn't it. Two people carry on an affair, and one of them is less than faithful. Perhaps they had a lovers' spat, and it got out of hand."

Caroline refused to be drawn into speculation, but Wendy persisted.

"Happens all the time in the movies, lovers quarreling, getting into fights. Roger finds himself a new girlfriend and wham! The battling begins." She paused, then added, "Couldn't expect him to stay with her forever, now could you? Good looking man like him wants a younger woman than Angela."

Caroline recalled the way Wendy shivered when Roger touched her earlier that day. At the time she'd thought it was a sign of revulsion, but perhaps she'd been wrong. Maybe the girl saw Roger in a romantic light.

"I'd forget about Roger if I were you, Wendy. The man's old enough to be your father."

Wendy paled at the thought, but before she could protest, Michelle Devine joined the conversation.

"I agree with Caroline. You're way too immature for Roger." Michelle gave Wendy an appraising look, then sank her fangs deep in the other girl's heart. "American men prefer a few curves on their women, Wendy. You're nice looking in a foreign sort of way, but there's not much to you, if you know what I mean."

Wendy's horrified expression faded from her mind's eye as a new thought struck Caroline. Where had Mavis Taylor been last night? At home crying on her husband's shoulder, or in Angela's apartment confronting the woman who'd stolen her job?

Unpleasant questions, but ones that needed to be answered. Pulling over to the curb, Caroline picked up her cell phone and dialed Mavis' number.

CHAPTER TWENTY-THREE

June 15th
5:20 P.M.

.   A radio was on in Krista's apartment, the music loud and pulsating. The unmistakable voices of the Beach Boys beckoned to Caroline, lifting her spirits as she circled the house and climbed the stairs to the second floor.

Beach music had always appealed to the kid in her. She'd grown up with it, and although she'd never ridden the waves at Malibu or hot-rodded down the street in a little deuce coupe, in her heart Caroline would always be a surfer girl, one of the gang with Brian and the boys.

She found herself singing alto harmony to Brian's tenor as she stepped into the apartment's tiny kitchen.

"Help me, Rhonda! Help, help me...Maddy!"

"Help me, Cari! Help, help me, Cari!" Madeline Moeller scooted across the kitchen floor and hugged Caroline. "Let's show 'em how it's done," she purred, winking at her friend.

Caroline grinned. "The old chorus line kick, right?"

Arms around each other's waists, the two women danced their way into the living room, belting out the song at the top of their lungs.

"Help me, Jake! Oh, help, help me, Jake!" Maddy batted her eyes at her police chief husband. Comfortably ensconced on the sofa, Jake blew her a kiss but refused to join the line.

"I'm having too much fun watching you," he hollered above the music. "Haven't seen so much leg since I closed down that strip joint over on Burley Street."

"One of the more enjoyable moments in Jake's professional career," Maddy commented dryly. She collapsed on a chair next to Krista and fanned herself with one ring-bedecked hand. "He spent an entire week 'gathering evidence' before I caught on and put my foot down."

Jake's face reddened. "Now, Maddy. You know I had to build a case that would stand up in court."

Laughing, Krista reached over the back of her chair and lowered the volume on the radio. "You have a couple of wild friends here, Mom."

"They're full of surprises," Caroline agreed. She sat down next to Jake and patted his arm. "Like turning up here at the apartment. Maddy said you were driving into town today, but I didn't expect to see you so soon."

"We couldn't stay away once we heard about the murder of Angela Horowitz."

"We caught the news on our car radio and figured you'd need our help," added Maddy.

"You're not involved in the investigation, are you, Mom?" Krista asked sharply.

Caroline hedged. "Not directly, Krista, but the police seem to think Molly O'Neal had something to do with Angela's death. I can't just sit by and watch her take the heat for a crime she didn't commit."

"Are you sure this O'Neal woman is innocent? If the Chicago PD..."

Caroline interrupted Jake with a vehement shake of her head. "I've known Molly since we were kids. She couldn't harm a fly."

"But your friend is in trouble now," Maddy said.

"The worst kind of trouble," Caroline replied. She launched into a concise summary of the day's events. When she got to the part about her conversation with Brenda and Tom Evans' sudden appearance on the scene, Maddy broke in with a comment.

"I thought we'd seen the last of that insufferable man."

"Sorry, Maddy, but if you recall, he's stationed here in Chicago. He's teaching a course at the Police Academy. He said he was doing other work, too, but he didn't elaborate on what it was."

"Hmm," murmured Jake. "Strange he'd be hanging around a murder investigation of this type. Not really FBI material, is it."

"Not as far as I can see." Caroline got up and walked into the kitchen. She rummaged inside the refrigerator for cold cans of cola. "But then I don't know a lot about the murder. The news reports have been sketchy so far, and it seems like everyone in the ER has clammed up. Everyone, that is, but Roger MacGuffy and Vic Warner."

She carried the drinks back to the living room and passed them to the others, then mentioned the confrontation she'd had with the Medical Director. "It was stupid of me to blast away at him like that, but I wasn't thinking clearly at the time. Knowing Roger, he ran straight to Vic with the story. By tomorrow morning, Vic Warner's twisted version of the facts will be spread all over the hospital."

"They can't fire you for that, can they?" asked Krista

"I suppose they could if they wanted to," Caroline answered lightly. "After all, I did sign the NESA form."

She told them about the document that allowed the hospital to fire employees with or without cause, with or without notice.

"That's terrible!" Krista sputtered. "You need a union, Mom. Ascension could never get away with that garbage if the nurses would organize."

"Now don't get worked up, Krista. This is only a temporary job, so it really doesn't matter if administration gets its shorts in a knot over the incident. Molly's the one we have to worry about."

"I don't understand why the police seem so interested in your friend," Jake said. "Did she say something to incriminate herself?"

"I don't know," Caroline replied. "I never got a chance to talk to her. After she finished with Dom Gianni, she left the department with Roger and Josephine Rose. Apparently the three of them were called upstairs to meet with the hospital lawyers."

"Probably a public relations thing. I imagine they were warned to keep their mouths shut and say nothing to the press."

Caroline agreed with Jake's assessment. "The police asked for Roger when they first arrived in the ER. They must have known about his relationship with Angela because they questioned him at length before tackling the rest of the staff."

"And he pointed a finger at Molly O'Neal."

"That's what Brenda told me. She said Josephine Rose backed Roger's accusations. Evans thinks Molly was about to lose her job. He figures that's motive enough for murder."

"But he has no proof."

"I don't know, Maddy. The cops may have found something at Angela's apartment that ties Molly to the crime."

Jake grunted. "I doubt it, Cari, or they would have coming looking for Miss O'Neal instead of Dr. MacGuffy. Whatever they found pointed to him, not her. Your friend only came to their attention because of MacGuffy's allegations."

The police chief's words made sense to Caroline, but her relief was short lived when he added, "Still, I'd advise Molly to get a lawyer. Circumstantial evidence has convicted many an innocent person."

"Don't say that," Caroline groaned. "Molly is no murderer."

"We may know that, but the jury won't. You'll have to convince twelve individual people, and that's not an easy thing to do."

Maybe so, Caroline thought, but the case against Molly would never get to the jury stage. She, Caroline Rhodes, would see to that.

CHAPTER TWENTY-FOUR

June 16th
5 A.M.

.   Caroline awoke to the sound of rain drumming on the roof. Unpredicted, a front had swept through the city around midnight leaving thunderstorms in its wake and dropping the temperature into the sixties. The storm hadn't broken the back of the heat wave, but it had bent it enough to provide a slight measure of relief to the city.

Delighted with the change in the weather, Caroline slipped out of bed and threw open the window. The sky to the east sparkled with lightening as the storm made its way over the lake. The heaviest rainfall had passed through Evanston an hour earlier. What fell now was a steady shower that showed no signs of letting up. Raindrops pinged off the boulders guarding the driveway entrance and puddled in the dips of the cracked sidewalk, spilling onto the sun-baked ground beside the house and flooding the bed of hostas growing there. In the garden next door Caroline spied a patch of dirt freshly spaded and ready for planting. Enriched by autumn's debris and darkened to the color of coal by the downpour, the newly turned soil gave off a pungent odor that mingled with the sweet fragrance of wet grass to tickle her nose.

Cleansed by the storm, the damp air vibrated with the scent of nature. Caroline closed her eyes and savored the aroma as it wafted through the open window. It felt good to breathe something other than recycled oxygen. Krista had turned off the air conditioner sometime during the night, and the breeze now flowing through the bedroom quickly banished the musty smell left by the overworked machine.

Caroline's peaceful mood evaporated as a sudden gust of wind hurled a fistful of raindrops against the screen. The chilly spray caught her full in the face and drenched the neck of her nightshirt. Reeling back from the window, she caught her toe in the rag rug, stumbled sideways, and hit the edge of the dresser with her shoulder. The rug skittered across the linoleum, and she plunged to the floor, her left knee bent and her foot twisted beneath her.

"Ow!" she yelped as she slid to a halt near the bed. Grabbing at her ankle, she rolled onto her side and massaged the injured limb.

"Damn, damn, damn!" The words rolled off her tongue and slipped past clenched teeth to echo off the walls of the empty apartment. Dragging herself to a sitting position, Caroline gingerly flexed her left leg. The kneecap stung from the impact with the floor, but the ligaments seemed in working order.

Her ankle was another matter altogether. Broken in a fall at Christmas, it still lacked strength, aching at times and swelling up after long hours of walking. It was already puffing up, and Caroline knew she had to get ice on it soon. When she tried to stand, though, pain shot up her leg.

Taking care not to awaken Krista, she hopped into the kitchen on her good foot and filled a plastic bag with ice, then hobbled back to her room. She flopped down on the bed, wrapped the bag around her ankle, and elevated her leg on a pillow.

Disgusted with herself, she closed her eyes and thought back on the visit with Jake and Madeline. The three of them had gone to a restaurant for dinner, leaving Krista back at the apartment waiting for her teacher friend. The two had a date, and while Caroline would have liked to meet the young man, she resisted the impulse to hang around until he arrived. The last thing Krista would have appreciated was an over zealous mother checking out her boyfriend.

"A good way to wear out your welcome," Maddy had warned.

How true, Caroline had thought as she'd kissed her daughter's cheek and followed Jake and Maddy out the door. The evening had been pleasant enough with the three of them cruising the downtown area before finally choosing a spot for dinner. Still, Caroline had found it difficult to concentrate on any other subject but the murder. Distracted by thoughts of Molly's predicament, she listened only halfheartedly to Maddy's enthusiastic evaluation of Emma Reiser's estate.

"I'm sure the tapestries alone will bring in a good sum of money. Considering their age, they're remarkably well preserved."

Jake reached over the table and touched his wife's arm. "I don't think Cari's in the mood to talk about tapestries, Maddy. Perhaps we ought to call it an evening."

Caroline blushed. "I'm sorry, but I can't stopping thinking about what happened today. I'll be better company tomorrow, I promise."

Maddy waved off her apology. "Silly of me to go on about Emma when you're obviously worried about your friend. I wish we could help in some way, Cari."

Little chance of that, Caroline thought as she opened her eyes and stared at the ceiling. Jake's offer to contact a friend in the Chicago PD was appreciated, but she didn't see what good it would do. Dom Gianni was in charge of the case, and friend or not, she couldn't see him giving out information to a small town cop who was buddies with a potential witness.

She'd tried to contact Molly when she'd arrived home last night, but either her friend wasn't answering the phone, or she was out for the evening. Mavis hadn't called back either. Caroline had left a message on her answering machine, and she wondered now if the other nurse was purposely avoiding her. Caroline had been back in the apartment by nine o'clock, early enough for Mavis to call.

There had been one message awaiting her return. Carl had called from West Virginia. Eager to talk to him, Caroline picked up the phone and dialed the number he'd left. Atwater answered on the second ring.

"Still raining in Heaven?"

"It's monsoon season here," Carl grumbled. "One more day of rain and I'm calling it quits. So what's new with you?"

Caroline sensed his surprise when she told him of Angela's murder. She gave what details she knew, then waded through a barrage of questions from the professor.

"I wish I could tell you more, Carl, but I'm as much in the dark as you are right now. Molly isn't home, and Mavis hasn't returned my call. Until I talk to one or both of them, I'll have to rely on the TV for information."

But the ten o'clock news had relayed few details on the murder. Either Detective Gianni was playing his cards close to his chest, or Ascension's administrator had pulled some strings down at the TV stations. Angela Horowitz's death was dealt with in a perfunctory manner before the newscasters moved on to more important stories.

Caroline tossed restlessly from side to side. She was scheduled to work the p.m. shift, and while the thought of putting in eight hours on a sprained ankle was depressing to say the least, she was not about to call in sick. Molly had enough problems without having to find a replacement for her. Determined to be in better shape by three o'clock, she closed her eyes and drifted back to sleep.

It was nine o'clock when she awoke for the second time. The rain had stopped, and the sun was creeping out from behind a thick band of gray clouds, ready to do battle again with the sweat glands of Evanston's citizenry. Already the humidity was unbearable. Pushing herself off the bed, Caroline limped to the window and closed it.

Krista had left for work by the time her mother entered the kitchen. Lacking company for breakfast, Caroline settled on a quick meal of buttered toast and orange juice, then went off to shower.

The ice had reduced some of the swelling in her ankle, and the hot water felt good as it cascaded down her legs and swirled around her toes. Ten minutes later the heat had loosened her muscles to the point where she could move her foot with only a minimum of pain.

After dressing, she applied a hard plastic air splint to her ankle. She'd used the splint after the cast had been removed from her leg last winter. It came in handy when walking aggravated the old injury, and she'd brought it with her from Rhineburg just in case it was needed. Its presence in her suitcase now proved invaluable.

She was about to call Mavis again when the doorbell rang.

"Who's there?" she asked. Leaving the chain on, she opened the door an inch.

"Sorry to disturb you, Mrs. Rhodes, but I'm here on behalf of my employer, Mr. Adam Horowitz. Mr. Horowitz would like to meet with you today."

Caroline peered at the man standing on the stairway. He was well over six feet tall and weighed close to three hundred pounds. His suit fit superbly, his shoes were polished to a fine sheen, and his hair was neatly combed. He could have passed for a choirboy in his Sunday best if it hadn't been for the dark glasses and the distinctive bulge under his left armpit.

"Is your employer related to the late Angela Horowitz?"

The man nodded. "She was his daughter." He slid a business card out of his pocket and passed it through the crack in the door.

Caroline took the card and examined it. Printed on thick creamy paper, one side was heavily embossed with the words "Adam Horowitz, Horowitz and Sons, Jewelers". The other side bore a scrawled message.

"Mrs. Rhodes -- I wish to meet with you about a personal matter. Mr. Moshe Goldstein will accompany you to my home at your earliest convenience. Our visit must be confidential - I trust you to keep it so. -- Adam Horowitz."

"I am Moshe Goldstein," said the man as he flashed his driver's license.

"So I assumed," murmured Caroline. "I also assume that by 'your earliest convenience', Mr. Horowitz means now."

The man nodded solemnly.

"I'm not dressed for an outing," Caroline said, indicating her shorts and tee shirt. "You'll have to give me a few minutes to change."

The man nodded again. "I'll be waiting downstairs by the car. It's parked behind your garage."

Caroline raised her eyebrows, but said nothing. If Goldstein preferred to hide in the alley, he obviously took this cloak-and-dagger thing a bit seriously. Perhaps she ought to think twice before going off with a gun-toting stranger.

Sensing her hesitation, Moshe Goldstein smiled. "You have nothing to worry about, Mrs. Rhodes. I've been Mr. Horowitz's driver for over five years. I'll see to it that you get to his home safely."

Driver? More like his bodyguard, Caroline guessed, but she only nodded before closing the door. Her curiosity piqued by the odd invitation, she changed clothes in record time, choosing a khaki skirt and a short sleeved hunter green blouse. She slid her feet into sandals, swept a comb through her short haircut, then headed downstairs to meet Goldstein.

"Where does Mr. Horowitz live?" she asked as Moshe helped her into the back seat of a black Lincoln Continental.

"Highland Park." Goldstein closed the door and climbed into the driver's seat. "Do you like rock gardens, Mrs. Rhodes? Mr. Horowitz has a beautiful one behind his house."

They drove east on side streets until reaching Asbury, then headed north to Green Bay Road, all the while discussing gardening. Caroline felt a bit like Alice in Wonderland, but she listened politely to Moshe's descriptions of the various plantings on the Horowitz property. Occasionally she offered a question or comment, but mainly she just sat back and listened to the muscular Mr. Goldstein expound on the beauties of nature.

The trip took less than twenty minutes and ended at the gates of a walled off estate on the outskirts of Highland Park. The wooded entrance gave way to rolling lawns that extended several hundred yards to a modern two-story brick house set back on a hilly incline. Sweeping windows and a raised flagstone patio graced the front of the house, but Caroline had little time to appreciate the architecture as Moshe nosed the Lincoln down a side drive towards an outlying building at the back of the grounds.

This second house was simpler in design. A single level structure of stone with a sloping roof of gray tiles, it sat in a hollow protected by massive pine trees and thick hedges. The front door of the house was guarded by two men of similar build and dress to Moshe Goldstein. Three other men patrolled the grounds adjacent to the building, each with a leashed Doberman at his side.

Moshe pulled around the building and braked near a side entrance. Stepping out of the car, he opened Caroline's door. "This way, Mrs. Rhodes."

She followed him up a shrub-lined path to where a woman wearing a maid's uniform stood holding the door. Goldstein motioned to her to enter.

"Hello, Caroline. I'm pleased you came on such short notice."

It took a moment for Caroline's eyes to adjust from bright sunshine to the subdued lighting of the house. Squinting, she looked past the maid and down a long hallway paneled in knotty pine.

At the far end stood an elderly white-haired woman, her trim figure accented by black linen slacks, an apricot silk sweater, and a black linen jacket. A pale yellow scarf streaked with darker shades of lemon encircled her throat, one end of it tossed over her shoulder, the other falling almost to her waist.

The woman listed slightly to the right as she leaned on a battered wooden cane, the head of which was carved in the form of a cobra. In her left hand she grasped a leash attached to the collar of a short gray-haired dog. The dog's pointed ears were tilted towards Caroline, but he stood rigidly at attention next to his mistress.

"Alexsa? Is that you?"

Caroline could hardly believe her eyes. Alexsa Stromberg Morgan, the ninety-year-old matriarch of the Morgan clan, hadn't left little Rhineburg, Illinois, in years. Why she was here in Adam Horowitz's house was a mystery that required a great deal of explaining.

"When... what..." Caroline stuttered to a stop.

"I've just come in from a walk with Harold." Alexsa reached down and tousled the thick coat of hair between the dog's shoulders. "I had to leash the poor beast since the men are out walking their animals. Here, Maria." She extended the leash to the Hispanic maid who took it and led Harold away to the kitchen. Crooking her finger at Caroline, Alexsa turned and entered a room off the corridor, still talking as she walked.

"Harold is a Norwegian elkhound. My husband gave him to Adam as a present for his seventy-fifth birthday. Harold was just a puppy back then; now he's thirteen years old."

"Alexsa..."

Mrs. Morgan put a finger to her lips. "Adam is tied up with business right now. While we're waiting for him, why don't I show you the garden?"

Alexsa opened a set of French doors that led onto a flagstone patio. Caroline followed her outside, careful to keep her voice neutral as she remarked on the weather they were having.

"It's been hotter than Hades around here," she said as she bent to smell one of the many roses growing alongside the patio. "Unfortunately, the rain last night only added to the humidity."

"Come see the pond, Caroline. Adam stocked it with fish and built a lovely rock garden around it."

The two women walked in silence until they entered a wooded area surrounding a large pool of water. Sunlight streamed through the tree-top canopy dappling the pine needles layered on the path.

"It's beautiful here," Caroline murmured. She gazed in admiration at Adam Horowitz's handiwork. Backed by a dozen ostrich ferns, cheddar-gold trollius bloomed near one edge of the pond. An arrangement of river rocks separated them from the feathery plumes of a Bridal Veil astilbe just beginning to whiten behind the plum colored foliage of flowering coral bells. Nearby, bell-shaped lily of the valley bordered a patch of violet blue monk's cap while Siberian iris stood tall in scattered groups around the pool.

A Mallard duck suddenly emerged from a bed of hosta planted next to the path, a string of fuzzy brown ducklings following in her footsteps. She stared at the two women, then guided her brood to the pond where one by one they flopped into the cool water. The two women sat down on a bench to watch them.

"This is not the best place to talk," Caroline said under her breath. "Someone could be listening behind those trees."

"I know. Unfortunately, I couldn't think of anywhere else to go."

Caroline glanced over at the old woman. Distress was written in every line on her face.

"What's happened, Alexsa? Why did you summon me here?"

"That was Adam's idea. When I mentioned that you worked at Ascension and had some experience as a sleuth..."

"Oh, Alexsa! You shouldn't have!"

"Forgive me, Caroline, but I wasn't thinking clearly. Adam was so upset when Ruben came to the house last night. All that talk of revenge." She shook her head. "Ruben was a hot-headed youth, and age has done nothing to improve him."

"Forget about Ruben," Caroline hissed. "Just tell me why I've been brought here. Who is Adam Horowitz? What does he want?"

Alexsa twisted her hands in her lap as she stared out over the water. "Adam's an old friend of my husband. They met years ago when both of them were young and still single. They worked together in Chicago before Adam went into his father's import business." She paused as if remembering those days." Adam was best man at our wedding, and when Thomas died, he was the chief pallbearer."

The old woman's eyes took on a far away look. "It seems so many years ago now. We stayed in touch after Thomas died, exchanging letters on birthdays, me sending him a card to celebrate Hannukah, Adam mailing good wishes at Christmas. He came to Rhineburg for Elizabeth's funeral," she said, recalling her granddaughter-in-law's sudden death the previous New Year's Eve. "When he called yesterday to tell me of Angela's murder, I took the first train out of Rhineburg. I knew I had to stand by him."

"Was she his only daughter?"

Alexsa nodded. "He turned fifty-one the day she was born. Angela was his baby, and her death is killing him." She turned and looked directly at Caroline. "Adam is desperate. He wants you to prove that Angela was murdered by someone she knew, someone from the hospital. He has to convince Ruben it wasn't a mob hit."

Caroline's jaw fell open. "A mob hit? Are you kidding me?"

"I wish I were," sighed Alexsa. "I wish I were."

CHAPTER TWENTY-FIVE

June 16th
12:30 P.M.

Spotting a police car parked across from the house, Moshe Goldstein circled the block, cut down the alley, and deposited Caroline at her back door.

"Sorry you couldn't join us for lunch," he said, a sudden hint of Texas in his voice as he helped her from the car. "Maria cooks up a real mean chili."

"I'm sorry also, Moshe, but I have to work this afternoon. Maybe some other time."

"Of course," Goldstein replied. He dug into his pocket and drew out a slip of paper. "If you ever require assistance, Mrs. Rhodes, you can reach me day or night at this number."

Caroline took the paper reluctantly. "Mr. Goldstein, I don't think..."

Moshe interrupted her. "Look, ma'am. I work for Mr. Horowitz, and this is what he wants done. That number is for my pager. Call if you need me. I'll never be far away."

Now that was a consoling thought. A gun-toting bodyguard watching her every move. Caroline sighed. This was all Alexsa's fault.

"Thank you, Moshe." She pushed the paper deep in the pocket of her skirt. "Hopefully, I won't have to bother you."

"It's no bother," Goldstein said as he climbed back into the Lincoln. He adjusted his sunglasses, nodded at her, then threw the car into gear and drove off. Caroline watched him go with a sense of relief.

"As if this case could get any more complicated," she muttered as she walked up the path through the yard. She was almost to the stairs when out of the corner of her eye she saw a figure concealed behind the bushes near the driveway

"This is private property," she yelled, quickening her pace. "Keep out!"

She took the stairs two at a time, pulled out her key, and jammed it into the lock beneath the ornate doorknob. The lock stuck, giving her pursuer a chance to catch up. Footsteps echoed on the steps behind her, heavy and ominous as they drew ever closer.

"Ca-ro-line!"

The intruder panted her name in a raspy, singsong voice, but she refused to look back. Her heart beating double time, she twisted the key back and forth, frantic until she heard the tumblers click into place. The back door of the apartment swung open, and she plunged into the kitchen. Spinning around, she leaned her weight against the wooden barrier and shoved it closed.

"Ooow!"

The agonized howl brought her up short. Glancing down, she saw the scuffed toe of a familiar looking boot wedged between the door and the jamb.

"CAROLINE!"

Professor Atwater's roar filled her ears. Grimacing, she backed away. The door flew open, and Carl stumbled inside.

"Good grief, woman!" he sputtered indignantly. "Are you trying to kill me?"

Hobbling over to the table, he collapsed on a chair. The wooden legs creaked beneath the weight of his portly body, and for an instant, Caroline wondered if the garage sale relic would give way and send him toppling to the floor. She reached out to steady it.

"I didn't realize it was you out there on the stairs. Why didn't you say something?"

"I tried to, but you..." Carl's voice cracked, then soared to a pitch far above his normal range before fading out entirely. He shook his head, then pointed to his throat.

Caroline looked more closely at her friend. "Sounds like you've come down with laryngitis."

"It comes...and goes," the professor squeaked.

She couldn't help but burst into laughter. The poor man sounded like a candidate for the Vienna Boys' Choir with his newly acquired soprano voice.

"I'm sorry," she said after she'd regained control of herself. "It's just that...well...you don't sound like yourself."

Carl's bushy white eyebrows seemed to have a life of their own as they waggled up and down above his scowling eyes.

"Wouldn't...so funny...were you."

"Of course not. Here, let me get you something for your throat." She stifled a grin as she mixed salt and water in a glass and handed it to him. "Bathroom's that way."

Carl heaved his massive frame off the chair and limped to the bathroom. A few minutes of gargling improved the condition of his vocal cords but not of his mood.

"Thank you," he rumbled in a dignified tone as he rinsed out his glass in the sink. Turning off the water, he cast a baleful eye at his hostess. "Now, please explain why my presence outside frightened you so."

Considering the fragile nature of the kitchen chairs, Caroline thought it best to continue their conversation elsewhere. She led the professor into the living room and pointed to the sofa, a newer piece of furniture with sturdy springs. Taking a seat opposite him, she confessed shamefacedly, "I thought you might be a hit man."

"A hit man? Now what have you gotten yourself into?"

"I'm not really sure," she replied with a rueful smile. "I've had a very strange morning, and I'm still trying to process everything in my mind."

Carl's face softened. "Tell me about it, Cari. We'll work through it together."

She shot him a grateful look. "A man showed up here this morning with a note from Adam Horowitz, the father of our former Director of Nursing. Mr. Horowitz requested a meeting with me."

"A meeting? Whatever for?"

"To discuss strategy. Angela's father wants me to catch her murderer."

Carl stared openmouthed as she told him about the trip to Highland Park and her surprise at seeing Alexsa Stromberg Morgan at the Horowitz estate.

"Apparently Alexsa and Adam are old friends. She took the first train to Chicago after he called and told her about Angela's death." She related the conversation they'd had down by the pond. "I was sitting there trying to recover from Alexsa's little bombshell when one of Mr. Horowitz's men arrived to escort us back to the house."

She recalled her initial surprise at seeing her host. Unlike his daughter, the man was small boned and on the short side. He'd probably been described as wiry in his youth, but years of comfortable living had filled in the curves of his once lean face and replaced muscle with fat. His paunch was well hidden by expensive tailoring as he sat writing at his desk in the study. When he stood up to greet her, though, his belly spilled over his belt line.

"He got right to the point, not even waiting for me to sit down before he started in on his grand plan to expose the killer."

"Is he mad?" growled the professor. "Or just senile?"

"Neither," replied Caroline. "Alexsa described him as desperate, and that's exactly what he is. You see, Carl, Adam Horowitz has a son named Ruben who thinks his sister was killed by the mob."

"Hold on, Cari. Maybe I missed something along the way, but I thought the prime suspect in this case was Molly O'Neal."

"That's the impression I got from the police, but apparently Ruben Horowitz has other ideas."

"But why?"

Caroline stood up and walked to the window. She flipped on the air conditioner and turned the switch to high, all the time wondering how to tell the next part of her story without sending the professor into a fit of apoplexy. She chose her words carefully.

"Adam Horowitz is a rich man. He owns a diamond import company and several high profile jewelry stores. He's eighty-eight years old and retired now. His son Ruben runs the business."

"Cut to the chase, Cari. My voice may die out at any minute, and I have a feeling I'm going to need it to talk some sense into you."

Caroline walked over to the sofa and sat down. It was useless pretending with the professor. He knew her too well.

"According to Adam, over the years he's developed ties to certain organized crime figures. He claims he's done nothing illegal, dealing with these people on a business only basis. He says he merely provided them with jewelry for their wives and girlfriends."

"He sold diamonds to the mob." Carl passed a hand over his face. "OK, I can handle that. Now tell me the rest."

"When Ruben took over as president of the company, he not only continued the relationship with these customers, but he built on it. Adam was careful not to elaborate on Ruben's activities, but reading between the lines, I gathered his son made some deals with these people that weren't quite kosher."

"Skip the puns, Cari. I'm beginning to get nervous."

Caroline smiled. "Sorry about that. Anyway," she said, continuing the tale, "Ruben made a lot of money before deciding he no longer needed his friends. Last winter he tried to sever his links with them, but they weren't overly pleased with the idea. There were threats made, and in the end Adam had to intervene. He called in some favors, paid off a few people, and eventually settled the matter."

"Or so he thought."

"Yes, so he thought. Now Angela's dead, and Ruben is convinced his former associates did it. He figures it was their way of hitting the family where it hurts most, and he's swearing revenge."

"He wants to take on the mob?"

"He already has a small army protecting his house. These men carry guns and use Dobermans to patrol the property."

"Shades of *The Godfather*," Carl muttered. "So what's he plan to do? Start a war, or go to the government and turn state's witness?"

"Nobody seems to know. Either way, Ruben's a dead man and Adam's lost two children, not one."

"And you feel sorry for him."

Caroline got up and paced the floor. "I feel sorry for anyone who's lost a child. But that's not the point, Carl. The fact is, I agree with Adam. I don't think this was a mob hit. I think Angela Horowitz was killed for very personal reasons." She stopped pacing and turned to face the professor. "Adam spoke to Michael Bradford, the Administrator of Ascension Medical Center. He promised to underwrite the total cost of the ER renovation if Bradford would give me free rein to investigate his daughter's murder."

"Bradford didn't agree, did he?"

"I'm afraid he did."

Carl rested an elbow on the arm of the sofa and cupped his chin in the palm of one hand. He stared at Caroline disapprovingly.

"Don't look at me that way," she snapped. "You're the one who's ultimately responsible for this mess."

"Me?" Carl roared. "What have I done to deserve the blame?"

"You got me involved in the murders at St. Anne's last winter. You also encouraged me to stick my nose into Emma Reiser's death. If it hadn't been for those two cases, Alexsa never would have mentioned my name to Adam Horowitz."

"Neither one of those affairs involved the Mafia. Angela's murder is a different matter altogether."

"How, pray tell? Am I in any more danger in Chicago than I was in Rhineburg?" She sat down on a chair opposite Carl, crossed her arms over her chest, and glared at him, a mulish look on her face. "If I remember correctly, I've been the target of killers twice since moving to your quiet little town."

Caught by the truth of her statement, Carl tugged on his beard and glared back without speaking. The two friends sat staring at each other in silence for several minutes before the professor capitulated and threw up his hands in surrender.

"All right, Cari. I can see you're determined to go through with this madness, but I won't let you go it alone. I'm here now, and so are Jake and Maddy. Together, we'll work out a plan."

"I already have something in mind," Caroline replied. She told him about the scheme she'd worked out in her head during the ride back to the apartment. "I discussed it with Moshe, and he thought it might work. He called Mr. Horowitz on his cell phone, and Adam promised to relay my request to Mr. Bradford. I'm going to stop by the Administrator's office on my way into work and finalize the plan."

"What do you want me to do?"

"Call Jake and Maddy. Let them know what's happening. Then contact the Archangels and see if they can come to Chicago."

Carl nodded. "What time should I show up in the ER?"

"Around five o'clock. People start taking their dinner breaks after five-thirty. You'll be free to roam then."

Carl nodded again as he dragged himself to his feet. For the first time he noticed the air cast on Caroline's ankle.

"What happened to you?" he asked, pointing to the splint.

"I twisted my ankle this morning. We can be limping buddies, you on your right foot and me on my left."

The professor glanced down at his boot. "Another angle to capitalize on." His voice cracked again and he grinned at Caroline. "I think I'll save my foot for tomorrow. This laryngitis should be enough to get me in the door today."

Caroline went off to change into her uniform. By the time she'd finished dressing, Carl had completed a phone call to Rhineburg.

"The boys are working on it," he told her as she stepped out of the bedroom. "With the university practically shut down for the summer, at least two of them should be able to get away."

"You never told me why you came to Chicago," she said as she walked into the kitchen and began rummaging about for the makings of a sandwich. "Did all the rain finally get to you?"

Carl grunted. "That, and hearing about Jake and Maddy's trip. I figured I'd come north for few days and do the tourist bit with the three of you. Martin's got the research well in hand in West Virginia."

Caroline packed her sandwich in a cooler bag, then checked her watch. "I have to get going. Make yourself at home, Carl."

"Will do," he replied, his eyes straying to the refrigerator.

Seeing the direction of his glance, Caroline wondered if she shouldn't have worded her invitation differently. The professor had a voracious appetite and kept a well-stocked kitchen at home. He could wipe out the entire contents of Krista's refrigerator in no time flat.

Thank goodness for twenty-four hour food stores, she thought as she walked out the back door and headed for her car.

CHAPTER TWENTY-SIX

June 16th
2:30 P.M.

The trip to Ascension Medical Center took longer than usual due to a sudden downpour of rain. Traffic crawled on Oakton, and it was almost two-thirty by the time Caroline pulled into the hospital parking lot. When she entered the Emergency Room lobby, it was crowded with people, half of them sitting in wheelchairs and on sofas, and the other half wandering about as if suffering from claustrophobia.

Caroline could understand the discomfort of the latter group. The temporary lobby was tiny, dimly lit, and closed in on all sides by windowless walls. The smell of wet clothes and sweaty bodies clung to the furniture, and the sliding glass doors provided the only source of fresh air as they opened and closed on new arrivals. It was not the most inviting place to wait, but it was better than standing outside in the rain.

Vic Warner was filling out paperwork on a new patient when Caroline limped by the triage area. He hadn't appeared to notice her, but then she heard him call her name.

"Hey, Mrs. Rhodes! What happened to your leg?"

Surprised by his sudden interest in her, Caroline turned and glanced back. Vic was standing in the hallway, his eyebrows raised and a smiling playing at the corner of his lips.

"Twisted my ankle," she said. "I tripped on a rug at home."

The triage nurse stepped closer. "Maybe we ought to X-ray it. Make sure you didn't break any bones."

She shook her head. "I iced it. It's feeling much better now."

"Well, if it starts to bother you..." The sentence was left hanging in the air as Vic shifted his attention to a spot beyond her left shoulder. When he spoke again, there was a hard edge to his voice. "Do whatever you want."

Without meeting her eyes, he turned and stalked back into the triage office.

"Such a touching scene."

Caroline swung around. Brenda Berlein was standing a few feet away, arms folded across her chest and a look of cynical disbelief etched on her face. The EMS Coordinator put a finger to her lips and shook her head. Motioning to Molly's empty office, she waited for Caroline to enter, then slipped in and quietly shut the door.

"You know what that was all about, don't you?" she whispered. "Vic's trying to get on your good side."

"I wasn't born yesterday, Brenda. I'm sure that if I'd agreed to the X-ray, I'd be sitting right now in the triage room being pumped for information about Molly. Vic's methods are pretty transparent."

Brenda looked apologetic. "I'm sorry, Cari. Sometimes I forget who I'm talking to." She sat down behind the nurse manager's desk and fiddled with the seat lever. The chair rose an inch. "I assigned myself to gossip control today. I've been all over the hospital squashing the stupid stories circulating about Molly and Angela."

"What kind of stories?"

Brenda waved her hand in a gesture of dismissal. "You know the sort. Molly was overheard threatening Angela. Angela was overheard threatening Molly. None of them make sense," she sighed. "And none of them can be traced to a reliable source."

"Speaking of Molly, where is she?"

"Out in the room arguing with Roger. The medical floors are practically full, and there are no beds anywhere for monitored patients. Molly wants to go on bypass."

Bypass. The worst of all solutions for a Medical Director, but one that had to be employed when there were no heart monitors available for use in the ER or on the units. All ambulances would be diverted away from Ascension until monitors became available again.

"But what's happened? How did we fill up all the beds in the hospital?"

"It's the heat wave. Molly predicted we'd see more victims, and today they started coming in. Old people living in apartments without air conditioning. Young people overdoing it at work. It's been a mess since ten o'clock, and this rain hasn't helped. The humidity is playing havoc with folks bothered by breathing problems, and we've seen our fair share of motor vehicle accidents. The MVA's are mostly minor, but they take up space and they're time consuming"

"And Roger doesn't want to go on bypass."

Brenda shook her head. "Not yet, anyway. Some of the day staff is staying over to work the p.m. shift."

"So we may be bedding patients in the Cast Room tonight."

Brenda nodded, and Caroline groaned. Molly had told her about Angela's decision to hold patients overnight in a space usually reserved for the orthopedic surgeons. The bone docs rarely used the Cast Room in the evening, and when the supply carts were removed, four beds could be squeezed into the area.

"The night shift won't like that one bit."

"They'll call in another nurse if it comes to that." Brenda stood up and walked to the door. "Now tell me what happened to your ankle."

"I tripped on a rug and twisted it." Caroline hoped she wouldn't have to explain her injury to anyone else. The whole incident was one she'd rather forget. "Do you know anything more about Angela's murder? And how is Molly? I called her several times last night, but all I kept getting was her message machine."

"All I know about the murder is what I've seen on TV. There were no signs of forced entrance, and no witnesses to the crime. According to our Administrator who appeared on the late night news wearing a somber look and a black armband, Angela was so beloved by the entire staff of Ascension Medical Center that her death could in no way be related to hospital matters." Brenda rolled her eyes. "As for Molly, she stayed at her mother's house last night. Thanks to Vic Warner, the press got wind of Roger's accusations and camped out in front of her condo. She saw their camera trucks when she rounded the corner, and she didn't even bother to stop."

"Poor Molly."

"Poor Molly indeed," replied Brenda as the two women stepped into the hallway. "About the only thing she can be thankful for is that the cops haven't shown their faces here today."

"You spoke too soon," Caroline murmured, her eyes fixed on the ER lobby. Brenda turned to look, then let out a soft moan.

Tom Evans had just strolled in past the sliding glass doors.

CHAPTER TWENTY-SEVEN

June 16th
10:30 P.M.

.   "We have no choice. We have to go on bypass." Keeshon
Jones gripped the phone to his ear with one hand while motioning with
the other to a team of paramedics who'd just rolled through the door.
"Look, Dr. MacGuffy, I know you're opposed to this, but there are no
telemetry beds left in the hospital, and we're up to our ears in
monitored patients. The Niles paramedics just brought in another chest
pain, and I don't even have a cart to put the guy on. What do you
expect me to do?"

Caroline stopped charting and looked over at Kee. From
where she stood, she could see his jaw go slack.

"So you're overriding Dr. Daley's decision? Then I'll tell him
you're coming in. I'm sure he'll be happy to let you take charge of the
room." Kee slammed down the phone. Seeing Caroline staring at him,
he walked over to her and said, "That sonofabitch told me to wait. He's
coming here to personally assess the situation."

"But why?" Caroline asked unhappily. "Chan Daley wouldn't
recommend bypass if it wasn't necessary."

"Of course he wouldn't," Kee snapped. "Roger just wants to
prove he's the boss."

"Chan's not going to like this. He'll take it as an insult to his
professional judgment."

"Roger doesn't give a damn what Chan likes or dislikes. He'll
be gone in another week or two, and then..."

"Gone? Keeshon! What do you mean, he'll be gone?"

"Haven't you heard? MacGuffy refused to renew his contract. Come July first, it's adios, Chan." Kee shook his head and walked off, leaving Caroline to stare after him in wide-eyed disbelief.

First Mavis, and now Dr. Daley. Roger was certainly cleaning house. She watched as Kee broke the news to Chan. The veteran doctor seemed to take it in stride, simply shrugging his shoulders in a 'what-can-I-say?' type of gesture.

"Roger is one helluva stupid man," Caroline muttered as she returned to her charting. Chan Daley was one of her favorite docs. She wondered what he'd done to earn the wrath of Roger MacGuffy.

"Are we on bypass yet?"

Interrupted once again, she looked up into the worried eyes of Susan Kane, now permanently assigned to the p.m. shift.

"Not yet. Roger wouldn't approve the move."

"I don't understand why it's such a complicated process. Of course, I've never been on duty when it's happened."

"Lucky you," Caroline said with a grin. She made a final entry on the chart, then laid it aside and gestured to the room at large. "All the people you see on these carts will stay overnight in the ER. It's not the most comfortable arrangement for them, but the care they need is unavailable elsewhere in the hospital."

Susan rolled her eyes. "Can't Dr. Daley make the decision?"

"The Medical Director has the final word on the matter. Roger's coming in to check things out for himself. Hopefully, when he sees the mess we're in, he'll agree to the plan."

The telemetry radio crackled into life. "Ascension, this is Niles Ambulance Two. Do you copy?"

"I'll get it," Caroline called to Keeshon. She smiled at Susan. "It's been a wild night, but don't let it fluster you. You're doing fine."

But Susan wasn't listening. Head bowed, she stared unseeing at a spot on the floor, her thoughts two decades in the past.

CHAPTER TWENTY-EIGHT

June 16th
11:20 P.M.

.   Caroline limped over to the desk and slumped down in a chair. Leaning her elbows on the crowded surface, she cradled her head in both hands. "This is madness, pure madness," she muttered in an exhausted voice.

"Theirs not to reason why, theirs but to..."

"Do and die." Caroline raised her head and glanced over at Wendy Moss sitting in her place at the computer. "What an appropriate line. What made you think of it?"

The unit receptionist looked up from her work. "When I was a child, my mother would sit by my bedside each night and read poetry to me until I fell asleep. Mostly she read narrative poems, and *The Charge of the Light Brigade* was one of her favorites."

"Alfred Lord Tennyson had a way with words."

Wendy nodded. "And my mother had a way of bringing those words to life. I could almost see the English soldiers marching through my bedroom, their sabers flashing in the moonlight. Mother said that war was folly, but she admired the courage and self-discipline of those soldiers. She said that if I developed those two traits alone, I could accomplish anything I ever wanted to do."

Caroline rubbed her tired eyes. "So you think we should all quit complaining and just play the cards we've been handed tonight."

"Oh, no," Wendy protested. "Please don't think I'm criticizing you and the others." The young woman rolled her chair closer to Caroline and whispered, "Personally, I think Roger's idea is crazy."

'Crazy' was putting it mildly as far as Caroline was concerned. Roger's decision to keep the ER open by moving four patients to the Cast Room and placing three others in cubicles in the Outpatient Department was simply insane. Alerted by Kee and arriving on the scene only minutes after the Medical Director, Molly had argued vehemently against the plan. Her objections were promptly overruled.

"Tell the supervisor to call in an agency nurse," MacGuffy had said airily. "That nurse can watch the four in the Cast Room, and you can shift one of your own people to the Outpatient Department."

"If I place a night nurse in Outpatients, there'll be only two people to cover the room."

"That's your problem, Miss O'Neal, not mine. Have someone work a double shift."

"I can't do that," Molly had snapped. "These people have had a rough night, and all of them are due to work tomorrow."

"Then you'll have to figure out some other way of handling it, won't you?" Roger had turned his back on the angry nurse manager and addressed the rest of the staff. "We wouldn't want anyone here accused of patient abandonment, now would we?"

"Roger..."

"I'll be in my office, Miss O'Neal. Let me know when the room is cleared."

Without a backward glance, Roger had exited the ER, leaving Molly to do the dirty work of explaining the move to their patients.

Now, thirty minutes later, the night shift was in place, and four unhappy people were being transported to the Cast Room. Erlinda Torres had been assigned to watch the patients relegated to Outpatients. With the help of Susan Kane and Patrice Woodson, she was clearing out three examining rooms, preparing them as temporary boarding areas. Kee was giving report to the night charge nurse while the remaining staff members prepared to go off duty.

Caroline had volunteered to work until 3 a.m. She would leave earlier if things settled down, but there was little chance of that happening. The rain had begun in earnest again, causing slippery streets that boded ill for drivers and paramedics alike.

"You look beat, Cari." Molly slipped into a chair and gave her friend an appraising look. "Are you sure you want to stay?"

"I'll be fine after I rest this ankle for a few minutes." Caroline explained about the fall she'd taken. "Of course it had to be the ankle I broke last winter. But enough about me. Tell me how *you* are. I saw Tom Evans arrive earlier today. Was he here to question you again?"

Molly glanced over at Wendy, but the girl didn't seem interested in their conversation. She pounded away at the computer keys entering orders for supplies.

"He talked to Kee and Patrice first, then asked me a lot of questions about hospital security."

"Security? Whatever for?"

"I'm not sure," she replied, her voice lowered to just above a whisper. "He wanted to know about keys. He asked if anyone outside the Security Department had access to Roger's office."

"What does that have to do with Angela's murder?"

"I have no idea. Evans also asked about the green scrubs our doctors wear. I explained how they arrive on the laundry cart each morning and are placed in the doctors' lounge by one of the techs. He asked if the lounge is a secure area, and I said of course not. Since every doc has a locker for personal belongings, it's unnecessary to lock the room itself."

Caroline leaned back and stared at the ceiling, her bottom lip caught between her teeth as she pondered the possible reasons for Tom Evans' questions. The police had coming looking for Roger within hours of the discovery of Angela's body, so obviously they'd found something linking the Medical Director to Miss Horowitz.

What could it have been? A pair of green scrubs bearing Roger's name? But the scrubs weren't personalized with names. What other piece of hospital paraphernalia could tie Roger to the scene?

"A name tag."

"What did you say?"

"Hmm? Oh, I'm sorry. I was just thinking aloud." She straightened up in her chair. "Tell me something. Did you see Roger wearing his name tag yesterday?"

Molly looked confused. "I...I don't remember, Cari. It's not one of those things I would have noticed."

"Probably not." Caroline stood up as the Niles paramedics rolled past the desk with an empty stretcher. They'd dropped off another victim of the wet roads and were on their way back to the station. "Time for me to get back to work. Are you going to hang around here for a while?"

"Definitely," Molly said with a grim smile. "I have no intention of leaving the ER until Roger's safely out of our hair. God only knows what he'd do behind my back."

"That's that," Wendy said to no one in particular as she signed off the computer. "I'm out of here."

"You, girl, are becoming way too Americanized. Shouldn't you be saying something British, like 'tally-ho, old chaps'?'" Dr. Chan Daley strolled over to the desk and squinted at Wendy through the thick lens of his Harry Carey-styled glasses. Faking an English accent, he added, "Or am I being bloody rude to even suggest such a thing?"

"Of course not, doctor," Wendy purred as she circled around Chan and headed for the hallway. "Bloody silly perhaps, but never bloody rude. Bye, everyone!"

"What a comeback," remarked Caroline with a grin. She punched Chan on the shoulder, then limped off towards the west wing. "I'll go see about our new patient."

"Forget it," Chan called out. "I already examined him, and Brenda's taking his vitals. He'll need a cervical spine X-ray and a tetanus shot for the scratches on his knees."

Caroline turned back, surprise written across her face. "Did you say Brenda's back there? What's she doing here tonight?"

"She probably came in to do paperwork," said Molly. Rising, she added, "She won't mind helping out a bit. Why don't you man the desk while I go see how Erlinda's doing in Outpatients."

Caroline was happy to oblige her boss. Eight hours of walking on a sore ankle had taken its toll. Her calf muscles ached, and her lower back was beginning to spasm.

"I'm getting too old for this job," she complained to Chan as she handed him a lab report spit out by the printer. "Has the workload gotten heavier since I left, or am I just imagining it?"

Dr. Daley tugged on his black Fu Manchu mustache. "It's this damn temporary room. It's so split up that you spend half your time walking back and forth between wings. The nurses in the west wing don't know what's happening in the east wing, and vice versa. It's a disaster."

Chan Daley was not a man given to complaining. The son of a Chinese woman exiled from her homeland by war and an Irish playwright with dubious political leanings, he'd inherited the stoical nature of his maternal ancestors along with the silver-tongued eloquence of his father. He was a bright, good-humored man who played his cards close to his chest. He confided in no one, and while freely discussing medical matters with the nurses, he rarely gave an opinion on hospital politics. Some people considered this a fault, but the truth was, Chan really didn't care about the internal wrangling that consumed the time and energy of some doctors. As long as he could practice medicine as he saw fit, Dr. Daley was content to let others battle for the positions of power at Ascension.

Because she was one of the few people in the ER who understood Chan Daley, his words came as a surprise to Caroline. She wondered if he was truly disgusted with the present working conditions, or if Angela's murder had shaken the man into revealing more of himself than usual. There was only one way to tell.

"Dealing with the police is no fun either. Have they been bothering you with their silly questions?"

There, thought Caroline. I've given you an opening.

But Chan was too wily to rise to the bait. Winking at Caroline, he chose a chart from the rack and sauntered over to the doctors' desk. She swiveled her chair in a half-circle and glared at him.

"What's that wink supposed to mean?" she demanded.

Pretending to study the chart, Dr. Daley took his time before answering. "I have a friend working at St. Anne's Hospital in Rhineburg. She told me about the murders there and your part in solving them."

"Really?"

"Yes, really. I suspect you're going to try your hand at sleuthing here at Ascension."

When she didn't answer, he raised his eyes to meet hers.

"As me sainted mother used to say," he quipped in a heavy Irish accent that faded to broken English, "Man who stands beneath tail of elephant must prepare for much dung to drop on head."

"Your sainted mother was very wise."

"Yes, she was, Cari." He paused, then continued in a more serious tone of voice. "Do me a favor, my friend. Stay away from the elephant."

Caroline smiled ruefully. "I can't do that, Chan, but if it makes you feel any better, I promise to carry an umbrella."

Chan Daley just shook his head.

CHAPTER TWENTY-NINE

June 16th
11:45 P.M.

Roger MacGuffy drained the last of the thick brown liquid in his cup and grimaced. Whoever had made this coffee certainly had botched the job. It was bitter, nothing at all like the stuff brewed by the day shift nurses. Perhaps it was an inferior brand, or maybe it had been left to simmer too long. The only good thing that could be said for it was that it lacked caffeine. He knew that for a fact because he couldn't stop yawning.

Roger was addicted to decaffeinated coffee. He drank ten or twelve cups a day on the average, and he'd been pleased to see someone had left a steaming pot on his desk when he'd entered his office tonight. At least there was one person on the p.m. shift who knew how to satisfy him.

It hadn't been Keeshon Jones, that was for sure.

Roger scrawled Keeshon's name on a scratch pad. He drew three circles around it, then scratched a thick black X through the word. Like Mavis and Chan Daley, Kee would have to go. He couldn't keep a man in the department who hated his guts like Kee did.

It was all the fault of that bitch Patrice. If she'd only been civil when he'd approached her at the picnic, none of this mess would have happened.

Angela would take care of Patrice, he thought as he stifled another yawn. Angela would kick her...no, wait a minute. Angela. Angela. What had happened to Angela?

He reached for the phone, but the receiver slipped from his

hand. He stared at his fingers poised above the desk. Five fingers. No, ten. Now five again.

"What the hell!"

He tried to stand up. His legs felt like worn out rubber bands, no pull left in them, no push, no anything. His knees wouldn't lock in place. He was slipping.

"Let me help you, doctor."

Roger felt the edge of the chair hit his spine as he slid to the floor. He looked up and blinked. Someone was standing over him, but the face was blurry, distorted. "Something wrong. Something..."

"Shh. It's all right now. I'm here, and I'll take care of you."

"Take care of me. Yes, I need you to take care of me."

He staggered to his feet, strong arms pulling him up. He felt wobbly, the room spinning around him. A chair nudged his legs and he collapsed backward.

"There now. Let's take you somewhere safe."

A blanket was thrown over his lap, another around his head and shoulders. He closed his eyes and yawned as the chair rolled out of the office.

"Did you enjoy your coffee?"

"Bitter." He heard a door swing open. Cool air hit his face. "I want Chan."

"Oh, he'll get around to seeing you. Eventually."

He forced his eyes open. He was in a short, dimly lit corridor, another door a dozen feet in front of him. "Where are we?"

"On our way to the Emergency Room."

"Not this way. Take me back."

A sigh, impatient and purposely drawn out.

"You're not in charge here, Roger. I am. Now be quiet." The second door was propped open, the chair propelled through. "Here we are, Dr. MacGuffy. Home at last."

CHAPTER THIRTY

June 17th
2:00 A.M.

Kate Lodash had worked the night shift in ER for twelve years. At first it had meshed nicely with her policeman-husband's schedule, then when the babies came along and Frank moved permanently to days, Kate found it easier to work at night when the kids were asleep. Frank handled breakfast with the quick competence of a man who'd spent more years living as a bachelor than as a husband, but the more complicated facets of child care were totally beyond his abilities. Kate always got home in time to dress the girls and send them off to school. She was there when they came bounding through the door at three o'clock, there when they ate supper at six, and there when they finally went to bed just after nine p.m. It was a way of life she was used to, and she couldn't imagine it ever changing.

The night shift wasn't for everyone, though. There were people whose internal clocks rebelled against the topsy-turvy world of eleven to seven. She could see that Caroline Rhodes was one of them. Thankful that she'd stayed behind to help, Kate took pity on Caroline and sent her on a break at 2 a.m.

"The coffee shop stays open round the clock now," Kate told her. "You can cut through the old ER and check out the renovations on your way upstairs. I hear the cubicle walls are finally going up."

Caroline smiled gratefully. "Thanks, but I'll take a pass on the coffee shop. I'll just go to the lounge and put my feet up for awhile. If I'm not back in fifteen minutes, you'll know I fell asleep."

Kate Lodash laughed. "Don't worry. I'll come wake you up."

Caroline limped out of the room, grateful for a chance to rest her ankle. The air splint had provided much needed support, but it would be days before the ligaments totally healed. Until then, she'd have to put up with some pain.

She was almost to the nurses' lounge when she heard someone call her name. Turning, she saw Erlinda Torres standing in the doorway at the north end of the hallway.

"I can't leave here," Erlinda said, thumbing over her shoulder towards the Outpatient Department where her three patients were tucked away for the night. "But I sure could use some coffee."

"I'll bring you a cup when I get off break," Caroline promised.

"Thanks. Have you seen the old ER yet? They put up some of the walls today."

Caroline sighed. In her mind a wall was a wall, nothing more and nothing less. To the other nurses, though, the placement of the walls meant their ordeal in the temporary ER was coming to an end. Obviously she'd have to tour the renovations or be considered an uncaring jerk by her coworkers.

"I was just about to go take a look," she lied, waggling her fingers at Erlinda as the night nurse signaled her appreciation and disappeared back through the doorway.

Damn, she thought. There goes my fifteen minutes of rest.

A makeshift corridor leading to the old ER lay just beyond Roger MacGuffy's office. Separated from the main north-south hallway by a door, it extended only a few yards and ended at a second less solid appearing door that opened into the construction area.

Trudging back up the hallway, she decided she'd eyeball the work in progress from the safety of the corridor, then hightail it back to the lounge for a cup of coffee and five minutes on the couch. Her plan would have worked if Chan Daley hadn't walked up behind her.

"Shall I give you the grand tour?" he said, taking her by the arm. He opened the door off the hallway and stepped aside, motioning for her to go first. "It's going to be quite a place once it's finished."

"I'll bet," Caroline grumbled. She slipped past Chan and entered the short corridor. The second door was only a few paces away Pulling it open, she stepped into the old ER.

It took a few seconds for her eyes to adjust to the dim light. When she was able to focus on her surroundings, she was surprised to find her curiosity piqued by the complexity of the renovations.

The walls had been stripped away and the floor bared to the original concrete. The ceiling tiles were gone, and in their place she saw a checkerboard pattern of aluminum crossbars supporting wiring of every type and color. Pipes of various sizes sprouted from the floor and crisscrossed the ceiling, some capped off, others open ended as if awaiting the addition of a sink or a faucet.

A fine layer of concrete dust lay over the entire room. It covered the denuded floor and the battered toolboxes piled against the stripped down center support. It covered the hacksaws and hammers lying on the tool bench, the wooden horses standing in a row in the corner, and the bright orange electrical cords that seemed to snake across the floor everywhere one looked.

"It certainly is dirty in here," she said as she swiped at the gritty film masking one of the pipes. "I feel sorry for the poor guys who have to clean up this mess."

Chan laughed. "Would you like to see how the room will look when it's done? The blueprints are spread out on a table over there." He pointed to a darkened area at the far end of the old ER. "I'll turn on the lights."

Pulling a pen flashlight from the pocket of his lab coat, he aimed a steady beam at the half dozen on/off switches secured to the center column. Caroline left him to it and wandered off towards the back section of the room.

The wall there was hidden by a mass of scaffolding extending the entire length of the room. Canvas drop cloths lay beneath and around the metal latticework, and one particularly stained sheet of canvas had been flung over and around the top crossbar. The material fell in uneven folds, the lower edge a bare two feet off the ground.

"Chan! Come here!"

"That's better," Dr. Daley said triumphantly as light flooded the room. He strolled over to where Caroline stood rooted to the floor. "They ought to label those darn things. It's hard to..."

She grabbed his arm and pointed to the scaffolding. "Please, Chan. Tell me those aren't shoes sticking out from beneath that cloth."

Chan's body stiffened. Caroline heard him suck in his breath, then he walked over and tugged on the fabric. The canvas fell in a heap on the floor.

"Oh my God," groaned Caroline. "It's Roger."

Ascension's Medical Director hung suspended from the metal framework by a bright orange electrical cord wound around his neck. The cord had crushed his larynx, and his down-turned face was grayish-blue and swollen above the binding.

Trained to respect the integrity of a crime scene when medical intervention was obviously futile, neither Caroline nor Chan made a move towards Roger. There was no doubt in either of their minds that the man was dead. Lowering him from the scaffolding might seem aesthetically appropriate, but doing so would definitely contaminate the surroundings. Further examination of the body would have to be left to the police and the medical examiner.

"Let's get out of here," said Caroline, backing up a step.

Chan tore his eyes away from the body. "Watch your footsteps as you go," he warned. "There's concrete dust everywhere in here, and if we left footprints, then so did the murderer. The police might find some useful prints if we don't track right over them."

Picking their way through the construction area, they arrived at the little corridor leading back to the main hallway outside ER.

"I'll notify the police," said Chan, taking charge. "You tell the others what's happened."

Caroline nodded as they passed through the second door. "We ought to seal off this entrance so no one else goes in."

"Or comes out," muttered Dr. Daley. "Although I'm pretty sure our killer is long gone. Roger looked like he'd been hanging there awhile."

He didn't expand on the statement, and for that she was glad. The picture of Roger hanging from the scaffolding was still fresh in her mind. She wasn't ready to discuss lividity or body temperature or any of the other symptoms that indicated time of death. Better to wait until the shock had worn off.

"I was beginning to think the two of you were never coming back," Kate joked when they walked into the room. "Thought I'd have to...hey! Wait a minute. Something's happened, hasn't it?"

"Your husband is a detective with the Niles police, isn't he?" Chan asked, disregarding the nurse's question.

Kate glanced at Caroline before answering slowly, "Yes, but he works the day shift."

"Then I'll call 911. Fill her in on the news, Cari." Chan walked over to the doctors' desk and picked up the phone.

"What's going on?" Kate whispered. "You two look like you've seen a ghost."

"You'd better sit down. If you think the past few hours have been bad, just wait. The worst is yet to come." Caroline told her about Roger. "It's possible he's been dead for several hours."

"Are you sure it couldn't have been suicide?"

"It's pretty hard for a man to drape a canvas sheet over himself after jumping off a scaffold."

Kate shuddered. "I'd better call Frank," she said, reaching for the telephone. "He'll want to know about this."

"While you do that, I'll page the supervisor."

Caroline punched in the code on the wall phone, then glanced in on her patients.

"Sleeping like babies," she murmured to herself as she walked back to the desk. She checked the main heart monitor, pushed a couple of buttons on the machine, and ran off a telemetry strip on each of the patients. Chan was still on the phone, and Kate had just hung up from her husband.

"Did the supervisor call back?"

Kate shook her head. "There was a problem earlier up in ICU. She's probably tied up there still. I'll wait for her call while you go tell the others."

Caroline walked back to the west wing to speak with Annie Singh. The Indian nurse took the news more calmly than Caroline expected.

"I never liked that man," Annie said, her long black braid swinging from shoulder to shoulder as she shook her head. "Not that I ever wished him dead, but I did wish him gone from here. Do you know he made a pass at me the month after he arrived here?" Seeing the surprise on Caroline's face, she shook her head again. "He thought I was just off the boat and wouldn't complain, but I did. I went to see Josephine Rose as soon as my shift ended."

"And what did she say?" Caroline asked, curious to hear how the Assistant Director of Nursing had handled the problem.

"She told me Dr. MacGuffy was just kidding around with me. She said not to take it seriously."

"She didn't send you to Human Resources? Didn't tell you to fill out a formal complaint?"

"Oh, no. No Human Resources, no paperwork, no nothing. I should have known she wouldn't do anything, but I was mad, so I went to see her."

"What exactly did he do to you?"

Annie wrinkled her nose in distaste. "He kept asking me to go out with him, and when I refused, he made a nasty remark about my body. He only said it because he was angry I'd turned him down. Still, it was unpleasant because he said it in front of several other nurses."

"Did you tell Molly about this?"

"No. She was having her own problems with Dr. MacGuffy. I didn't want to make things worse for her. But I told him I went to see Josephine Rose. After that, he left me alone."

Caroline pondered Annie's story as she made her way to the Outpatient Department. The Assistant DON's response didn't surprise her. Despite the high number of sexual harassment cases pending in the courts and all the publicity given those cases, hospitals still tended to protect their male doctors rather than their female nurses. Caroline thought it all came down to a matter of money. Doctors brought money into the hospitals; nurses didn't.

Erlinda Torres was camped out on a chair in the Outpatient hallway. Portable monitors rested on folding chairs on either side of the corridor, their wires extending into four separate examining rooms. Erlinda looked bored as she sat with her head against the hallway wall, her eyes roving from one monitor to the next.

"How's it going?" Caroline asked as she approached the nurse.

"All my patients are mad at me," Erlinda responded with a rueful smile. She motioned towards four partially closed doors. "They blame me for having to sleep in those tiny rooms. I told them it was not my idea," -- she shrugged her shoulders -- "but they have to take out their anger on someone, and tonight, I'm that person. Tomorrow they can all yell at Dr. MacGuffy."

"I'm afraid they won't get the opportunity to do that." Caroline related the news about Roger. Unlike Annie Singh, Erlinda was visibly shaken.

"Someone murdered him right here in the hospital?"

Caroline nodded. "I'm afraid so, Erlinda. The police are on their way as we speak. They'll probably want to talk to you."

"Why me?" Erlinda asked, her voice becoming shrill. "I didn't have anything to do with it."

"Of course you didn't. The police will just want to know if you witnessed anything suspicious going on here tonight. They may ask if you saw any strangers in this hallway, or heard any odd noises coming from the corridor by Roger's office."

"I heard nothing and I saw nothing," Erlinda stated emphatically. "I want nothing to do with the police."

"I'm sorry, Erlinda, but you may not have a choice in the matter. The police will question all of us."

Leaving her to ruminate on that unwelcome thought, Caroline walked back to the ER. She found Kate Lodash sitting at the desk, but Dr. Daley was nowhere to be seen.

"Have the cops arrived?"

Kate nodded. "Chan took them to the old ER. I'm waiting for the Chief of Staff and Mr. Bradford. Chan notified them both."

Despite her intentions, Caroline hadn't found time to confer with the Administrator that afternoon. She wondered how Roger's death would affect the deal Bradford had made with Adam Horowitz.

"And the supervisor knows what's happening?"

"She called right after you went to talk to Annie. I thought the poor woman was going to have a heart attack when I told her Roger had been murdered. She was down here in under a minute, and she was not a happy camper."

"None of us are," retorted Caroline. "Did you call Molly?"

Kate nodded again. "She's on her way in. So is Josephine Rose."

Caroline groaned. "The last thing we need is Josephine flitting around the department."

"I agree, but the supervisor felt it was necessary to notify her."

"A gathering of eagles."

"More like buzzards, if you ask me," grinned Kate.

"I notice you're not too broken up over Roger's death."

"Why should I be? Very few of us around here were fans of the Medical Director. We all knew what he was trying to do to Molly. And don't tell me he didn't have a hand in Mavis Taylor's ouster."

"Then you're not surprised someone killed him."

Kate thought for a moment. "I'd be very surprised if anyone from the department had a hand in his death, but no, I'm not surprised by his murder. Roger was a nasty man. I'm sure he made enemies in his private life just as he did in the ER."

But nastiness wasn't reason enough for murder. Roger had died in a most unusual and vicious way indicating that his killer was not someone simply ticked off by the man's behavior. Whoever had strung him up from that scaffolding had hated Roger deeply and, thought Caroline, for some period of time. Hate of that magnitude didn't spring up over night. It took months or even years to evolve.

So who had known Roger long enough to develop such a loathing for the man?

Unbidden and unwanted, Molly O'Neal was the first person who came to mind.

CHAPTER THIRTY-ONE

June 17th
6:00 A.M.

Someone had alerted the press to the murder of Roger MacGuffy. The first lot descended on Ascension Medical Center before dawn, a scruffy looking band of sleepy-eyed newsmen who yawned into cell phones as they relayed the story to all-night radio stations. Their numbers were small at first, then grew by leaps and bounds as word of the murder spread. By six o'clock the parking lot outside the ER was crowded with multicolored TV vans, silver satellite dishes sprouting from their roofs like overturned mushroom caps. Reporters stood at the ready, microphones in hand, while print journalists with tape recorders prowled the hospital exits seeking unwary employees to interview.

Ascension's security force had their hands full keeping the press at bay. With the help of the Niles police, they managed to clear the ER driveway. Outside of locking all the doors, though, there was little they could do to prevent enterprising newsmen from slipping into the hospital. The building had too many entrances, and while they patrolled the corridors searching for unwanted visitors, they'd received orders not to antagonize the members of the Third Estate. The unpleasant job of ejecting intruders was left to the Niles police.

Security was made more difficult due to a decision by Michael Bradford. Although he was told repeatedly that the media were getting restless waiting about outside, Ascension's administrator refused to make a public statement until the hospital lawyers arrived. It was an unwise move on his part, but Michael Bradford was a stubborn man.

Caroline's shift was to have ended at three a.m. Roger's death delayed her departure, but by six the police had finished their interviews with the night staff, secured the construction area, and given everyone permission to leave the building. Caroline took a circuitous route to the parking lot, hoping to avoid the crush of people standing outside the ER. Her plans were thwarted by a local reporter who recognized her as she dashed to her car.

"Mrs. Rhodes? Caroline Rhodes?" The young woman ran after her waving a notebook in the air. "Please, Mrs. Rhodes, will you give me an interview?"

Caroline dragged out her keys, but before she could unlock the Jeep, the woman caught up with her. She put a hand on Caroline's arm.

"Wait a minute, please, Mrs. Rhodes," the reporter panted. She brushed a lock of sand-colored hair out of her eyes and smiled. "I'm Jackie Fields from the New Day Neighborhood News. I wrote a piece for my paper about your return to Chicago and your role in solving those crimes in Rhineburg."

Caroline's eyes narrowed. "I saw your article, Miss Fields. You made me out to be more than I am."

Jackie Fields grinned. "My editor loved it."

"I'm sure he did." Caroline reached for the door handle. "Now if you'll excuse me..."

"No, wait!" Jackie glanced over her shoulder. "Damn! They've seen us. Please, Mrs. Rhodes, just give me a quote for my paper before the others arrive."

Caroline looked past Jackie Fields, already certain she knew who "the others" were. Sure enough, a group of newspeople had spotted them and were hotfooting it across the parking lot.

"I have nothing to say," she muttered, pushing Jackie aside and tugging on the handle. She slid into the car, but got no farther as another reporter forced his body between her and the door.

"Do you work in the Emergency Room?" the man asked.

"No comment," Caroline growled. "Now get out of my way."

"Did you see what happened?" "Can you tell us about the doctor who died?" "Was it a suicide, or murder?" "Do the police have a suspect?"

The questions came fast and furious as a mass of bodies crowded around the Jeep. Caroline saw a camera flash and she ducked her head.

"I have nothing to say," she shouted. "Now please get away from my car."

"Don't you believe her," yelled Jackie Fields, turning to the other reporters. "This is Caroline Rhodes, famed crime-solver from Rhineburg, Illinois. She came to Ascension because of the trouble here, and she knows much more than she's telling."

The man standing next to Caroline backed off to catch Jackie on microphone. Caroline quickly slammed the door and turned on the ignition. The crowd fell back as she gunned the engine.

"Hey, look!" Jackie shouted, pointing to the ER entrance. "Someone's coming out to speak."

The others tore off for the ER, leaving Jackie alone by the side of the Jeep. She turned and grinned at Caroline who rolled down her window angrily.

"Why the hell did you say that? Now they'll all be hounding me for interviews."

Jackie shrugged. "You should have talked to me when I asked for a quote, Mrs. Rhodes." Pulling out her notebook, she added, "Of course, I could always tell my colleagues that I was wrong, that you aren't the person I thought you were. Just give me the inside story on the murder and I'll be glad to admit my mistake."

Caroline bit back a few choice words as she threw the Jeep into drive and tore out of the parking lot.

PART FOUR

*Man who stands beneath tail of elephant
must prepare for much dung to drop on head.*

Dr. Chan Daley

CHAPTER THIRTY-TWO

June 17th
8:00 A.M.

Miguel Ramos swallowed his last spoonful of corn flakes and pushed the cereal bowl aside. Reaching for the remote control, he turned up the sound on the TV.

"...and all of us at Ascension Medical Center would like to express our deep sorrow over this unfortunate incident. We would like to assure everyone in the community that our Emergency Room will remain open to the public during this time."

A reporter interjected his body between the speaker and the camera.

"That was Michael Bradford, Administrator of Ascension Medical Center, making a statement concerning the murder of Dr. Roger MacGuffy, the Director of Ascension's Department of Emergency Medicine. As we told you earlier, the body of Dr. MacGuffy was found at approximately two-thirty this morning in a construction area in the suburban hospital. According to police, MacGuffy was discovered hanging by the neck from a network of scaffolding in the partially renovated Emergency Room. The cause of death is assumed to be strangulation, although the Medical Examiner has not yet made a formal report.

"The body was discovered by two members of the hospital staff. Although police have not released the names of these people, I have been told they are Dr. Chan Daley and ER nurse Caroline Rhodes. Neither Dr. Daley nor Mrs. Rhodes have consented to interviews at this time."

The scene switched to footage taken earlier in the morning outside the hospital. A nurse dressed in navy scrub pants and a white polo shirt was shown climbing into a late model Jeep Cherokee. A stethoscope hung around her neck, and the metal end pieces glinted in the sun as the woman waved off reporters massed around her car.

Miguel clicked off the TV set and pushed himself back from the kitchen table. Ignoring the empty cereal bowl, he slipped on his gym shoes and ran out of the house.

Leaping the fence, the boy pulled out a key for his neighbor's back door. He let himself in and tiptoed through the kitchen to the hallway leading to the back bedroom. He needn't have worried about waking Mr. Harris; the old man was sitting up in bed staring intently at the blank screen of the TV set perched on his desk.

"Did you see the news?" Miguel asked as he entered the room.

Walter Harris motioned to the boy with one blue-veined hand while he turned up his oxygen with the other. "Damn plastic piece won't stay in my nose," he grumbled as he adjusted the prongs of the cannula. "Falls out at night, and then I can't breathe."

"Did you see the news?" Miguel shifted from foot to foot, impatient for an answer. Harris turned his head, his pale blue eyes twinkling mischievously as he glanced up at his young neighbor.

"That sonofabitch finally got what he deserved, didn't he."

A grin split Miguel's face. "I knew it was him! As soon as I heard the name, I told myself that had to be the guy in the files."

Harris threw back the covers and pulled himself upright. "Looks like we have a busy day ahead of us, son. You help me get dressed, then after I eat a little something, we'll dig into my records."

Miguel's heart raced as he snatched clean clothes from the closet. After a dull start to the summer, things were beginning to look up for the twelve-year-old.

Chapter Thirty-three

June 17th
10:00 A.M.

Krista was sound asleep when Caroline arrived at the apartment a little after six a.m. It was the young woman's day off, and she'd planned to go shopping and to lunch with her mother, but of course that was out of the question now. Caroline scrawled a hasty message on a sheet of paper and left it on the kitchen table where Krista was sure to see it, then hobbled off to bed for a few hours sleep. Four hours later, Krista woke her just as she'd requested in the note.

"I can't believe it," the girl exclaimed as she sat on the edge of the bed watching her mother rub the sleep from her eyes. "First Angela Horowitz, and now Dr. MacGuffy. I've been listening to the radio, and they're saying he was found hanging by his neck from the scaffolding in the old ER."

Caroline yawned. "Did they happen to mention who found him?"

"No, but… Oh, no, mom. Not you!" Krista's eyes widened as her mother nodded. "No wonder you were so late getting home. I suppose the police asked you a million questions."

"A million and one," Caroline responded wryly. She threw the covers off and sat up in bed. "I have to go to the police station this morning and sign a formal statement, then be back at work at three o'clock."

"Can't you take the day off? You must be exhausted after yesterday."

"I wish I could, but we're so short staffed that it would be hard to replace me." She yawned again. "I need to shower, but first I want to call Carl and tell him what's happened."

"He knows about it already," Krista said. "He called here an hour ago after seeing a news report on TV. I told him you'd be up at ten, and he said he'd stop by around eleven to talk to you. He said to tell you he'd contact Jake and Maddy."

"Good. Carl checked into the ER last night, ostensibly because of his laryngitis. He was actually there to do a little snooping around."

"Yes, he told me about that. He was here when I got home from work yesterday. I was surprised to see him sitting in the kitchen when I opened the back door. I was even more surprised when he told me about your visit to Highland Park."

"All in all, yesterday was a very strange day." Caroline stood up and walked over to the closet. She pulled out a pair of khaki slacks and a short sleeved tangerine blouse and tossed them on the bed. "I hope you understand why I agreed to Adam Horowitz's request."

Krista picked at the blanket, silent for a moment.

"I was upset when I first heard about the plan," she finally admitted. "Then I started looking at it from your viewpoint. You're caught between two friends, Alexsa and Molly. You don't want Molly to be arrested..."

"Molly O'Neal is no murderer."

"It would be to her advantage if Angela was killed because of something her brother did. On the other hand, you'd be helping Alexsa and Adam, and maybe stopping a mob war, if you could prove someone at the hospital was responsible for Angela's death."

Caroline placed her hand on her daughter's shoulder. "I promise you, I won't put myself in danger. Roger's murder has to be connected to Angela's, and that points to the killer being someone who works at Ascension. It's the only sensible answer."

"Then Roger's death cancels out the Mafia connection."

"I think so, but what I think doesn't matter. What matters is what Ruben Horowitz thinks."

"Where does Molly stand in all this?"

Caroline frowned. "Deeper in trouble, I'm afraid. Molly was in the ER around the time of the murder. The Niles police may not be aware of her role as a suspect in Angela's death, but I'm sure they'll hear about it very soon. The Chicago PD is bound to contact them."

"And you feel obligated to help her."

"She's my oldest and dearest friend, Krista. Of course I'll try to help her."

"All right, then," Krista said with an emphatic nod of her head. "If you believe that strongly in Molly's innocence, I have to believe in it too. I want to help you, mom. Tell me what I can do."

"First of all, you can scramble a couple of eggs for me while I shower. I went straight to bed when I got home, and now I'm absolutely famished."

"No problem." Krista smiled as she got to her feet. "Breakfast will be ready in fifteen minutes."

True to her word, Krista was waiting with French toast, eggs, and bacon when Caroline entered the kitchen a few minutes later. She poured her mother a glass of orange juice, then sat down at the table.

"Kerry called while you were in the shower. I told her what's happening, and she wants to help also."

"Is she coming over here?"

Krista nodded as the doorbell rang. "Maybe that's her now."

But it wasn't. Instead, Carl stood at the back door, two bags of groceries in his arms.

"I thought we'd need some sustenance to see us through the day," he said, then added somewhat sheepishly, "I had a bite to eat yesterday before Krista came home. I'm afraid I wiped out some of her supplies."

Krista took the groceries and set them down on the counter. "You've more than made up for it, Professor," she said, glancing at the array of food in the bags. "We could feed an army with all this."

"Well, the Archangels are arriving this morning, and those boys are hearty eaters."

"All three of them are coming?" Caroline was amazed they'd been able to get away. Michael, Gabriel, and Rafael Bruck ran the security department at Bruck University. Triplets, the men were direct descendants of the German immigrant who'd founded the school.

Carl nodded. "Their dad used to run the department, so he offered to watch over the place while they're gone. They're bringing their wives along with them."

The thirty-year-old brothers had married the previous year in a joint ceremony. Faith, Hope, and Charity were also triplets. Unlike the Brucks, the sisters were of Irish descent, redheads with flashing green eyes and creamy complexions. Their quick wit and easy-going approach to life tempered their husbands' Teutonic sobriety.

"Would you like something to eat, Professor?"

Carl, who'd been eyeing Caroline's plate with some degree of envy, turned to Krista with a smile. "A stack of French toast would be greatly appreciated. I had an early breakfast today, and I must admit my stomach is beginning to rumble a bit."

Krista whipped up another batch of eggs and milk, dunked four slices of bread in the batter, and laid them on the skillet to brown while Carl unpacked the groceries.

"The Moellers should be here any minute," he said. "Jake had a few calls to make, and Maddy had an appointment at one of the auction houses. They know about Dr. MacGuffy's murder."

"I found the body," Caroline said between bites.

Carl gave her a sidelong glance. "Not a pretty picture, I'm sure."

"Chan Daley was with me -- he's an ER doc -- and I'm not sure which of us was more shocked when we saw Roger's feet sticking out from under that canvas drape."

"The TV reports didn't mention anything about a drape," said Carl as he settled himself at the table. "The murderer covered MacGuffy with something?"

The doorbell rang before Caroline could reply. Mindful of his French toast sizzling on the skillet, Carl waved Krista back to the stove and got up to answer it. As he'd predicted, it was Jake and Maddy.

"My goodness, Cari. What an exciting life you lead!" Maddy Moeller swept into the room. She planted a kiss on Carl's cheek and patted Krista on the shoulder, then plopped down on a chair across from Caroline. "The reports on the radio have been sketchy at best. I'm relying on you to give us all the gory details."

"Now, Maddy. Let the poor woman eat in peace. There's plenty of time for talk once she's finished." Jake Moeller snatched a piece of French toast from the plate Krista was handing to Carl and wolfed it down. Shaking her head, Krista turned back to the stove and dipped more bread in the batter.

"Actually, I don't have a lot of time this morning," Caroline said. "I'm due at the Niles police station in an hour. I have to sign a formal statement."

"Then let me tell you what Carl and I have been up to," said Jake, drawing a chair up to the table. The burly policeman looked over at the professor. "Unless you've already filled her in on yesterday."

Carl shook his head, his mouth full of French toast.

"Good. I hate to repeat things," Jake said, hitching up his belt.

Years of living with the man had taught Maddy that belt hitching was a sure sign Jake was about to launch into a long involved speech. She quickly intervened.

"Dr. MacGuffy's death changes things a bit, doesn't it, Cari? The professor told us about your visit with Adam Horowitz, but I don't see how his son can blame this murder on the mob."

"I think whoever killed Angela also killed Roger," Caroline replied. "I also think that person works at Ascension Medical Center."

"All the more reason for us to cooperate with Mr. Horowitz," Jake said with a frown aimed at his wife. "You told us your friend, Miss O'Neal, was having problems with MacGuffy. Since she's already a suspect in Angela Horowitz's murder, she's bound to come under suspicion for this one, too."

Caroline pushed her plate away and fought back a yawn. "Sorry, folks. It was a long night. As for Molly, I'm sure she'll face some stiff questioning today, especially since she was at the hospital around the time of the murder."

She told them about the argument between Molly and Roger over the ER going on bypass.

"Molly said she was going to stick around until Roger left the hospital, but no one in the department remembers seeing her leave. No one saw him again either after he went to his office. Dr. Chan Daley and I discovered the body just after two o'clock this morning. From the looks of it, Chan thinks Roger died a couple of hours before we found him."

"So he was killed sometime between eleven p.m. and two a.m. According to what you've told us, there were more than a few people present on the scene who disliked Roger MacGuffy."

"That's right, Jake. Patrice Woodson was there. So was Keeshon Jones. I can't see Patrice as a murderer, at least not Roger's murderer. But Keeshon was very angry last night, not only about the bypass issue, but also because of Roger's treatment of Patrice. Keeshon is strong enough to overwhelm anyone, and Roger had to have been subdued somehow before he was killed."

"No one in their right mind would willingly let somebody put a noose around their neck." Maddy touched her own throat, then shivered. "It's creepy just thinking about it."

"We'll have to wait for the autopsy," said Carl. "The police will know if Roger tried to fight off his assailant."

Jake nodded. "Did you notice anyone missing from the ER during those hours, Cari?"

"Not really. I was pretty busy with my patients, and frankly, the long hours were getting to me. I'm not used to double shifts, and I wasn't as alert as usual. Beside that, we were all split up. Erlinda was in Outpatients, and Annie Singh was in the west wing. Kate was coming and going between the two. Patrice moved patients to the Cast Room before the evening shift ended, but I don't recall seeing her after that. I assumed she left with Keeshon. Wendy was working on the computer and left a little after eleven-thirty, as did Susan King. And like I said before, I never saw Molly again after our conversation at the desk." Caroline frowned. "I almost forgot about Brenda, the EMS Coordinator. She came in late in the evening to do paperwork, but I never really saw her. Chan mentioned that she was in the room and helping out with a patient."

"Any one of those people could have killed MacGuffy," said Krista. "Even the ones who left at eleven-thirty could have come back and attacked him."

"You're right," said Carl. "At least three people we know of had motives, and who's to say the others didn't."

"Couldn't it have been someone who worked days? Some other employee who hated him?"

"Doubtful, Maddy," replied Krista. "Only those working the p.m. and night shifts were aware of Roger's presence in the building."

Caroline nodded. "Krista's right again. It was ten-thirty when Kee phoned Roger. We were the only ones who could have known."

"Unless Dr. MacGuffy was with someone when Kee called," Maddy reminded them. "If he was half the lady's man you claim he was, then Angela Horowitz wasn't the only woman he was seeing."

"You have a point. I'm almost positive he was dating Michelle Devine, an ER tech at Ascension. I overheard a conversation between the two of them the day before Angela died. Michelle was livid over the fact that Roger had apparently been chasing after Patrice Woodson."

"Jealousy might have driven her to kill him."

"Somehow I doubt it, Maddy. I got the impression Michelle saw Roger as a potential husband. Why would she kill the goose that laid the golden egg?"

"Let's find out where she was last night before we rule her out," said Jake. "If she has no alibi for the time of the murder, it's possible Maddy is right. Michelle could have been at Roger's place, then accompanied him to the hospital. Maybe they argued on their way over. Maybe that argument was continued in Roger's office and things got out of hand."

Caroline remained dubious. "I'll admit she was upset when Josephine Rose hinted that Roger and Angela were lovers. I'll also admit she didn't appear too happy when Roger made a pass at Wendy the other day. Still, I think Michelle figured she was head and shoulders above the competition. She's young, clever, and beautiful. That's a deadly combination in a woman with marriage on her mind."

"Who's Wendy?" Carl asked as he finished his last bite of food.

"She's a unit receptionist, new to the department." Caroline told them about the English girl. "Wendy was convinced Roger killed Angela Horowitz. She had a whole scenario built up in which Dr. MacGuffy grew tired of Angela, tried to ditch her for some other woman, then killed her when she refused to go quietly."

"Sounds like she's been watching too many B-grade movies," Carl muttered.

"Actually, it wasn't a bad theory until this morning," said Jake. "Roger's murder cancels it out, even if the police had been taking all the clues in Angela's apartment seriously."

"What clues?" asked Caroline. "What have you found out, Jake?"

"Yesterday morning I got in touch with a buddy of mine on the Chicago P.D. We met years ago in the Army, and we've been friends ever since. Andy's in narcotics, but when I told him I was interested in the Horowitz case, he said he'd find out what he could and give me a ring. He called back in the afternoon, and the story he told was very interesting. It seems the police found several clues in the apartment that implicated Dr. MacGuffy in the murder."

"I knew there had to be a reason they came to Ascension looking for Roger."

Jake nodded at Caroline. "Angela had a visitor the night she died. The police found a champagne bottle and two glasses on the bar, and an address book opened to Roger's phone number. Other items indicated a man had showered and shaved in the bathroom that evening."

"Were Roger's prints on one of the glasses?"

"The report wasn't back yet, Maddy, but Roger admitted to being in the apartment earlier that evening. What he didn't admit to was wearing green scrubs and his hospital lab coat."

"Those were found in the apartment?" asked Krista.

Jake shook his head. "A neighbor claims she saw someone come out of the brownstone, walk to the end of the street, then take off a coat and throw it in the trash can at the corner. The police checked the can and found a gray lab coat with MacGuffy's name embroidered on the pocket. They also found his name tag in an umbrella."

"An umbrella? Where?" Maddy's astonishment was matched by the others as they echoed her question in rapid succession. Jake held up a hand for silence.

"The umbrella was in some kind of fancy stand near the inside door of the apartment. One of the cops noticed it because the tie had come undone and it was half opened. He looked a little closer and saw a rectangular piece of plastic wedged between the ribs. It was the name tag."

"Quite a bit of evidence pointing to Roger."

"Too much evidence, Carl," said Caroline. She turned to Jake. "Murderers are usually more careful than that, aren't they? Even if a crime is committed in the heat of the moment, one would think the killer would be concerned about leaving traces of his presence."

"That's exactly what the police thought after they talked to Dr. MacGuffy. A man like him doesn't rise to a position of power without giving careful thought to his every move. Andy said the investigating officers thought the stuff was planted after the murder. MacGuffy had no reason to wear hospital scrubs when he went to the apartment. He'd left Ascension hours before the murder, and anyway, according to other employees, he wasn't wearing scrubs in the ER that day."

"Someone tried to frame him," said Carl. "A few less clues and it might have worked."

Jake nodded. "Maybe that's why Roger was murdered."

"What do you mean?" asked Maddy.

"What he means is, the killer wanted Roger executed by the state. Since the state didn't appear eager to do that, the killer took matters into his own hands." Caroline looked around at the others, her expression grim. "Someone hated Roger MacGuffy more than any of us can imagine."

Chapter Thirty-four

June 17th
12:00 P.M.

Kerry arrived just as Krista and Maddy were clearing the table of the breakfast dishes. She brought with her a large white box clearly labeled with the name of the local bakery.

"Thought you might be hungry after your long night at work," she said after kissing her mother on the cheek. "Are you OK?"

Caroline smiled at her youngest. Kerry could occasionally be trying, but her heart was in the right place.

"I'm fine, dear. And thanks to Krista, I'm also well fed. It was thoughtful of you, though, to stop at the bakery."

"What have you got in there?" the professor asked as he eyed Kerry's offering with a longing that belied the casual tone of his voice.

"A cherry coffee cake," said Kerry, opening the lid of the box and glancing inside. "Plus some jelly bismarcks, a few long johns, a half dozen apples slices, and a couple of chocolate eclairs. I wasn't sure how many people would be here this morning."

Carl's eyebrows wagged up and down faster than a hound dog's tail at supper time as he fought to control his baser instincts. He might have given in and snatched a bismarck if he hadn't seen the disapproving look Caroline shot him. Abashed, he took refuge in his pipe, studiously tamping down the tobacco in the bowl.

Seeing Jake unmoved by the expression on her friend's face, Maddy moved in to rescue the baked goods. "The Bruck boys will be here soon enough," she said crisply as she picked up the box and placed it on the counter. "We can put these out when they arrive."

"I'm afraid I can't hang around here any longer," Caroline said, getting to her feet. "I'm due at the Niles police station at one o'clock to sign a formal statement. I'd like to see Mavis Taylor before I talk to the police again. She hasn't answered my phone calls, but she lives just a few blocks from here near Northwestern University. I'm going to drive over to her place now. Maybe I'll get lucky and find her at home." She turned to Kerry. "You'll be happy to know we've assigned you top billing in the little drama we're planning to put on in the ER. Krista will fill you in on your part."

"We'll see you later," Jake said as she picked up the bag with her work clothes in it and walked to the back door.

"Six o'clock sharp," she replied, giving her friends the thumbs up sign before heading downstairs to her car.

It took only a few minutes to navigate the streets leading northeast to the university. The Taylors lived in one of the older brick houses just west of the school, and Caroline found a parking spot not far from their home. When she rang the bell, she half expected it to go unanswered, but Mavis herself appeared at the door only seconds after the high pitched peel faded away.

"I saw you come up the walk," she said as she motioned Caroline inside. "It's been quite a week, hasn't it?"

If Caroline had expected to see apprehension in the black woman's eyes, she was mistaken. Mavis appeared calm, collected, and even a bit amused as she guided her guest into the living room.

"I've been waiting for the police to arrive. They questioned me after Angela's murder, you know."

"They questioned us all," said Caroline as she took a seat on the ivory and green striped sofa. She glanced about the room. "You've redecorated since I was last here."

"I got tired of the old look. Do you like it?"

"Absolutely," Caroline replied with enthusiasm.

The blue flowered wallpaper that had once graced the large room had been stripped off and replaced by cream-colored paint. The overstuffed couch and chairs had been removed as well. In their place stood an assortment of lean looking furniture of a more modern design. Low backed and elegant, the chairs were covered in a deep burgundy material to offset the ivory and forest green sofa. Each one was flanked by a glass-topped table bearing either a shaded reading lamp or a small vase of flowers. The gleaming wood floor was dotted with various sized rugs in shades of cream, tan, and brown while stark black and white prints hung on the walls, each one depicting a Chicago scene from the past.

"Very stylish," proclaimed Caroline. "And very different from what I remember."

Mavis shrugged. "The kids are all grown and gone now. No need for throw pillows littering the living room and scratch-proof tables for the cola cans and pizza boxes. I've always wanted this kind of room, and on Harry's salary we can afford it." She shifted in her chair. "But you haven't come to exchange small talk, have you?"

"No. I wanted to talk to you about the murders. The police seem to be concentrating on Molly as their prime suspect."

"Molly? Why, that woman wouldn't hurt a fly." Mavis stood up, a frown destroying her previously tranquil expression. "Much as I like this room, it's more for light-hearted gossip than serious talk between friends. I do most of my problem solving in the kitchen, so let's go back there and have a cold drink while we try to figure out this mess."

Caroline followed the other nurse down a corridor leading to the back of the house. The kitchen was a large, sunny room with honey-colored cabinets and a long wooden trestle table set against one wall. She settled herself on a high-backed chair and accepted the glass of lemonade Mavis handed her.

"So the police talked to you already."

"They came here after Angela's murder, but I had an alibi for that one. Harry and I were attending a bank function along with several hundred other people. It didn't end until close to midnight, and then we drove another couple to Schaumburg when their car wouldn't start. We had a drink at their place before coming back here. It was after two when we finally arrived home."

A wave of relief swept over Caroline, and it showed. Mavis threw back her head and laughed.

"Thought I might have done the dastardly deed, did you?" Her eyes sparkled as Caroline blushed in embarrassment. "Oh, don't apologize, Cari. I was mad enough to kill when I stomped out of Angela's office, but on the way home I got to thinking that Miss Horowitz had done me a favor."

"A favor? What do you mean?"

"For several months now I've been thinking of quitting my job. Like I said before, the kids have finally left the nest. The last one graduated from college last month and took a job in Michigan. We've no extra bills to pay, nothing to do with our money but spend it on ourselves." She paused for a sip of lemonade. "Harry's in a position where he travels to Europe several times a year. Between the kids and my job, I've missed out on ninety-nine percent of those trips."

"But now you can go with him."

Mavis nodded. "He was overjoyed when he heard I'd quit. He's going to Paris in a couple of weeks, and he's been urging me to come along. The night Angela died we were celebrating the fact that we'd be traveling together to the most romantic city in the world."

"You had more of a motive to kiss Angela than kill her."

"And I have no motive at all for killing Roger. Lord knows the man was an egotistical pain in the neck, but up until my last day at Ascension, I'd managed to work around him."

"Do you know of anyone in the ER who hated him enough to want him dead?"

"No," replied Mavis firmly. She began ticking off names on her fingers. "Vic was using him to climb the management ladder. Vic's working on his Master's degree and thinks he's ready to take over as nurse manager of the department. Fawn was less obvious than Vic, but she buttered up to Roger, too. She knew he was thick with Angela, and Angela was the key to Fawn's success at Ascension."

"Molly gave her your job as charge nurse."

"I figured she would. Fawn's been there a while, and she knows her medicine. I don't like her as a person, but I have to admit she's smart."

"What about the others?"

"All the people who left the ER got jobs in other hospitals. I can't see any of them bothering to come back and kill Roger. As for the new folks, it was clear to me that Susan was scared stiff of Roger. She avoided him like the plague, but I can't say I ever saw him hit on her. Maybe it was his reputation that frightened her, or maybe I missed something between the two of them. Either way, she was always more relaxed working with the other docs than when Roger was in the Room."

"What about Michelle? Could jealousy have driven her to murder?"

"Michelle? You have to be kidding!" Mavis snorted. "She was after a wedding ring, which just goes to show how naïve she was. Roger wasn't the sort of man to settle down with one woman. He was a user, nothing more and nothing less."

"But could she have killed him?"

"She doesn't have the need to commit murder. Michelle's clever, and she's got the kind of body men like. She made a mistake with Roger, but mark my words. She'll hook up with someone soon."

"That leaves Keeshon, Patrice, and Chan Daley. I heard that Roger gave Chan his walking papers."

"What you didn't hear was that Chan was hired by another hospital the very next day. Dr. Daley has no motive, Cari. As for Patrice, she was miserable over the incident with Roger, but she's far too gentle a person to provide any physical threat to the man. Kee might have killed Roger in a fit or rage, but he would have beaten him to death, not hung him. He's a direct sort of person, not one who plans ahead."

That didn't leave him out as a suspect, thought Caroline. He was present that evening, and although Mavis didn't know it, Kee was angrier than hell over the bypass issue. An argument about that could have led to words over Roger's treatment of Patrice. Kee might have gone for Roger's neck, then hung him in the old ER to cover his tracks.

"I hate to ask this, but what do you think about Molly's state of mind? The change in her is alarming, and it worries me."

"I think Molly is on the verge of quitting her job. I only stuck around this long because I felt sorry for her. Roger drove so many nurses out of the department that she was having a terrible time staffing the place. My leaving would have made things even worse."

"I saw that the first time I looked at the schedule. There just weren't enough people assigned to each shift."

"In my opinion, Molly's on a downward slide. She's burned out, a nervous wreck. She's been working too hard, and the problems with the renovations just added to her worries."

"Do you think it's possible she cracked under the pressure?"

Mavis stared out the window, considering her answer. When she looked back at Caroline, the doubt showed in her eyes.

"I said before that Molly wouldn't hurt a fly, but God only knows how each of us would react to the kind of stress she was under. I can only hope she has an alibi for the time of both murders."

CHAPTER THIRTY-FIVE

June 17th
1:10 P.M.

Caroline was late for her appointment at the police station. She didn't notice the boy sitting on the bench in the waiting area when she hurried through the main door, but his eyes followed her as she made her way to the desk.

"I'm here to sign a statement concerning the death of Dr. Roger MacGuffy," she told the officer behind the glass partition.

"Your name?"

"Caroline Rhodes. I work at Ascension Medical Center."

"Wait over there, please. Someone will come for you in a moment."

The officer picked up a phone and spoke quietly to someone on the other end of the line. Caroline moved away, her eyes straying to a bulletin board on the lobby wall. Pictures of lost pets were pinned to the board along with an official looking directive warning residents of the legal hours for watering lawns. The postings spoke louder than words of a suburban community unused to murder.

"Must seem like home to you, Mrs. Rhodes."

She turned and saw a heavy-set balding man walking towards her. He held out his hand.

"I'm Frank Lodash, Kate's husband. Kate tells me you've just returned to Ascension."

"That's right, detective. I'm back for the summer. And yes, this place does remind me of home. People post all kinds of notices in Rhineburg's police station. You'll find everything from pictures of missing dogs to announcements for yard sales tacked to the bulletin board, and occasionally you'll even see a wanted poster hanging there."

Lodash smiled. "What I meant was, I've heard you spend a good deal of time with Rhineburg's Chief of Police. I've been told you were involved in a couple of murder investigations in your town."

"I helped out a bit," Caroline said hesitantly, wondering what Lodash was leading up to. It didn't take long for her to find out.

"The Niles police are on top of this case, Mrs. Rhodes. We're working hand in hand with the Chicago PD, and we'd rather not have any civilians messing about in it."

"I hear you loud and clear, detective." But that doesn't mean I'm going to back off, she added silently.

"Are you in charge of the murder investigation? The one at the hospital?"

Caroline and the detective turned simultaneously. A young Latino boy was standing a few feet away, his gaze concentrated on Lodash.

"I'm one of the investigating officers," Frank answered. "Why do you ask?"

"I have a message for you." The boy pulled a folded piece of paper from his pocket and handed it to Lodash. "Mr. Harris wants to talk to you."

Frank glanced at the note before stuffing it into his pocket. He nodded at the boy who turned and ran out of the station.

"Everyone wants to get in on the act," he said with a sigh. "All right, Mrs. Rhodes. Let's go get your statement on paper."

Chapter Thirty-six

June 17th
2:30 P.M.

"Hey, you! Young woman! Come over here."

Caroline had just entered the ER when the white-haired man in the wheelchair called out to her. She glanced around, then looked at him, her eyebrows raised as she pointed to herself questioningly.

"That's right. I mean you!"

"Can I help you, sir?"

"I've been waiting here for hours," the man said gruffly. "You'd think a simple X-ray shouldn't take all this long."

"I'll go check on what's holding things up."

"No! I want to go outside. I need a cigarette."

Fawn Phillips circled the desk and walked over to the man. Her face was set in its usual stern expression. "I'm sorry, sir. We're looking for your X-rays, but they seem to have gone missing. I'm afraid you'll have to go back for another picture."

"I want a cigarette first." The old man crossed his arms, raised his chin, and stuck out his bottom lip. "I'm not going anywhere until I've had one."

"I'm not on duty yet," Caroline told Fawn. "I'll wheel him outside for a smoke, then take him back to X-ray."

"Thanks," Fawn said grudgingly. She turned away, then added, "Don't be long. I'd like to get him out of here."

Caroline nodded. She slipped the brakes on the wheelchair and pushed it down the corridor to the ambulance entrance. Once outside, she parked the chair under a tree.

"So what did you do with your films? Throw them away?"

Carl Atwater grinned at her. "I told that young fella in X-ray I could wheel myself back to ER. He gave me the pictures and I stashed them under the mattress on one of the carts."

Caroline rolled her eyes.

"I talked to Vic Warner," Carl said. "He signed me in for my laryngitis yesterday, and he was back in the triage room again today when I rolled in with my sore foot."

"Did he say anything useful?"

"Yesterday, all I had to do was mention the subject of Angela's death and Vic was off to the races. He talked about Angela like she was some kind of saint, but outside of hinting that Molly was behind the murder, he didn't say anything we already didn't know."

"What about today?"

"Vic was a different man altogether. I think Roger's murder really has him shaken. He talked like the two of them were old buddies. When I asked if he had any ideas on the identity of the murderer, he replied in the negative. He did say, though, that lots of people here hated Dr. MacGuffy. He said it was because Roger ran a strict department, and some nurses didn't like that."

"That's a load of..."

"What your language, Cari. It doesn't fit your position."

Caroline shot him a look, but she managed to hold on to her temper. "What else did he say?"

"I made a few sympathetic noises, then mentioned how some women used work as an excuse to hate a man when it really boiled down to sex. Vic took the bait, hook, line, and sinker. He said there was a woman working here who had lived with Roger years ago."

"What!"

Carl nodded. "Surprised me, too, since you'd never mentioned anything about it. I tried to worm a name out of him, but he resisted."

"So we don't know who it was."

"All Vic had to say was that this woman is married now and her husband doesn't know about her relationship with MacGuffy."

Caroline mentally listed the married women in the department. Brenda Berlein, the EMS Coordinator, was one of them. Annie Singh and Kate Lodash had husbands also, as did Mavis Taylor. Mavis had an alibi for Angela's murder, but she'd never said a word about her whereabouts last night. Had Roger threatened to expose one of them? Reveal a secret that could ruin a marriage?

"Vic said there were a couple of young women after Roger, girls who hounded him for dates because he was a wealthy doctor."

"That would be Michelle Devine, and maybe Wendy Moss. I can't quite figure out Wendy's feelings for Roger. I saw him touch her once, and I thought she was repulsed. I may have been wrong, though. She asked a couple of questions that led me to believe she might be interested in him romantically."

"The girl's new here, isn't she? Maybe she just wanted your opinion on the man."

Caroline shrugged. "Could be. It doesn't really matter, anyway. Wendy hasn't worked at Ascension long enough to develop a hatred for Roger, so she's not on our list of suspects." She turned the wheelchair around and headed back to the ER. "Better get you to X-ray or Fawn will start wondering what's up. Behave yourself this time, will you?"

"I'll be a good little patient," Carl replied with false meekness. "Before we go in, I want to tell you that everything's been arranged with Adam Horowitz and your administrator, Mr. Bradford. Jake and I were on the phone to Alexsa yesterday afternoon and this morning. She told us that Michael Bradford has agreed to keep quiet about our presence in the hospital. The police won't hear a word about our plan."

"Have the Archangels arrived?"

"They're in the hospital's security office getting fixed up with uniforms even as we speak. One of them will be assigned to the ER for each shift."

"Good," said Caroline. "Let's pray this works. I have a feeling the police are close to charging Molly." The automatic door opened and she rolled the wheelchair into the corridor. "Detective Lodash had a whole new set of questions for me when I visited the police station this afternoon. Ninety percent of them were about Molly's relationship with Roger."

"Detective Gianni was here when I arrived. I saw him go into Miss O'Neal's office, and he didn't look happy."

"I hope we're not too late with our snooping, Carl."

But it appeared they were. They were half way down the corridor when they saw Dom Gianni lead Molly out of her office. She was wearing handcuffs.

CHAPTER THIRTY-SEVEN

June 17th
3:10 P.M.

"The police had a search warrant when they arrived," Brenda said bitterly. "They said they had Michael Bradford's permission to search Molly's office, but they wanted to make sure everything was done legally."

"Sounds like they don't want to jeopardize the case," Caroline remarked.

"They found a letter in Molly's desk. She wrote it the other day after that fiasco with the renovations in the old ER. She listed all the problems she'd been having with Roger and said she couldn't work with him any longer."

"It was a letter of resignation."

Brenda nodded. "Unfortunately, she never finished it. The police think that's because she decided to kill Roger."

Caroline groaned.

"Molly tried to explain she was just letting off steam, but then she couldn't prove where she was at the time of the murder."

"How did you hear all this?"

"I took over the triage office when I saw that detective grilling Molly. The walls are so thin you can hear right through them."

"So you tossed Vic out and took his place."

"He still hadn't handed in his monthly review test, so I made him go into the ER and fill out a new one. He didn't like it, but at least I knew he didn't have any fish with him today."

"Fish? What's that all about?"

"Last week I threatened to have Vic's ERCN status withdrawn if he refused to complete the monthly tests. He retaliated by tossing a dead fish on my desk. He put it there sometime on the weekend, and when I arrived here Monday, my office stunk to high heaven." Brenda shook her head. "I still don't know how he got into my locked office, but I can tell you it won't happen again. I made maintenance change the lock, and I told the head of security that if any of his people ever again opened my door while I was away, I'd have them fired."

"Then the security department has keys for all these offices."

"Of course," replied Brenda. "They need them in case of an emergency. I have to get back to work, Cari. I'll let you know if I hear anything more about Molly."

She turned to leave, but Caroline placed a hand on her arm.

"Brenda, I need to ask you something before you go. Were you ever romantically involved with Roger MacGuffy?"

The color faded from Brenda's cheeks. Lips compressed in anger, she pulled her arm away.

"I can't believe you'd ask me that," she hissed. "Who told you I had an affair with Roger? Was it Vic?"

When Caroline didn't answer, she stalked out of the room.

"What's the matter with her?" asked Keeshon as he walked up behind Caroline.

"She's upset over Molly's arrest. What about you, Kee? Do you think Molly killed Roger MacGuffy?"

She looked into his eyes, watching for some sign of fear or remorse, but there was none. Instead, Kee appeared angry.

"Damn fool police. It won't be the first time they've arrested the wrong person." He walked over to the desk and sat down. "They worked me over pretty good this morning. I was home alone when Angela Horowitz was killed, but I had an alibi for last night. I took Patrice out for something to eat after work."

"So you were together when Roger died."

Not that it really mattered, thought Caroline. They could have committed the murder as a pair, then rushed off to a restaurant where they'd be seen and remembered.

"That's right. Hey, Susan! What's wrong?"

Susan Kane appeared aggravated as she approached the desk. She was waving an X-ray folder. "You know that old geezer in the wheelchair? The one with the injured foot? Well, I just found his first set of X-rays tucked under the mattress on cart ten. When I asked him about it, he just smiled at me and said, 'So that's where I put them!'"

Kee reached for the folder. "At least you found them. I'll have a doc look at the films so we can get this guy out of here."

"Sorry, Kee. It won't be that easy. Mr. Atwater tried to stand up and he fell. Now he's complaining that his back hurts. He's stretched out on a cart refusing to leave until a doctor looks him over again."

Kee sighed. "Since he fell while under our care, you'll have to make out an incident report. Have you done one of those yet?"

Susan shook her head.

"I'll help her, Kee. I don't have any patients at the moment."

"That's 'cause nobody's coming in, Caroline," Kee replied darkly. "The murders have scared people away. Even the ambulance patients are requesting diversion to other hospitals."

That was good news to Caroline's ears. Fewer patients meant more time to snoop around the department and talk with the staff. She accompanied Susan back to the west wing, instructing her on the paperwork to be filled out as they walked.

"Keep it simple and stick to the facts," she said, handing the form to the other nurse. "Report only what you saw and did."

Susan nodded and pulled out a pen.

"While you're busy with that, I'll go check on Mr. Atwater."

Caroline walked over to cart ten where Carl lay in apparent agony. He was moaning as he tried to shift his weight from one side to the other on the hard mattress.

"I know you don't want to leave," she said in a low voice, "but did you have to fake a fall? You could have hurt yourself."

"I didn't fake it," growled the professor. "And I did hurt myself. I wrenched something in my back, Cari. I'm afraid I'm no good to you now."

Caroline patted her friend's hand. "One of the docs will be here to see you shortly. I'll see if we can get you something for pain."

"Get me a chocolate bar," Carl called out as she turned away. "I'm hungry!"

Shaking her head, she returned to where Susan sat writing at a little desk in the corner of the room. "How's it coming?"

"It's an easy enough form to fill out." She handed the completed paper to Caroline who looked it over, then handed it back.

"Give it to Kee. He'll see that the supervisor gets it."

She watched Susan go, then picked up the desk phone and dialed the apartment. "Krista? It's mom. The professor fell and hurt his back, so he's out of commission for awhile. Tell Jake to move up the time on our other 'victims'." She listened for a moment, then said, "Fine, dear. Now give me Alexsa's cell phone number. I may need it later tonight." She scribbled the number on a pad of paper, tore off the sheet, and stuffed it into her pocket. "Thanks, Krista. See you later."

Hanging up the phone, she went back to check on Carl.

"Have you got my chocolate?" he grumbled, gritting his teeth as he turned his head towards her.

"Sorry, not yet. I do have some butterscotch with me, though."

She dug in her pocket and extracted two pieces of hard candy along with the paper she'd just written on. The paper slipped out of her hand and floated to the floor.

"What's that?"

"Alexsa's phone number," Caroline said, picking up the paper and handing it to the professor. Atwater stared at it for a moment, his brow wrinkled in thought

"You've written the name Scotty above the number."

She glanced at the scrap of paper and shook her head. "Not my writing. I tore this off a pad on the desk. Susan must have been doodling on it."

'Scotty' was penned in bold letters at the top of the page. Susan had boxed in the word with thick, black lines that looked for all the world like the outline of a coffin.

"Did you know that Scotty was Roger MacGuffy's nickname? Vic called him that several times when he was talking to me yesterday. He was trying to impress me, show me how buddy-buddy he was with the late doctor. He said only Roger's closest friends knew him by that name."

"Are you saying that Susan Kane was tight with Roger?" Caroline shook her head. "I find that hard to believe. She always seemed to avoid him when he was in the room."

"Maybe she had good reason to avoid him. Maybe she was one of his cast-offs." Carl's eyes swiveled to the left. "Here she comes now. I'll find out what I can about this."

Caroline nodded and moved off as Susan and Dr. Chan Daley walked up to the cart. Chan gave her a smile before drawing the curtain and starting his examination of the professor.

"I imagine Chan's pretty worn out today," she said to Susan. "The police kept him here late with all their questions."

"One of them showed up at my door this morning. I live alone, so it was impossible to prove I'd been in bed all night and not here knocking off Roger."

"Scotty's as troublesome dead as he was alive."

Susan didn't blink at the mention of Roger's nickname.

"I didn't know him all that well," she said, turning away and walking to the desk. "Still, I hear that a lot of people didn't like him."

"Apparently someone liked him even less than the rest of us," said Chan Daley as he left Carl's side and walked over to join them. He looked at Caroline, one eyebrow raised questioningly.

"Can't stay away from the elephant's tail, can you, Cari."

She smiled ruefully. "Not with Molly in custody. But don't worry, Chan. Now I'm carrying more than one umbrella."

And each one had a name: Jake, Maddy, the Archangels. With these people at her side, Caroline felt she could survive anything the elephant dumped on her.

CHAPTER THIRTY-EIGHT

June 17th
5:00 P.M.

"Why don't they call? I gave that detective the note hours ago."

"You're sure he was the one in charge of the investigation."

Miguel Ramos nodded. "He was talking to the woman, the one we saw on TV outside the Emergency Room."

"And his name is Lodash."

Miguel nodded again. "Frank Lodash. He introduced himself to the woman right in front of me. I heard everything they said."

Walter Harris drummed his fingers on the table. "Maybe I should have said more in the note. Maybe he didn't take it seriously."

"You should call him," Miguel urged. "Tell him what's in the file."

Harris shook his head. "Can't do that, boy. He has to see it to get the whole picture."

The telephone rang, startling them both.

"It's got to be him," Miguel said excitedly. Harris shushed him as he leaned across the table to answer it.

"Hello? Oh, it's you, Maria. Yes, Miguel's here. Hold on and I'll put him on the line."

Miguel took the phone, disappointment etched on his face. "Yes, mamma, I understand. Don't worry, I'll make supper for him and tell him you'll be late." He placed the receiver back on its cradle. "The funeral was this morning. Lots of people came to the house, so mamma was cooking all day. She's staying to help with the clean up."

"I'm sure she had her hands full. Adam Horowitz is still the head honcho, even if he supposedly retired from the business. I'll bet there was a procession of mourners visiting the estate today. I'll also bet the FBI guys were there recording license plate numbers."

The boy's eyes clouded over. "I know what you think of Mr. Horowitz, but he's been good to my family. My mother respects him."

"I'm not criticizing your mother," Harris sighed. "Horowitz is a crook, but he's treated her fairly, and for that I give him credit. Look, Miguel..." He broke off, suddenly tired of having to explain himself to his young neighbor. The rebellious set of Miguel's chin told him that while the boy could believe the information in Roger MacGuffy's file, the copious details Harris had compiled on Adam Horowitz were another matter altogether. "You'd better go home. Your father will be there soon, and he'll be expecting his supper."

Miguel gave him a troubled look, but he didn't argue. Harris watched him walk out the door, then he picked up the phone and dialed the Niles police station.

"I'd like to speak to Detective Frank Lodash, please. My name is Walter Harris, and I have some information concerning the murder of Roger MacGuffy." He listened as a polite voice explained that all the investigating officers were unavailable at the moment, but if he'd like to leave a message on the special line set up for people calling in about the murder, he was welcome to do that.

"I'm not some crank calling in a bad tip," he growled. "I have solid information...aw, forget it." He slammed down the receiver, than sat catching his breath. It was never good to get angry. His heart raced when his temper flared, and that made it even harder than usual to breathe. He turned up the oxygen on the portable canister and readjusted the prongs of the cannula tickling his nostrils.

"I guess there's only one thing I can do," he muttered to himself. He reached for the phone and dialed the local cab company.

CHAPTER THIRTY-NINE

June 17th
5:15 P.M.

"You're new here, aren't you?"

"Just started working for the Security Department today." Michael Bruck stuck out his hand. "I was told you're the evening charge nurse here in ER."

"Name's Keeshon Jones. Everyone calls me Kee."

The two men shook hands.

"That's quite a grip you've got there," Michael said, smiling. "I bet you lift weights."

"Every day. I used to box back in my Army days."

"Oh, yeah? I was in the Army. 91st Engineers, Ft. Hood, Texas."

"Spent a little time there myself," said Kee. "When were you in?"

The two men fell to reminiscing, each one describing in vivid detail his best and worst experience in the service.

"Nice to meet a fellow vet," Michael said as the stories wound down. "Maybe you could help me out here. I was told some doctor was killed in the old ER the other night. My boss told me to keep an eye out for strangers wandering the corridors. He thinks this weirdo -- the guy who did the killing -- might return."

"Guess you didn't hear," Kee replied as he settled back in his chair. "The cops arrested our boss today. They think she's their murderer."

"Sounds to me like you might disagree with them on that."

"Sure do. Molly O'Neal had cause for murder what with the hell Roger put her through, but she didn't do it."

"How can you be so positive?"

Kee shrugged. "I know the woman. There's not a bad bone in her body."

"Then maybe my boss was right. Maybe it was some nut case who just wandered in off the street."

"I doubt that. If you ask me," said Kee, lowering his voice, "Detective Lodash has the right idea, but the wrong person. Somebody in this department killed Roger, but it wasn't Miss O'Neal."

Michael feigned surprise. "Who do you think did it?"

"Just between the two of us, I'm putting my money on that woman over there." He pointed to a nurse working in the east wing. "She arrived here the day before Angela Horowitz was murdered, and she was working the night of Roger's death."

Michael tried to hide his amusement. "Really," he said.

"Yeah, man. Her name's Caroline Rhodes, and she used to work here. She claims to be a friend of Molly's, but I don't know about that. I heard she spent some time in a psych hospital before she left Ascension. I'm wondering if Molly didn't have to let her go, and she's taking her revenge by framing our boss for those murders."

"Hmm." Michael stared at Caroline's back. He didn't know if the psych part was true, but he figured Caroline would be interested in hearing Kee's evaluation of her. He glanced at his watch. "Hey, I got to get going. I've got rounds to make, you know."

"Sure. Stop by on your break and we'll have a cup of coffee together. It doesn't look like we'll be busy in here tonight."

"Thanks, Kee. I'll remember that."

He surely would, he thought as he walked away. The Army connection had allowed him to form a bond with the only other male working the shift. He was determined to use it for all it was worth.

CHAPTER FORTY

June 17th
5:30 P.M.

"You're a dear," whispered Maddy, patting Patrice Woodson's hand. "One more pillow ought to do it."

Patty placed a third pillow under Maddy's head. "Would you like me to turn off the overhead light?"

"Oh, no," screeched Maddy as she sat bolt upright on the cart. "And please don't leave me! I was so afraid to come here what with the murders and all. But Jake said it was the only thing to do. This migraine headache has been getting worse all day, and now it's killing me. Oh! I didn't mean to use that word. I hope I didn't upset you."

She reached out and grabbed the paramedic's arm. Patty tried to pry her loose, but she was fighting a losing battle.

"My husband can't stand to see me in pain, so he went back to the lobby. Please don't leave me alone."

"There, there," Patty said in her most soothing voice. "You'll only make your headache worse if you keep this up. You've got to relax, Mrs. Miller."

"Moeller. It's Moeller, dear." Maddy fell back on the cart. She placed one hand on her forehead and tried to groan convincingly.

"Are you sure you wouldn't like the light turned off?" Patty had never seen a true migraine sufferer who wasn't affected adversely by light. She wondered how bad Mrs. Moeller's headache really was.

Sensing she'd made a mistake and her fakery was about to be discovered, Maddy made an about-face on the lighting issue. She covered her eyes with both hands and said, "I'd probably feel better with it off. I'm being silly, I know, but I'm afraid of being alone in the dark with a murderer at large."

"I'll leave the curtain open a bit so you can see the rest of the room," Patty said, hitting the light switch. Glancing back at the little woman on the cart, she thought how miserably frightened she looked. She decided it wouldn't hurt to stay with her, at least until the doctor arrived.

"Thank you," Maddy mumbled as Patty sat down on a chair next to the cart and took her hand. "You're such a nice young woman."

Patty softened a little more. "The doctor will order something for pain after he sees you."

"That would be nice. Perhaps you could talk to me until he comes. Sometimes just listening to someone talk puts me to sleep. Then, when I wake up, the headache is gone."

"What shall I talk about?"

"Tell me about yourself. Do you have a young man?"

Patty smiled at the quaint expression. "I'm seeing someone, if that's what you mean. He's a nurse, and he works here, too."

"Are you going to marry him?"

"Yes, I am. He gave me this last night." Patty held out her hand for Maddy to see. "We went out to eat after work, and he popped the question right there in the restaurant exactly at midnight."

"Oh, what a lovely ring. I bet you came back here to show it off to your friends."

Patty shook her head. "I didn't have to. Most of my friends are paramedics, and a lot of them hang out at the restaurant where we went for dinner. It's one of those sporty places with five or six TV's hanging from the ceiling and all of them tuned to ESPN. There was a crowd of paramedics there last night, and every one of them bought us a drink to celebrate."

"How nice," said Maddy, and she sincerely meant it.

Chapter Forty-one

June 17th
6:00 P.M.

"Have you met our new unit receptionist?" Patrice asked Caroline as they headed to the nurses' lounge for their dinner break.

"No, I haven't. They've hired another one?"

"Wendy gave notice today. She said she couldn't work in a place where a murder had been committed. 'Too creepy' is the way she put it."

"Is she going to another hospital?"

"No, she's going home to England. Going to work at her parents' hotel in Cornwall. She says her mom could use another hand in the kitchen."

"That's too bad. She just finished training, and she seemed to be adept at the computer."

"The new girl's name is Faith McGinty. She's Irish as the day is long, red hair, green eyes, the works." Patty opened the door to the lounge and walked in. "You'll get to meet her in a few minutes. She's coming on break with Wendy."

Caroline went to her locker and pulled out a brown bag containing two nectarines and a bagel.

"That's all you're eating?" Patty looked at her in horror. "I'd starve if that was my dinner."

"You don't need to lose weight. I do." She sat down at the table and watched Patty unpack her own meal. "Looks like you have a healthy appetite tonight. You also seem more relaxed than I've seen you in days. Roger's death hasn't affected you, has it."

"Actually, it has, but it's affected me in a good way." Patty played with the wrapper on her sandwich, appearing unsure whether to continue her comments or leave it at that. In the end, her need to confide in someone overcame her reticence. "I was worried about Kee when Angela's body was found. You know how angry he was that day in Brenda's office."

"I remember. He seemed close to losing it at the time."

"Sometimes his temper gets the best of him. Please don't tell him this, but for a while there I was afraid he'd killed Miss Horowitz."

Caroline nodded. "I can understand your fear, Patty."

"But now I know he didn't do it. We left the hospital together last night, and we stayed together until this morning when we heard the news on the radio."

"Are you sure Kee never left the department before the shift ended?"

Patty shook her head. "No way, Caroline. He was too busy overseeing the transfer of patients to the Cast Room and giving report to Kate Lodash. There wasn't time enough for him to confront Roger, kill him, then rig up that scene in the old ER."

Caroline had to admit Patty had a point. They'd all been busy with patients between ten-thirty and eleven-thirty. The murder had to have been committed during the night shift.

"I can't believe Angela and Roger died at the hands of different people," Patty continued. "It's too much of a coincidence."

"I'll agree with you there. I also think the same person killed them both. Apparently the police do, too."

"Then that clears Kee." Patty smiled. She was a woman at peace with herself and the world, and it showed on her face.

Cross those two off the suspect list, thought Caroline.

The door opened and Wendy Moss walked into the lounge followed by Faith Bruck, Michael's wife.

"Caroline Rhodes, meet Faith McGinty. Faith will be taking my place as UR for the evening shift."

Caroline stood up. "Welcome to the ER, Faith."

Faith kept a straight face as they shook hands. "I'm pleased to meet you, Miss Rhodes."

"It's Mrs. Rhodes, but please, call me Cari."

"I'm going back to England," Wendy said as she pulled a chair up to the table. "Faith has worked in a hospital before, so this job isn't new to her."

"That's right," said Faith, nodding her head. "My last job was on a medical floor back home."

"Where's home?" Patty asked between bites of her sandwich.

Faith's eyes flew to Caroline who was staring at her bagel with an intensity that defied description.

"Ho...home?" she stuttered. "Why..."

"Lincoln, Nebraska," Wendy answered for her. "Faith's a farm girl just like me."

"That's right," Faith said again. "Just a farm girl come to the big city."

Caroline groaned.

"Are you all right?" Patty asked, staring at her with some concern. "Did you choke on your bagel?"

"I choked on something," Caroline answered, rising to her feet. She went to the sink and poured herself a glass of water. Faith had better pull her act together, she thought, or they were done for. "Where do you live, Wendy? In England, I mean."

"I come from a little town in Cornwall called East Looe."

"You told me it was West Looe," said a surprised Faith.

Wendy laughed. "Same thing, actually. The town is divided by a highway, East Looe on one side, West Looe on the other." She stood up. "I think I'll go get a soda from the machine. Anyone want one?"

"No thanks," said Patty, rising from her chair. "I need to make a phone call, so I'll see you all back in the room."

Neither of the other women wanted a soda. Wendy and Patrice left the lounge together, much to Caroline's relief.

"You almost blew it, Faith."

"I know," the young woman replied. "I'm not used to lying to people!"

"It's not lying, it's acting. Think of yourself as a movie star with a role to play. It's much easier that way."

"I'll do better," Faith promised. "The hardest part is seeing Michael and not being able to say hello."

"You can say hello. In fact, why don't you flirt with him a little? Pretend you're smitten by his good looks and wavy blond hair. It might get Wendy talking about men, and then you can find out if she was interested in Roger sexually."

Faith's eyes widened. "I thought he was an older man!"

"About as old as I," Caroline replied dryly. "Just do your best to get her talking, Faith. Find out what you can about Michelle Devine, also. Michelle's coming in at seven o'clock. She's working a twelve-hour shift, so she'll be here until morning. Which Bruck brother is coming in for the night shift?"

"Gabe pulled the short straw."

"Tell Gabe to concentrate on Michelle. We need to find out if she argued with Roger the night he died. We know she was jealous of his other women. She'd fought with him over it before. It could be they had it out that night and somehow Roger ended up dead."

"You can count on me, Cari. I'll pull the truth out of both of them."

Caroline's face was grim as she replied, "Don't pull too hard, Faith. Remember, there's a murderer walking around the ER, and we have no idea who it is."

Chapter Forty-two

"You're here early," Kee said as Michelle entered the room dressed in her blue scrubs. The girl was less than her radiant self this evening. Her black hair was tied back in a loose ponytail from which long strands had escaped and lay curled against her damp neck. She wore very little makeup, and dark circles showed under her eyes. Her scrubs were worn thin, and although clean, they looked as if they'd been bunched up in a drawer somewhere, pulled out at the last minute, and thrown on with no thought to appearance or decorum.

"The power's out on our block. It was so stuffy in the house last night without air conditioning that I hardly got any sleep. Couldn't do my laundry either." Michelle tossed her purse in a drawer under the desk. "Figured I'd might as well come in to work. At least it's cool here."

Caroline looked up from her charting. "We have a new unit receptionist," she said, pointing to Faith. "Wendy is leaving us. She's going back to England."

Smiling, Faith turned from the computer and extended her hand. Michelle ignored it as she zeroed in on Wendy.

"Making nice to Roger last night was nothing but a waste of time, wasn't it, Wendy. Before you could get your claws into him, someone...someone..." The girl broke into tears. Pressing her hand to her mouth, she whirled and fled from the room.

"Whoa!" said Kee. "She really did have the hots for him, didn't she."

"Perhaps I'd better go after her," Caroline said, rising from the desk. "She's pretty distraught. Will you keep an eye on my patient, Kee? Mrs. Moeller refused in IV. She's resting pretty comfortably, though, with Patrice at her side."

Kee grinned. "Patty's been talking an arm and a leg off that woman. Strangely enough, Mrs. Moeller's headaches ease up when Patty's with her, then return when Patty leaves. Personally, I think her migraines are psychosomatic."

"You could be right," murmured Caroline. She glanced over at Wendy Moss. "Are you all right? That was quite a tongue lashing Michelle gave you."

Wendy wrinkled her nose. "She never did like me, and I'll admit, the feeling's been mutual. I'll be glad to see the end of Michelle Devine."

I can't blame her, Caroline thought as she hurried off to find Michelle. The tech had been riding Wendy ever since Roger made a pass at the girl. Rudeness was consistent with Michelle's attitude towards other women. She'd aimed plenty of snide remarks at Wendy, and more often than not, hit her target dead center.

She was not in the nurses' lounge when Caroline went looking for her there, nor was she in the triage office or lobby. Caroline was about to give up when she saw Jake Moeller standing outside the ER doors. She walked towards him, and the doors slid open automatically.

Jake was on his cell phone, and she waited for him to finish the call, using the few minutes to search the perimeter of the hospital for Michelle. Dusk was settling over the city, but the air was still warm and muggy. Caroline felt like she was breathing in pure water instead of oxygen. It was an uncomfortable sensation, and it caused her to hurry her search.

The once green lawn outside the ER had been torn up by the construction vehicles parked there. Deep ruts dotted the landscape.

"Ow!" Caroline winced as she slipped on a clod of dirt, wrenching her already damaged left ankle. She stepped back and tested her weight on the leg. The air splint had saved her this time, but further excursions on the uneven ground were out of the question. Straining her vision in the gathering gloom, she surveyed the area around the construction company's trailer, but saw no one. Where Michelle had gone was a mystery.

"How's Maddy doing?" Jake had walked up behind her, and he stood now with an amused grin on his face. "Is her headache any better?"

"It comes and goes as needed," Caroline replied, a smile tugging at the corner of her lips. "What about you? Were you able to look around the old ER?"

"I sneaked past the police tape about an hour ago. Looks like they went over the scene with a fine tooth comb."

"Did you see the scaffolding?"

Jake nodded. "I also saw two parallel chalk lines drawn on the floor. They extended almost from the doorway to the scaffolding, then twisted around and ended off to one side. There were a few circles drawn between the lines, each one surrounding what looked like a thin layer of cement dust."

"Footprints?"

"Or what was left of them. The dust wasn't as obvious there as in other parts of the room. I think the killer may have dragged a rag or a broom behind him as he left the room. Whatever he used, he made a good attempt to wipe out his tracks."

"Parallel lines. I wonder what they could mean." She turned and walked back towards the building, Jake at her side.

"I don't know, Cari, but I put in another call to Andy. I'm hoping he can tell me something more about the case. They might have a preliminary autopsy report by now."

"That would be helpful. I still can't believe that Roger would willingly allow that noose to be slipped over his head. He had to have been knocked out first."

"I'll let you know what I hear. Meanwhile, take good care of my wife."

Caroline threw him a smile as she walked back through the sliding doors of the ER. She passed through the waiting room and was almost to Molly's office when she spied a wheelchair abandoned at the end of the corridor. She stopped dead in her tracks, remembering how she'd wheeled Carl outside earlier that afternoon.

"Two parallel lines with footprints between them. Of course!"

It was clear to her now. Roger had been taken to his death in a wheelchair, which meant he'd been unconscious at the time. No wonder he hadn't objected when the electrical cord had tightened around his neck. He hadn't even known what was happening.

CHAPTER FORTY-THREE

June 17th
7:10 P.M.

The telephone rang, short, repeated bursts of sound that indicated the call came from the registration desk. Kee lifted the receiver and listened as the registrar asked for a triage nurse.

"Wish we had enough people scheduled on the p.m. shift to keep the triage office open," he said as he rose from his chair.

"It would be a waste tonight," replied Susan. "We've hardly any patients in the room."

"Well, I'll take this one." Kee circled the desk and headed for the waiting room. "I'm getting bored sitting here doing nothing."

He passed Detective Dominic Gianni in the hallway.

"Is Mrs. Rhodes in there?" Dom asked, thumbing towards the room. Kee nodded and kept on walking. The detective watched him go, then shook his head and continued into the main part of the ER. He saw Caroline standing next to the desk talking to Chan Daley.

"Evening, doctor. Mrs. Rhodes." His expression was grave as his eyes met Caroline's. "I need to speak to you. In private."

"We can talk over there," she said, pointing to the deserted front section of the east wing. "Or, we can go to the nurses' lounge."

"Over there is fine." Gianni turned and walked away. Chan raised his eyebrows quizzically, but Caroline only shrugged in response. She had no idea what Dom wanted with her.

"I understand you had a visit with Adam Horowitz yesterday," Dom said when the two of them were safely out of earshot of the others.

"News travels fast, doesn't it."

"Don't play with me, Mrs. Rhodes. Tom Evans was furious when he found out about it. He wanted to arrest you for obstruction of justice."

"Arrest me? Whatever for?" Caroline asked in astonishment.

Dom took her by the arm and led her even further into the empty section of the room. "Adam Horowitz is under surveillance by the FBI," he said quietly. "That's why Evans was in on the initial investigation into Angela Horowitz's death."

"I thought there was something strange about his presence on the case. Why is the FBI watching Mr. Horowitz?"

"Come on, Mrs. Rhodes. You know I can't give out that kind of information." He looked at her impatiently. "But you're a smart woman. Figure it out."

Caroline blushed. "I'm sorry, Dom. I don't mean to make things harder for you, but you've arrested my best friend."

"I didn't arrest her, the Niles police did. Frank Lodash believes Miss O'Neal had both motive and opportunity in the case of Roger MacGuffy. There's no solid evidence linking her to Angela's death, but it's logical to believe that the same person committed both murders."

"I agree with you on that last point, but I'm convinced of Molly's innocence."

"Why? Because she's an old friend? Old friends sometimes change, Mrs. Rhodes."

"Plenty of other people in this department hated Dr. MacGuffy."

"And we've been checking out all their alibis. If you have any solid leads to give me, then do so."

"Did you know that Brenda Berlein was involved with Roger? Or that Susan Kane apparently knew him better than she's admitting? Had you heard that Michelle Devine was deeply jealous of Angela?"

Gianni cocked his head to one side. "This is news to me, Mrs. Rhodes. Perhaps you should fill me in on the details."

Caroline told him everything she'd discovered about the ER staff. Gianni listened intently, interrupting her only once or twice for questions.

"Perhaps you should call the electric company and find out if the power was really off on Michelle's block last night."

"I'll do that," said Dom. "But first I'd like to speak to the young woman. The Niles cops didn't find her at home today, and she hasn't answered the phone messages I've left."

"She was in the ER earlier, but she had words with Wendy Moss, then ran out of here crying. I had no luck hunting her down, and as far as I know, she hasn't returned to the department."

"Took off, did she? That's interesting." Dom pulled a card out of his pocket and handed it to her. "I'll be around for a while talking to your coworkers, but if you need to reach me later tonight, or at any time for that matter, you can call me at this number. It's for my cell phone."

Caroline took the card and put it in her pocket.

"I know Roger was transported to the old ER in a wheelchair. Can you tell me if he was dead already when the killer strung him up from the scaffolding?"

"So you saw the wheelchair when you discovered the body. Frank didn't tell me that."

"Actually, I just figured that part out."

Dom's eyes narrowed, but he didn't comment on her statement. "Who makes the coffee around here?" he asked.

"The coffee? No one in particular. We keep two pots going in the nurses' lounge, one decaffeinated, one not. If you pour the last cup, you're supposed to put a new pot on to brew."

"And what about the pot in Dr. MacGuffy's office?"

"I don't know," admitted Caroline. "I've heard he drank tons of decaffeinated coffee when he was working, but I don't know if someone made it for him or he brewed it himself."

"See if you can find out, will you?"

"Is that how... was he drugged?"

Dom Gianni nodded. "We think so. The preliminary tests on stomach contents revealed he'd been drinking coffee shortly before he died. I haven't heard anything on the results of the blood work, but since there was no trauma to the body, other than signs of strangulation, we're assuming he was drugged first, then carted off to the old ER. The Niles police are no slouches. Lodash suspected drugs as soon as he saw the body, and he confiscated MacGuffy's coffeepot as evidence."

"But you don't know which drug it was."

"Not yet. Hopefully we'll learn more tomorrow."

"I'll ask around about the coffee," Caroline promised.

"Do something else for me, Mrs. Rhodes. Give up this silly plan of yours to load the ER with fake patients. And stay away from Adam Horowitz. You could get yourself in big trouble, and maybe mess up more than one case."

Dom walked away before a surprised Caroline could respond. How had he uncovered their plan? Had Jake let something slip to his friend on the Chicago PD? Or had the FBI bugged the Horowitz house. If they were watching the estate, they'd obviously witnessed her arrival there yesterday. It would have taken a listening device, though, to overhear her conversation with Adam.

I can't worry about that now, she thought. Alexsa should be appearing any minute, followed in another half-hour by Kerry and Krista. They would learn what they could tonight, then reevaluate their plan in the morning.

Despite Tom Evans and his threats, the show would go on.

CHAPTER FORTY-FOUR

June 17th
8:15 P.M.

Miguel Ramos finished drying the supper dishes and tossed the towel over a chair.

"I'm going next door to check on Mr. Harris," he called to his father as he slipped on his gym shoes. "Be back in an hour."

Lost in a made-for-TV movie, his father simply grunted. Miguel took that for an acknowledgment and ran out of the house, letting the screen door bang behind him. He jumped the fence and used his key to let himself into his neighbor's home. A light was on in the kitchen, but when Miguel called out, Walter Harris didn't answer.

He's asleep already, the boy thought as he crept quietly down the hallway to the bedroom. The day had been a tiring one for the old man, and Miguel wasn't surprised that he'd gone to bed before the evening news.

But the bedroom was empty. Miguel backtracked to the living room, then checked the bathroom and basement. Harris was nowhere in sight. Worried now, he made a second search of the house, checking even the closets this time.

"Mr. Harris! Please answer me!"

He ran out to the yard, looked in the garage, then circled the building and hurried back inside.

Where was he, Miguel wondered as he stood alone in the silent kitchen. He couldn't remember the last time his neighbor had left the house. Walter Harris never went anywhere due to his bad heart. People came to him, even his doctor.

"The file! He must have taken it to the police."

Miguel ran to the bedroom and switched on the light. They'd spent the morning there arranging the papers, sorting the information gathered so laboriously over so many years. Harris had made notes, and when he'd finished, Miguel had taken the file to the corner drug store and duplicated every page on the copy machine there. When he'd returned with the papers, Harris had handed him a message. He'd biked to the Niles police station, waited for Frank Lodash to notice him, then given the policeman the folded note.

But the detective had never called.

I shouldn't have left him, the boy thought as he rummaged through the desk looking for the file. I shouldn't have gone home to cook supper.

But he'd had no other option. His mother was not the kind of woman one argued with, and although his father was an easy-going man, he expected a meal on the table when he came home from work. There was no doubt about it; he'd had no choice in the matter.

Unfortunately, he'd been angry when he'd walked out on Harris, and that fact bothered him.

"Where is it?" he muttered as he rifled through the metal cabinet where the retired investigator stored all his papers. "It's got to be here somewhere."

After ten minutes of looking through every drawer, he gave up. The file was gone, as was Walter Harris.

Miguel locked the back door and jumped the fence separating the two houses. Grabbing his bicycle, he tore out of the yard and headed for the Niles police station.

CHAPTER FORTY-FIVE

June 17th
8:20 P.M.

The paramedic stood to one side of the cart giving report as Caroline connected her patient to a heart monitor.

"His portable oxygen ran out. It was on empty when we arrived at the police station. The guy at the desk said he'd been sitting on the bench for hours waiting for one of the detectives to talk to him. Guess the officers were all busy or gone home already."

"Any meds or allergies?"

"He had this list in his pocket." He handed her a slip of paper. "How are you feeling now, Mr. Harris?"

"Better," the elderly man whispered. His voice was barely audible through the plastic oxygen mask covering his mouth. "Thanks."

"No thanks needed," replied the paramedic with a smile. "Just remember to keep your oxygen tank filled from now on."

The color was returning to her patient's face. Caroline glanced at the monitor, then hit the button for the automatic blood pressure cuff before attaching the twelve leads that would record Mr. Harris' EKG. She was just finishing the procedure when Chan Daley pushed back the curtain and stepped to the side of the cart.

"Any chest pain?" he asked as he examined the EKG report.

Harris shook his head. "Just a little breathless. It was stupid of me to forget to fill the tank."

Chan smiled. "We all forget things at times. This will serve as a good reminder for you in the future."

"That's for sure." Harris smoothed his graying hair with a trembling hand. "Scared the life out of me. Thought I was a goner for sure."

"How long have you had heart trouble?"

Caroline slipped past Chan as Harris launched into a recitation of his medical history. She'd heard the story from the paramedics, and she knew Chan would request a cardiac work-up on her patient. She went off to order the lab work.

"You're back," she said in surprise when she saw Michelle Devine standing by the computer. The tech was talking with Faith. Wendy was nowhere in sight.

"I was upset over Roger," the girl said, her eyes defying Caroline to make something of it. "I'm fine now."

"Then perhaps you can draw labs on our new patient. Mr. Harris needs a cardiac work-up." She glanced at Faith as Michelle walked off to gather her equipment. "Where's Wendy?"

"On break." Seeing they were alone, Faith motioned to a chair. "Sit down. I have news for you." She waited for Caroline to settle herself, then continued in a hushed voice. "First of all, Alexsa is here. She arrived a few minutes ago, and she has Bricole with her."

"Bricole Gregori? I didn't know she was in town."

"She arrived unexpectedly this afternoon. She had one of her premonitions, and she persuaded Alexsa's grandson to drive her here."

Caroline frowned. Bricole was Alexsa's ten-year-old ward and the granddaughter of the murdered Maria Gregori. An orphan since the age of seven, the little girl had traveled the carnival circuit with her gypsy grandmother, pulling in customers for their fortune-telling booth. Like Maria and her ancestors before her, Bricole had the Rom gift of second sight.*

*See SOMETHING WICKED IN THE AIR

"What kind of premonition?"

"She thinks Mrs. Morgan is in danger," Faith replied darkly. "She wants her to leave Highland Park and go home to Rhineburg."

"Why did Alexsa bring her to Ascension? She knows that one of the people working here tonight may be a murderer."

"Bricole wouldn't leave her side. She's sitting next to Alexsa's cart watching everyone who passes. She says she's here to protect Mrs. Morgan."

Caroline rolled her eyes. "The last thing we need is a child in our midst. I'd better go talk to her."

Faith put a hand on her arm as she started to rise. "Wait a minute. I have something to tell you about Wendy and Michelle."

She hesitated. "Make it fast, Faith."

The young woman did. When she finished, Caroline sat back and stared at her. "So you think Wendy's been lying about her family. But why?"

Faith shrugged. "Maybe she's trying to build herself up to be more than she is. Her accent is genuine, that's for sure, but she sounds more like London than Cornwall. You can check it out with Mrs. Morgan if you like. I asked Wendy to show me around the department, then I stopped to tie my shoe right in front of Alexsa's cart. I made sure Mrs. Morgan heard Wendy's voice."

"You Bruck women are pretty sharp," Caroline said as she got up from the chair. "I'm off to see Alexsa. Call me if Chan orders anything else on Mr. Harris."

She walked the few yards to the front end of the east wing where Kee was checking Mrs. Morgan's temperature.

"Still normal," he reported cheerfully. "Perhaps you have a touch of the flu."

"I never throw up, young man, but I've been doing it all day. I know this is a gall bladder attack."

Alexsa crossed her arms over her chest and dared Kee to disagree with her. Experienced as he was, the male nurse didn't take up the challenge.

"Let's see what your X-rays show before we go jumping to conclusions. I'll have Michelle wheel you over for the films." Catching sight of Caroline, he moved away from the cart and murmured under his breath, "Is it a full moon tonight, or what? Between Atwater, Moeller, and this one, we have our hands full."

"They're all giving you trouble, are they?"

"Chan just ordered Demerol for the first two. Atwater refuses to leave until he can walk without pain, and that Moeller woman," -- he shook his head -- "she gets hysterical every time Patty leaves her side. Chan's thinking of calling in a psych consult on her if the Demerol doesn't do the trick."

Oh-oh, thought Caroline. She'd better warn Maddy to lighten up a bit. The last thing she needed was a head doctor hovering over her. One of them would end up totally confused, and her money was on the psychiatrist.

"I noticed your patient has a child with her. I thought I'd offer her some ice cream."

"Good idea," Kee replied with a nod. "That ought to keep her occupied while her grandmother's in X-ray. Don't worry, though. I'll be at the desk if the kid gives you any trouble."

Caroline wondered why Kee had added that last part. She found out soon enough when she walked over to where Alexsa sat bolt upright on a cart, two pillows propped behind her back.

"How's everything going?" she asked, her gaze traveling from the elderly matriarch of Rhineburg to the child at her side.

"We're fine," Alexsa said firmly.

"We are not," hissed Bricole in an equally adamant voice.

Caroline sighed. "Perhaps you shouldn't have come tonight."

"I'm doing this for Adam, whether the child likes it or not."

'The child', as she'd been called, let out an epithet more fitting of a longshoreman than a ten-year-old.

"Bricole! I told you I would not put up with that kind of language! What would your grandmother think if she'd heard you say that?" Alexsa turned to Caroline. "Unfortunately, my ward learned some unsavory words during her carnival days. It's her only vice, and one that shall soon be behind us."

"I don't have much time now," Caroline said, eyeing the unhappy little girl. "But maybe we can talk while Mrs. Morgan is in X-ray."

The child stared at her shoes without answering. Undisturbed by her behavior, Caroline turned her attention to Alexsa.

"I understand you had a chance to observe Wendy Moss, our unit receptionist. Wendy claims to come from a village in Cornwall called Looe. She told Faith she's a farm girl, but she told others in the department that her parents own a hotel in the town. Faith thinks her accent doesn't fit the area."

"I haven't been to England in years," Alexsa admitted. "I'd have to trust Faith on the accent. She has family in Northern Ireland, and I know she's traveled there numerous times. She'd know how the English sound since there are so many Brits stationed there.

"As for Looe, I visited that town with my husband a long time ago. It was a fishing village then, set on both sides of a channel inlet from the ocean."

"An inlet? Wendy said it was divided by a highway, East Looe on one side and West Looe on the other."

"Unless it's changed greatly since we were there, East and West Looe are separated by water. There's a bridge that joins the two, and the houses are built up on the hills that flank the inlet."

"Doesn't sound like farming country to me."

"There may be small farms nestled in the hills. I'm not really sure of that. I do know there were several nice hotels, all family run, in the area. I suppose Wendy's parent could own both a farm and a hotel."

"Perhaps," agreed Caroline. "Or Faith may have hit the nail on the head when she suggested Wendy made up the story. She thinks Wendy's covering up a less than ideal background." Switching subjects, she asked, "What do you think of Michelle?"

"I tried to engage her in talk when she came to draw my blood, but she seemed distracted and quite nervous. She nearly jumped out of her skin when I mentioned Dr. MacGuffy's murder. I asked if she knew him, and she said, not really. Then I said it was a pity the hospital had lost Angela Horowitz." Alexsa smiled ruefully. "I guess I should have waited until she had the needle out of my arm. She jabbed me so hard that I'm sure I'll have black and blue marks for weeks."

"I didn't like her," muttered Bricole. The little girl pushed a strand of brown hair out of her eyes and looked up at Caroline. "She's sneaky and mean."

"I'll tell her to stay away if you'd like."

Bricole shrugged her shoulders. "It doesn't matter. She's going away soon."

"Actually, Michelle's working a twelve hour shift. She'll be here all night. I have to go, Alexsa, but I'll stop by to see you later."

With a last troubled look at Bricole, she turned and walked away. The child had changed since her grandmother's death in May. Mrs. Morgan had provided her with a stable home, but the loss of her last family member was a wound too deep to heal quickly. Bricole was suffering, and the present situation only aggravated the problem. Something told the little girl that she was going to lose Alexsa too.

They'd have to alter their plans, Caroline decided. The old woman and the child would have to be sent home.

CHAPTER FORTY-SIX

June 17th
9:00 P.M.

Walter Harris was resting comfortably when Caroline left his bedside. Chan Daley had wanted to admit him to the telemetry unit, but the grizzled veteran of numerous hospitalizations was resisting the ER doc's efforts.

"I want to go home," he insisted. "I've work to do, people to see, especially the police."

"You should stay here at least overnight," Chan counseled. "Nothing's as important as your health."

"This is," Harris declared, waving a manila envelope in the doctor's face. "This holds the key to your murders."

Chan's eyebrows soared. "Our murders?" he laughed. "What are you anyway? Some kind of detective?"

Sensing he'd made a serious mistake, the old man tucked the envelope under the sheet and refused to say another word.

Chan was still laughing when he told the others about it. "That guy thinks he's Sam Spade. He's hiding a thick envelope that he claims contains evidence of -- drum roll, please -- Who Done It."

Caroline was amazed by the various reactions of her coworkers. Kee appeared angry while Michelle visibly paled. Free, for the time being, of the demanding Mrs. Moeller, Patrice seemed nonplussed by the announcement. Her perplexed expression was shared by Susan Kane. Only Wendy seemed unmoved by Chan's story.

"I don't care what's in that envelope," she stated. "I'm out of here tomorrow, and I never want to hear another word about murder."

"Wouldn't it be nice if we could all just walk away."

The group turned as one as Brenda Berlein walked through the doorway.

"I thought you'd want to know that Molly O'Neal was formally charged with murder tonight. My husband, Bill, will be defending her."

Kee stood up and walked around the desk. He gathered a shaking Brenda in his arms and hugged her.

"I know how close the two of you are," he said as she began to sob. "I also know Molly didn't do it."

"Of course she didn't," cried Brenda as she pushed him away. "But someone here did." She stared at them, searching each face for some sign of guilt, then stated defiantly, "I know it wasn't me."

A silence enveloped the room broken only by the sound of someone snoring in the west wing. It lasted only seconds, but it seemed to stretch on forever until Chan stepped forward to put things back into perspective.

"We've all been affected by the events of the past week," he told them somberly. "I must remind you, though, that this is an Emergency Room. We treat sick people here, and they deserve our undivided attention. Regardless of our personal concerns and our loathing for whoever did this, we have to let go of our feelings while we're here. If we don't, our fear and anger will spill over into our work and cause us to make mistakes." He looked directly at the EMS Coordinator. "You of all people should know that, Brenda."

Brenda's eyes glistened with tears. "I'm sorry, Chan. You're right, and I apologize." She turned and walked out of the room.

"Go after her, Cari," Chan said as the others scattered. He tugged on his mustache to cover his discomfort. "She needs to talk to another woman right now."

Caroline nodded. "Call me if I'm needed."

She followed the corridor south to the EMS office. The door was closed, but when she knocked, Brenda answered.

"Want to talk?" she asked as she slipped into a chair.

"I made a fool of myself in there, didn't I?" Brenda sighed.

"You were upset, and with good cause."

"I shouldn't have come here."

"Why did you?"

Brenda fiddled with a pencil lying on the desk. It took her a moment to answer, and when she did, her words surprised Caroline.

"I told my husband about my affair with Roger MacGuffy. I figured I had to if he was going to defend Molly."

"That must have been difficult for you."

Brenda pushed the pencil aside. "It happened long before I met Bill. I'm not sure why I kept it a secret from him, but I did."

"Maybe it was because you were embarrassed."

"Embarrassed to admit I'd been taken in by Roger's charm? His sparkling personality? Yes, Cari, I was embarrassed. I was a fool to believe he could ever care for me as I thought I cared for him." Her eyes traveled to a spot beyond Caroline. "We were making wedding plans, even though he hadn't given me a ring yet. Then one day I came up to his apartment and found him in bed with another woman. She wasn't more than eighteen years old, and suddenly, at twenty-six, I felt old and used."

Caroline waited as her friend fought to retain her composure.

"I quit my job that same day and applied for the EMS position here." Brenda's voice grew stronger as she told the story. "I never saw Roger again until he took over as Ascension's Medical Director. That first day we met in the department, he looked at me like I was a stranger, then suddenly I saw a flash of recognition in his eyes. He smiled at me, a smirk actually, and my blood just ran cold. I could tell he wanted to take up where we'd left off, but I was having none of it."

"Did he pursue a relationship with you?"

"Hot and heavy for about a month. He knew I was married, but that didn't stop him. He only quit when I threatened to complain to the Chief of Staff." She stood up and began pacing the floor in the tiny office. "I hated the man, but I knew if I ever signed a formal complaint against him, the whole sordid truth would come out. You know how gossip travels through a hospital, Cari. My name would have been mud within a week."

"I don't blame you for wanting to keep it quiet. I'd probably have done the same thing in your place."

"Bill was out of town the night Angela died, so I have no proof that I was home at the time of her murder. And according to Frank Lodash, no one saw me leave the ER last night."

"But your husband can testify to the time you arrived home."

Brenda smiled sadly. "I didn't go directly home. I was one of the people Roger accused when the police came to interview him. I was afraid he'd tell them about us, and they'd think I'd killed Angela out of jealousy. I drove down to the lake and sat in my car until one in the morning trying to decide what to do."

The two women stared at each other in silence, then Brenda sank down in her chair again.

"I swear, Cari, I had nothing to do with either murder. I've told Bill everything, and I came here tonight to tell you."

"I believe you, Brenda," Caroline said, and she meant it. "I only asked you about your relationship with Roger because I wanted to help Molly. Somehow, we've got to discover the truth behind what happened here last night."

"I'm willing to do whatever is necessary to clear Molly of the charges. Tell me how I can help, Cari."

Caroline hesitated, then went with her gut instincts. "Susan Kane was afraid of Roger. I want you to find out why."

CHAPTER FORTY-SEVEN

June 17th
9:35 P.M.

Carl Atwater was snoring up a storm when Caroline went to check on him.

"The Demerol knocked him out," Susan said with a smile. "It had the same affect on Mrs. Moeller. I'm baby-sitting them both at the moment."

"Lucky you," Caroline replied, her heart sinking even lower. "Have you seen Mrs. Moeller's husband anywhere?"

"He and that new security guard were in here a few minutes ago, but I don't know where they are now. They seem pretty chummy for only having met a few hours ago. Maybe they're outside together having a smoke."

But neither man was in sight when Caroline walked into the waiting room and peered through the glass doors. She desperately needed to find Jake. He was the only man she knew of who commanded the total respect of Alexsa Stromberg Morgan. If he couldn't convince the old woman to leave the ER, then nobody could. God knows she'd tried her best and failed.

Caroline returned to the main room depressed and worried. Kerry had arrived while she was in Brenda's office, and even now the girl was putting on the performance of her life. A supposed victim of kidney stones, she'd attracted the attention of the entire staff with her cries of pain. Even Krista was impressed with her sister's acting. Playing the role of the concerned relative, Caroline's oldest daughter was busy demanding the immediate services of a specialist. It was enough to make Chan Daley tear his hair out as he struggled to calm both women.

Meanwhile, another scene was playing out near the bedside of Walter Harris. A young boy was standing by the cart talking earnestly to Caroline's patient. He was no more than twelve, yet his demeanor was that of a high school counselor speaking to a recalcitrant freshman. Harris was looking mulish, his arms folded tightly across his chest with the now famous manilla envelope tucked beneath his chin. At the foot of the cart, closely watching the two, stood Bricole Gregori.

"Is everything all right here?" Caroline asked as she approached her charge.

Three pairs of eyes stared at her in silence, then the boy suddenly said, "I saw you on the news. You're the lady who solved those other murders."

So Jackie Fields' comments had earned her a spot on television. She was thankful she hadn't seen it. She probably would have thrown a brick through the screen.

"I'm just a nurse," she replied quietly.

"No, you aren't," Bricole objected. "You caught the man who killed my grandmother."

Caroline was distracted by a particularly poignant groan that echoed through the nearly empty room. She looked over to where Kerry was being helped to the bathroom by her sister.

"Excuse me a minute." Turning her back on Harris and the children, she hurried off to intercept Kerry before her play-acting got out of hand.

"I'll help her," she told Patrice who was about to hand Kerry a specimen cup. "Would you take those children to the lounge and give them some ice cream? I think Mr. Harris and Mrs. Morgan would like a few minutes of peace."

"Will do," Patty said with a grin. "Both those kids have been watching their grandparents like hawks. You'd think someone was going to steal them away."

Kerry gave a low moan and stumbled into the bathroom, Krista right behind her. Caroline threw Patty a smile, followed the girls into the john, and slammed the door shut behind her.

"How am I doing?" Kerry asked, straightening up from her kidney stone posture.

"A little less groaning would help," her mother said. "You're in pain, not dying."

Kerry took the criticism in stride. "So who do you want us to question?"

"Concentrate on Michelle Devine. She's the tech with the gorgeous body and the inflated ego."

"The white girl, not the black one."

Caroline nodded. "The black tech is Patrice Woodson, the paramedic. I've more or less ruled her out as a suspect."

"Good," said Krista. "I was hoping she didn't do it. I saw the diamond on her finger and I asked her about it. She said she just got engaged to Keeshon Jones."

Caroline nodded again. "It's a little tight in here, ladies, so why don't Krista and I leave while you do your duty."

"You actually want a specimen?" Kerry looked at her mother in horror.

"If we're going to make this look real, then yes, I do want a specimen." She pulled a finger stick needle out of her pocket. "Give me your finger."

"Why?" asked Kerry, tucking her hands behind her.

"Because kidney stone patients have blood in their urine." She grabbed her daughter's right hand and quickly pricked her finger.

"Ouch! That hurt!"

"Quiet down," she said as she pressed a drop of blood into the specimen cup. "Now if you want to convince Chan Daley that you're really in pain, you'll sit down and add a little something to this."

Kerry sucked on her injured finger. "The things I do for my mother," she grumbled.

Caroline blew her a kiss and opened the door. She and Krista waited outside until Kerry emerged with her golden offering.

"Thank you, Miss. You may return now to your cart."

Bent double and supported by her sister's arm, Kerry hobbled back to bed. Caroline took the specimen to the utility room, tested it with a dipstick, and recorded the results on a sheet of paper. She walked back to the desk and handed the form to Chan.

"Looks like she might have a kidney stone."

"Hmm." Chan chewed his lower lip, then turned to Kee. "Give her sixty milligrams of Toradol and order routine labs. If the lab results are normal, you can go ahead and order an IVP."

Caroline decided that Kerry would undergo a miraculous recovery before the intravenous pyleogram could be ordered. It would lessen her time in the ER, but it would save her a bit of discomfort.

"How are the kids doing?" she asked ten minutes later when she ran into Patrice again.

"I left them with their ice cream in the nurses' lounge," the paramedic replied. "Want me to look in on them?"

"I'll do it. First, though, I'll go check on Mr. Harris."

Harris was napping when she arrived at his side. She tucked a blanket around him and was about to leave when he opened one eye.

"Did Miguel give you the envelope?" he asked. Seeing her blank expression, he sat up straight on the cart. "Where is the boy? Where has he gone with the file?"

"What file, Mr. Harris?"

"The file on Roger MacGuffy. The one that names his killer."

CHAPTER FORTY-EIGHT

June 17th
10:15 P.M.

Caroline plowed into Michael Bruck as she tore out of the Emergency Room.

"Come with me," she said, grabbing his arm. "We've got to find the children."

"What's wrong?" asked a puzzled Michael as he ran down the corridor behind her. She slid to a halt at the door of the nurses' lounge and pulled it open. The room was empty.

She turned to Michael. "Get Jake and the others. Bricole and a boy named Miguel Ramos are missing. Miguel has an envelope that may contain proof of who murdered Roger MacGuffy."

"Then they're in big danger," Michael said soberly. "We'll have to spread out if we're to find them."

"I'll start at this end. You and Jake check the old ER while the others look...everywhere." Caroline threw up her hands, suddenly overwhelmed by a feeling of helplessness. The hospital was huge. The murderer could have taken them anywhere in it. "And call for the rest of security!"

Michael nodded and ran off to find Jake. Caroline went in the opposite direction, heading first for Molly's office, then for the triage room. The nurse manager's office was locked, but the door to triage stood open. She glanced inside, not surprised to find it empty.

"Where are they?" she muttered to herself as she passed through the waiting room. The automatic doors slid open and she ran outside, her vision quickly adjusting to the poorly lit exterior of the temporary ER.

Off to the left she saw the outline of the construction company's trailer. A back hoe was parked next to it flanked by a Dumpster filled with trash from the site. Two trucks stood behind the hoe, one of them a pickup, the other the size and shape of a small moving van.

To the right lay two parking lots, a private one for ER patients backed by a larger one for visitors. A wide strip of grass lay between the lots and the hospital itself. The lawn circled the building, dipped into a V-shaped crevice where a garden had been planted between two walls of the medical center, then disappeared near the front entrance.

"Mom!" Caroline spun around as Kerry emerged through the sliding doors. "Michelle's gone! She's vanished from the ER."

Caroline dug into her pocket and produced the cards from Dom Gianni and Moshe Goldstein. She handed them to her daughter.

"Call these numbers and tell them what's happened. We'll need an army to search these grounds."

"Don't do anything stupid," Kerry warned in a fierce voice. She gave her mother a hug and ran back into the building.

Caroline glanced in both directions before deciding to search the construction area first. She crossed the asphalt driveway and recalling her previous experience with the uneven ground, walked gingerly towards the trailer.

A few yards from the pavement lay a ditch newly dug for sewage pipes. Plastic wire fencing lined the trench, but as a protective device, it was a failure. The fence was torn in some places, bent to the ground in others. In one spot where it was missing altogether, wooden boards formed a bridge across the ditch. Using her penlight, Caroline headed for the gap. She had just stepped onto the planks when the thin stream of light glinted off something in the ditch. She looked down.

There in the dirt lay Michelle, a scalpel stuck in her chest.

CHAPTER FORTY-NINE

June 17th
10:22 P.M.

Only an inch or two of handle protruded from the wound in Michelle Devine's breast. The rest of the scalpel was buried deep in her heart.

Caroline checked for signs of life, but Michelle's blue lips and dilated pupils told her the girl was dead long before she lifted her fingers from the pulseless neck. She rocked back on her heels and stared at the body. She was sure now that she knew the name of the murderer. The question was, would she kill again?

Of course she would, she told herself as she scrambled out of the ditch. Three were dead already. What did another two matter?

Mindless of the air splint on her ankle, Caroline plunged over the rocky ground towards the construction trailer. A single unshaded bulb illuminated the door while the rest of the structure lay in total darkness. She slowed her steps as she approached the mud caked stairs leading up to the entrance.

The door should have been locked. Instead, the handle turned easily in her hand. She took a deep breath, conscious of her heart pounding against her ribs, and pushed the door open.

The inside of the trailer was bathed in shadows. A desk and several file cabinets took up most of the space, but towards the rear of the long, narrow room stood a folding cot. Sitting on it, their hands tied together and tape covering their mouths, were Bricole and Miguel Ramos.

Caroline rushed over to the cot. She heard the door slam

and lock behind her and she whirled, her right hand raised in a fist, her left extended in a protective gesture. After a moment of complete silence, she relaxed her stance. There was no one in the trailer besides her and the children.

She turned back to the cot and removed the tape from Bricole's face. The little girl broke into sobs as Caroline did the same for Miguel.

"It's all right," she told them as she untied their hands. "She's gone now, and we're safe."

"No!" screamed Bricole. "She said she was going to kill us!"

Caroline gathered the child into her arms and held her tightly. "Help me push that desk against the door," she said to Miguel. "We'll wait in here until the police arrive."

The boy nodded and rose unsteadily to his feet. He was as frightened as Bricole, but accustomed to discipline, he followed Caroline's instructions without protest.

"No! Don't do that!" Bricole beat against Caroline's chest until she released the little girl. "We're trapped if we stay here! Can't you smell it?"

Caroline smelled nothing, but she saw a flare of light outside the tiny window. The truth of their predicament hit her immediately. The killer had locked them inside because she intended to torch the trailer.

Praying that Kerry had reached Dom Gianni or Moshe, she yanked on the desk, pulling it back until she could reach the door. It was locked from the outside and despite her desperate efforts, it refused to budge.

She raced to the window. It was small, but the children could probably squeeze through. She'd be unable to follow them, though, and that meant they'd be at the mercy of the killer waiting outside.

If they got through the flames, she thought wildly.

The smell of gasoline fumes was undeniable now. The fire crackled against the walls making them hot to the touch, and the air grew heavy with smoke. Caroline drew the children into the center of the room and pressed their faces to her shirt.

"Breathe through the cloth," she urged them as they began to cough. "Slow and easy now."

She heard voices yelling in the distance and her hopes rose. Choking back tears, she saw a spray of water hit the window. Something banged against the door, again and again. It rocked on its hinges, then splintered into long pieces that fell at her feet.

Fresh air flooded the room as Michael Bruck rushed in. He scooped up the children, one in each arm, and bounded down the steps with them. Caroline stumbled after him.

"Are you all right?" A groggy Carl Atwater gathered her in his arms and led her away from the trailer.

"Where's Wendy?" she gasped.

"Over there." Carl pointed to a figure lying on the ground. "Alexsa ran her through with her sword cane when the girl charged at her with a scalpel."

"That's what she used on Michelle Devine."

"We know. Jake found her body when we came out looking for you and saw the fire."

"Mother!"

Kerry and Krista came running up. Both girls were crying as they threw their arms around her neck.

"Don't ever do that again," Kerry whispered, her voice tense with fear and relief.

"I had no choice," Caroline replied. "I couldn't let her have the children." She glanced over to where Alexsa was kneeling on the ground, her arms wrapped around Bricole. Moshe Goldstein stood guard over the two, and he waved to her.

A police car screamed to a halt in the driveway and Frank Lodash tumbled out. He shouted to an officer who had arrived minutes earlier and was clearing the way for the approaching fire engines.

"Keep those people out of here! Keep the area clear!"

But Jake Moeller was not to be denied. He flashed his badge at the policeman and hurried past with Maddy and Faith.

"I took Miguel in and left him with Dr. Daley," he told Michael. "The boy's parents are here now."

"How's Mr. Harris?" asked Caroline.

"He's fine now that Miguel is safe." Maddy pushed through the crowd and hugged her friend. "Thank God you're all right."

"Alexsa looks ready to collapse, Maddy. Let's get her out of here."

Michael lifted the old woman to her feet. Despite the ordeal, she was remarkably composed when Frank Lodash intercepted the group near the makeshift bridge.

"No one threatens my family," she told him firmly. "I'm sorry about Wendy, but I was defending myself."

Lodash held up a hand. "I don't think there will be any charges filed in her death. I will have to question you, though."

"Later, Frank." Dom Giannia approached them from the direction of the Emergency Room. He glanced briefly at Caroline, then switched his gaze to the other policeman. "We need to talk first. There's a patient inside the ER who may clear up a lot of our questions concerning these murders."

Lodash nodded and waved them on. When they reached the glass doors of the ER, Chan Daley was waiting for them.

"You told me you had several umbrellas, Cari," he said with a mischievous smile. "But I never guessed you had this many!"

"Let me introduce you, Chan. These are my daughters, Krista and Kerry, and these my friends, Carl, and Maddy, and Jake, and..."

CHAPTER FIFTY

July 4th
8:30 P.M.

"Fill in the blanks, Cari. The TV glossed over a lot of stuff." Sharon settled deeper in her lawn chair, eager to hear the gory details.

Caroline took her time answering as she recalled her promise to Dom Gianni the night it had all ended.

"Moshe Goldstein works for the FBI," Dom had said. "He told us about your meeting with Horowitz, and Maria filled in the details."

"Maria Ramos works for them too?"

"She has a great cover as Adam's cook." He'd taken her hand and held it tightly. "Never reveal what I've told you, Mrs. Rhodes. In fact, forget you ever heard of Moshe Goldstein and Maria Ramos. Mentioning their names in public could endanger both their lives."

"I give you my word, Dom." And she meant to keep it.

"Walter Harris held the key to the murders," she finally said. "Twenty years ago he worked as a private investigator. He was hired by a hospital Chief of Staff to check on the man's son-in-law. That son-in-law was Roger MacGuffy, also known as Scotty to his friends."

"He was probably a creep even back then," said Janie. Glad to have her former neighbor visiting, she was busy pouring wine and cutting cheese for the crackers. She wasn't missing a word, though.

"He was cheating on his wife, sleeping with a young student nurse." Caroline didn't say that the student had been Susan Kane, nee Witterson. "Harris gave the Chief of Staff proof of the affair, but Dr. Melmann died suddenly of a heart attack while Roger was in his office. The file on Dr. MacGuffy subsequently disappeared."

"He took it," Sharon concluded.

"Harris thought so. He also thought Roger might have saved Dr. Melmann's life, but chose not to. Walt Harris was suspicious, so he continued to watch Dr. MacGuffy, keeping a file on everything the man did. Roger's wife, Barbara, was pregnant at the time of her father's death. She left her husband soon after their daughter was born, going to live in England, and taking the child with her."

"She must have known about the other women in his life," said Sharon.

"She did. Harris said she cited the student nurse in her divorce papers."

"So Wendy Moss was really Roger MacGuffy's daughter."

"Yes, Janie, although her real name was Belinda. Belinda grew up hating her father, and after her mother died this past January, she decided to find Roger. She assumed the identity of Wendy Moss, a girl she'd met at school. The real Wendy was as emotionally disturbed as Belinda, so she had no problem going along with the hoax.

"How did she find Dr. MacGuffy?" Janie asked

"Apparently through her mother's solicitor." Caroline took a sip of her drink. "This is really good wine, Janie."

"Thought you'd enjoy it. I bought it up in Michigan."

"Let's stay on track here, ladies," admonished Sharon. "We know that Belinda found her father, then got a job at Ascension and bided her time. We also think she might have killed Angela and Michelle because they were sleeping with Dr. MacGuffy."

"We believe so," said Caroline. "The police in England have questioned the real Wendy Moss. She says Belinda worshipped her mother and saw Roger's other women as enemies to be done away with. Belinda framed Roger for Angela's murder, but it didn't work out as she'd planned. She then drugged his coffee with her own sedatives, hauled him off to the old ER, and strung him up to the scaffolding."

"I still say the man got what he deserved," Sharon insisted. "How did Belinda manage to steal Roger's lab coat and name tag?"

"That part was easy. She simply waited until he walked into the ER, then she went to his office and took it. Over the weekend Vic Warner paid off a security guard to let him into Brenda's office. The police heard about that and assumed Roger always locked his office when he stepped away, but he didn't. Chan Daley told them the door was always open."

"Then Belinda had no problem sneaking in and drugging his coffee," said Janie.

"It was common knowledge that Roger loved his coffee. Belinda made sure the pot was full so he'd be out of it when she strangled him. Unfortunately, Michelle must have seen her go into the office. Shortly before her death, she chided Wendy for playing up to Roger the night he was killed. I think that's what decided her fate."

"Thank goodness you were able to clear your friend."

"Walt Harris did that with his file, Janie. He gave it to the children to give to me, but Wendy waylaid them in the nurses' lounge. She must have been afraid there were notes on her in the file."

"And were there?"

"Oh, yes. Walter had kept track of both her and her mother."

"I still wonder how Belinda was able to get into Angela Horowitz's apartment," said Sharon.

"Angela probably let her in. She had no reason to distrust Wendy. The girl meant nothing to her, so why be afraid?"

"And now we know the rest of the story," Janie laughed. She handed Caroline another cracker, then bent down and hugged her. "Oh, Cari. You don't know how glad we are to see you again."

"I stayed away too long, but never again. You'll be seeing lots of me in the future." She glanced over the fence at her old back yard. "Your new neighbors look nice. I see they have children."

"Those kids have been waiting all day for the fireworks to begin," said Sharon. She pointed to the sky. "Look! There go the first ones now."

Caroline watched as the sky exploded in a mass of sparkling red and blue. The display faded, to be replaced moments later by another twice as colorful as the first. She leaned back in her lawn chair and closed her eyes, content to simply listen to the ohs and ahs of the neighborhood children.

Relaxing with her friends, Caroline figured she'd experienced enough fireworks for one summer.